"It's been years, Abby."

Reese stuck his hand out. "You wouldn't shake my hand last night. I thought I'd try again."

She relented, clasped his hand and stared at the long fingers wrapped around hers. Bits of twig and soil stuck to their joined palms.

"Cleaning the yard, I see."

She leaned on her rake. "You cops don't miss a clue, do you?"

Reese crossed his arms. "So how've you been?"

How have I been? Abby marveled at the casualness of his question in light of what her life had been like since she'd last seen him. But of course Reese never thought of that night.

He'd had thirteen years to forget.

She'd had thirteen years to remember.

And regret.

Dear Reader,

I'm something of a Christmas fanatic. Just ask my husband and son, who watch our house transformed each December with lighted garlands and holiday villages populated by dozens of miniature people.

I've always thought New England was the best place to experience traditional Christmas cheer. Then, two years ago, I spent part of my holiday in Key West, Florida. And believe me, what the people of "The Conch Republic" lack in tradition, they make up for in creativity. Picture storefronts with mounted sailfish twinkling in blue lights and statues of sailors twined with red and green lights on Mallory Square. And tall-masted schooners competing for the grand prize in the holiday boat parade. From the humblest shotgun house to the island's majestic Victorian mansions, Key Westers happily proclaim, "It's Christmas and we're making merry!"

So I decided Key West was the perfect locale for a Christmas love story. I hope you'll spend part of your holiday with Reese and Abby, both native "Conchs" whose fortunes have brought them back to the island at this magical time to face the regrets of the past and build a future in the paradise of their childhoods.

I love to hear from readers. Please visit my Web site, www.cynthiathomason.com, or write me at P.O. Box 550068, Fort Lauderdale, Florida 33355. And have a happy and magical holiday!

Cynthia

CHRISTMAS IN KEY WEST
Cynthia Thomason

TORONTO • NEW YORK • LONDON
AMSTERDAM • PARIS • SYDNEY • HAMBURG
STOCKHOLM • ATHENS • TOKYO • MILAN • MADRID
PRAGUE • WARSAW • BUDAPEST • AUCKLAND

ISBN-13: 978-0-373-71528-2
ISBN-10:   0-373-71528-5

CHRISTMAS IN KEY WEST

ABOUT THE AUTHOR

Cynthia Thomason writes contemporary and historical romances and dabbles in mysteries. She has won a National Reader's Choice Award and the 2008 Golden Quill. When she's not writing, she works as a licensed auctioneer for the auction company she and her husband own. As an estate buyer for the auction, she has come across unusual items, many of which have found their way into her books. She has one son, an entertainment reporter. Cynthia dreams of perching on a mountaintop in North Carolina every autumn to watch the leaves turn. You can read more about her at www.cynthiathomason.com.

Books by Cynthia Thomason

HARLEQUIN SUPERROMANCE

*Texas Hold 'Em

This book is dedicated to my mother,
Barbara Brackett, with love
for all the Christmases past, present and future.

CHAPTER ONE

REESE HUNKERED DOWN on one knee and burrowed his fingers into a patch of soft golden fur covered by a colorful neckerchief. "You have a good day, buddy," he said to the Labrador retriever. "Take a couple of naps for me." Giving the dog a goodbye scratch behind the ears, he walked outside and got into his patrol car. He'd already talked to the dispatcher on duty. The night had been a quiet one. Reese hoped the calm would continue at least for the next three days, at which point a new crop of tourists would descend upon Key West in the four-day Thanksgiving break.

He'd just backed out of his driveway when a message came through on his radio. Instantly tuning in, he hoped the call from the station would be nothing more important than a request to stop for doughnuts. "This is Reese," he said into the mic on his shoulder. He preferred using his real name instead of his official police-speak identity when he could. "What's up?"

His hope for continued calm evaporated when the dispatcher said, "It's Huey Vernay, Reese. He's at it again."

Reese gripped the steering wheel in response to the coiling in his stomach. Anything to do with Huey, his trinket business or the happenings at Vernay House produced this reaction. "Did we get another complaint from a tourist about his attitude?"

"Nope. This is worse."

The coiling resulted in an all-too-familiar pain in his neck. "What's he done now?"

"Edna Howell just called. She said Huey started another fire in his backyard and the smell came over her fence. She claims that if she opens her windows, she'll suffocate from toxic fumes."

"Here we go again," Reese muttered as he turned onto Duval and headed toward Southard Street, where the ten-room Vernay House had stood since the late 1850s. He leaned out the window, caught a whiff of burning rubber. "Shit."

"What's that?" the dispatcher asked.

"Sorry, Merlene. Call the fire department. I'm only a couple of blocks from Huey's now. I'll go on over."

"Roger that, Reese. Do you need backup?"

As much as he'd like to foist the responsibility on anyone else in the department who would take it, he declined. He didn't see flames shooting into the air, so that was a good sign. "Probably not. But I'll want a half bottle of aspirin when this is over, so make sure we have some."

The dispatcher chuckled before signing off, and Reese gave up hope of filling his thermal mug with coffee from Martha's Eye Opener Café. He flipped the switch on the car's light bar and sped toward Southard Street.

REESE PULLED TO A STOP in the plume of smoke drifting over the wraparound porch of Vernay House. He got out of the cruiser and waved his hand in front of his face to dispel the foul air. Walking around to the backyard, he spied Huey Vernay standing upwind from a smoldering pit of who knows what. Thank goodness the flames that still existed were minor, but acrid gray clouds hung over the old Classic Revival mansion.

Reese strode to the big man, who was bare-chested except for the apron of his denim overalls. Smudges of soot blotched his face and arms. A typical scowl creased his face.

"What the hell do you think you're doing, Huey?" Reese asked.

The man took a drag on the stub of his cigarette and released a long, wispy stream of smoke. He flicked the butt to the dirt and ground it in with the heel of his boot. Looping his thumbs through the straps of his overalls, he said, "What's it look like?"

Reese wanted to say, *Insanity,* but refrained, knowing that answer was too close to the truth.

Huey raised his bushy white eyebrows in the condescending smirk he'd perfected after years of boasting about his blue-blooded-Louis-the-Something background. Genetically speaking, French ancestry, even ties to royalty, didn't count for much in modern-day Key West, but Huey refused to accept that. "I'm abiding by the almighty Community Improvement Board and the code enforcement officer's order to clean my place up."

"You know darn well you can't do that by lighting a fire," Reese stated. "I warned you about this a week ago when you set that blaze in your garbage can."

"I'm doing it different this time," Huey retorted. "You complained that I didn't have a proper containment screen on the top of the can, so now I'm burning my trash in the open. There isn't a law against that as far as I've heard."

Reese looked down at the pile of garbage slowly disintegrating into spitting embers. "I've only been here a couple of minutes, Huey, and I've already come up with five codes you're breaking right now."

"Well, hell, Reese, you can't have it both ways. The island's gestapo can't tell me my home is an eyesore and then have you stop by and prevent me from sprucing it up."

Sirens sounded in the distance. Aware that even laid-back Key West was in the midst of rush hour, Reese tuned to the radio channel connecting him to the island's fire department. "Tell your boys they can slow down," he said to the dispatcher. "The fire's under control. I still need them here to do a damage assessment, but there's no immediate threat to property." He signed off and glared at Huey. "I'm going to my car to get the paperwork," he said. "You're getting citations this time."

Huey's eyes, as gray as the smoke around him, became slits. He tugged on the full beard that had earned him first place in the Ernest Hemingway look-alike contest four out of the past ten years. "What for? Doing my civic duty?"

Ignoring the sarcasm, Reese went around the house to retrieve the necessary reports. After he'd written the first citation, he walked back and handed a copy to Huey. "This is for burning household waste."

Huey stared at the paper that had been thrust into his hand. "Of course I'm burning household waste. That's exactly what that officious son of a bitch you sent out here told me to get rid of."

"You can't burn it, Huey. You can only set fire to lawn debris. I gave you a copy of the rules the last time I was here."

"You did? Guess I must have burned it in this pile by mistake."

Refusing to be goaded into making an equally sarcastic comeback, Reese studied the smoldering items in the widening circle of blackened weeds and said, "You've got a rubber tire in there, along with plastic and metal containers that, if I knew what they'd once held, might scare the crap out of me." He handed Huey a second ticket. "This is for not having your fire within the appropriate setback. You're too close to the fence line."

Huey stared at the fence separating his property from his neighbor's. "That damn busybody Edna Howell. The old biddy ratted me out—"

"And for not clearing an area around the pit to ensure containment," Reese continued. He wrote the third citation. "This is for not having a shovel and hose nearby in case the fire spreads."

He was starting a fourth ticket when Huey reached out and placed his big hand over Reese's. "You've made your point. Now we both know you can write."

Reese frowned at him. Huey was consistently the most difficult resident on the island to deal with. He held on to grudges longer than anyone Reese had ever known. And Huey had a hell of a lot of grudges to stew over, including one against Reese and his family that dated back a lot of years. "I thought I made all this clear last week when you had the previous fire," he said. "I should have ticketed you then."

Huey ruffled the papers in Reese's face. "I'll tell you what you can do with your citations, Mr. Big Shot."

Reese struggled to hold on to his temper. "You want me to arrest you, Huey? Because I will. You're threatening an officer of the law—"

"Phooey. I remember when you were still wet behind the ears. It wasn't so many years ago, Reese Burkett, that you were on the other side of the law more often than not, and don't you forget it. Many's the night I sat on my porch and watched the cops chasing you and that Cuban gang you hung out with."

Reese sighed, admitting to himself that Huey had a point. Reese had gotten into a lot of trouble on this island. That was why folks had been surprised he'd accepted a position with the Key West Police Department when he'd gotten out of the navy.

He started to remind Huey that both of them had episodes in their pasts that were better left buried, but his words were interrupted by a crew of firemen coming around the side of the house.

Larry Blanchard, fire captain and another Key West native, warned Huey about his reckless actions. "I should charge you for what this unnecessary call cost the citizens of this town," he said.

"Go ahead." Huey clasped his wrists together and held them in front of him, daring someone to slap cuffs on him. "I can't pay it. You know what it's like for a small, independent businessman these days. Can barely keep food on the table."

Blanchard rolled his eyes, and it was all Reese could do not to point out that Huey hadn't made a decent living in years. Having ruined his reputation as the local handyman by charging folks for inferior work, he now sold cheap souvenirs to tourists from a mobile vendor's cart during the nightly sunset festivities on Mallory Square. Still, Reese found it hard to believe that Huey had trouble paying his grocery tab. The six-footer tipped the scales at well over two hundred pounds.

"You've got fourteen days to pay these citations," Reese said.

Huey passed his hand over his collar-length white hair.

"Don't hold your breath. I won't have the money in fourteen *weeks*. And if I did, I wouldn't give it to you jackass bureaucrats."

"Then I'll be back to get you."

"Fine. I'll be waiting. The people of this island can provide me with a bed and three squares a day."

Although Huey had been an eyewitness to some trouble Reese had gotten into thirteen years ago, the last thing Reese wanted was to arrest the guy. He dreaded listening to Huey's complaints while he served time. And he certainly didn't relish providing Huey with any more excuses for not earning a living. But mostly Reese didn't want to haul Huey in because the Vernays had been on this island for more than a hundred and fifty years. Not all of their history here was good, but they were as much a part of Key West lore as Stephen Mallory, John Simonton or Samuel Southard, men who'd had streets named after them because of their illustrious contributions to the island. No street was named for the Vernays.

Regretfully, Reese had to accept that he was running out of options with Huey. The stubborn old guy wasn't giving him any choice other than jail. Reese scratched his head. Except for the option he'd used as a last resort once before in similar circumstances. Maybe Loretta could talk some sense into her ex-husband this time, too.

He stopped the fire captain as he circled the contaminated pile. "How's it look, Larry?"

"It's out, but there could still be some hot spots. To totally decontaminate the site, we should clear the whole pile out of here."

Reese nodded toward Huey's rusty old truck, which sat in front of the decrepit carriage house. "Never mind," he said loudly. "Huey's cost the city enough for one day." He glared at the man. "You haul this trash down to the sanitation site after it cools, or call the junk dealer to come take it away. You hear me?"

"I'm not deaf, Reese," he snapped. "Just pissed off, and that doesn't affect my hearing."

"I'm just making myself clear," Reese said. "I'm stopping back this afternoon to see that you've started cleaning this toxic mess up. And if it isn't all gone in two days, I'll slap you with another fine."

"That doesn't surprise me."

Reese got in his cruiser and headed to the station. He'd missed breakfast, but that wasn't the main reason he was already thinking about lunch. He'd made up his mind to go to Phil's Pirate Shack on Caroline Street. Hopeful about talking to Loretta Vernay, he could also order a grouper sandwich to go.

EVERY TIME A CUSTOMER opened the door at Phil's, a grease-smeared plastic pirate's head hanging on a hook over the entrance cut loose with a squawky rendition of "Ho, Ho, Ho and a Bottle of Rum." Reese entered the establishment at noon and glanced around at the usual crowd of locals who knew this was the place for the best seafood on the island. And unlike many of the restaurants in town, the prices were fair.

A few customers hollered at him, mostly construction workers building or remodeling ever-expanding resort hotels, or guides and charter operators from the area's marinas. These were guys for whom the fresh-catch scent at the Pirate Shack was cologne. Reese walked over to a table where the two mechanics from Burkett's Paradise

Marina were chowing down on fish and chips. "How's everything going?" he asked the men.

"Wouldn't do any good to complain," Bill MacKenzie said. He scooted a chair away from the table with the toe of his work boot, indicating Reese should join them.

He waved off the invitation. "I'm getting a takeout," he said.

Bill took a swallow from a long-necked beer bottle. "We wanted your father to eat with us, but your mom asked him to pick out some fabric for curtains or something."

Reese chuckled. His mother was always doing something to their Gulf-side stilt house—a fact that made Frank Burkett cringe. At this stage in his life, Reese's dad was basically content with a comfortable recliner and a television. The marina had provided a good living for the family since he'd resigned as a cop and opened the business twenty years earlier. And his wife was a major reason for that success. Ellen Burkett was an excellent manager.

"You guys enjoy your lunch," Reese said, scanning around the restaurant for Loretta. He spied her coming out of the kitchen with a platter of food skillfully balanced on her hand. Reese smiled at her. He didn't know Loretta's age, but he figured her for around fifty, sixteen years older than he was. She looked good. Kept her short hair a light blond, her figure trim and appealing. A lot of women who'd lived most of their lives in the unforgiving island sun showed the effects of ultraviolet rays in creases around their eyes and lips, as well as scars from skin cancer treatments. Not Loretta. Reese guessed she must have a closetful of wide-brimmed hats. And he knew for certain that she was one Vernay who would always have a smile for him.

She gestured with her free hand. "Be with you in a minute, Reese."

He propped his foot on the empty chair and talked with his friends until she was free. When she approached, her order pad at the ready, he led her away from the others.

"What can I get you, honey?" she asked him.

"A grouper sandwich to go, coleslaw instead of fries. But that's not the only reason I'm here."

"Oh?" She grinned. "Anything else, and you'll have to check with Phil."

Reese smiled. Loretta and Phil had been together for almost twelve years, once she'd finally given up on Huey, packed her bags and walked out of Vernay House for good. And since that time, the mansion had suffered twelve years of nobody caring about it.

"If I didn't know that Phil could beat me with one hand tied behind his back, I'd be tempted," Reese said. "But this has to do with an entirely different matter." He sobered, cleared his throat and watched Loretta's blue eyes narrow suspiciously. She was a smart woman and caught on fast.

"You're not here about Huey, are you?"

Keeping his expression resolute, he replied, "I know you're busy, but I need to talk to you."

She lowered her voice. "I asked you to leave me out of Huey's problems, Reese. Besides, Phil could come out of the kitchen anytime, and if he hears us discussing Huey, he'll blow a gasket."

Reese stated the obvious, hoping it would make a difference. "Huey's his brother, Loretta. He must care about what happens to him."

"He did once," she said, "but not anymore. Phil has vowed never to lend him money again or come to his rescue." She leaned in close and spoke in a whisper. "I know Huey was hurt when I left him for Phil, but darn it, Reese, it's been twelve years, past time for Huey to get on with his life."

Reese wasn't sure he agreed. In fact, the way the romantic triangle had ended up was one aspect of Huey's life that earned Reese's sympathy. Another was that Huey had said goodbye to his daughter shortly before Loretta walked out on him.

"Phil doesn't even like me talking about Huey," Loretta said, "and frankly, that's how I want it, too."

"I'm going to have to arrest him, Loretta."

She sagged against the bar. "Oh, come on, Reese. You don't mean that. Huey's a problem. Nobody knows that better than me. But arrest him? He's sixty-five years old. And he's not a criminal."

"Maybe not in the sense you're thinking, but he's a public nuisance and he's breaking the law. At least once a week I've got to drive over to his place and remind him that living in the Conch Republic doesn't mean that we're divorced from the rest of the country. We have the same laws here as on the mainland, and Huey seems to enjoy stretching them to the limit."

Her voice filled with resignation, she asked, "What did he do this time?"

Reese explained about the fire, Mrs. Howell's phone call and the complaints they'd gotten from tourists recently. "No wonder he doesn't make a living selling those cheap souvenirs," Reese said. "One encounter with Huey, and nobody wants to buy anything he's offering. All the tourists think about is getting away from him."

Loretta shook her head. "I don't know what I can do."

"I'll give you a chance to talk to him one more time. He has fourteen days to pay his latest citations, and a couple of days to dispose of a load of offensive garbage in the yard. If he does those things, and if you can convince him to abide by the laws around here, I'll cut him a break... again."

She sighed. "Huey doesn't like to listen to me, Reese. You know that."

Reese felt bad for putting Loretta in the middle of this situation, but he knew darn well she'd never forgive him if he arrested Huey without telling her first. She might claim to have given up on the man, but somewhere deep inside her, an affection for him still flickered.

"Okay," Reese said. "I understand your position, but I felt I owed it to you to tell you before I acted."

She tapped her order pad on the bar. "I appreciate that. You still want your sandwich?"

"I'm happy to say Huey hasn't ruined my appetite."

She turned to go to the kitchen, but stopped after a few steps. Turning back, she said, "Actually, there's one person, and one only, who might be able to get through to him."

Reese knew exactly who she meant, and an image of a cute, blue-eyed blonde filled his mind. "I didn't think it was my place to suggest Abby," he murmured.

"He still listens to her," Loretta said. "Not that he follows her advice. But if anybody can get him to behave himself, it would be our daughter."

Reese was beginning to see a way out of this dilemma. "So what are you saying? That you'll call her?"

"I hate to. She's got her career in Atlanta. She's busy. And she's really not comfortable being here."

Reese only nodded. He hadn't seen Abigail Vernay in

thirteen years. He was aware that she returned to the island sometimes. She still maintained a connection to Huey and her mother, but she stayed away from the public areas when she was here, and remained only a couple of days. Their paths hadn't crossed in the seven years he'd been back.

All that supported what Loretta had told him. Abby did seem to have misgivings about coming home. Reese just hoped the history between them wasn't one of the reasons.

What had happened was ancient history. She'd probably forgotten all about it. Still, Reese couldn't be certain. Women's memories were tricky things.

CHAPTER TWO

"HE'S GOT TWO WEEKS *to pay a bunch of fines, Abby, or Reese Burkett's going to arrest him.*"

Abby had been unable to get her last conversation with her mother out of her mind. When Loretta had informed her of Huey's latest trouble and its consequences, she had been furious. "Arrest him?" she'd practically shouted at her mom, though her anger had been directed at the island's arrogant police captain. "Reese had better not lay a hand on Poppy."

Now, two days later, as she neared Southard Street, Abby was ready to do whatever was necessary to protect her father. Once she'd calmed down, she had admitted that his behavior *had* gotten out of hand. She also recognized that she had the best chance of talking some sense into him and keeping him from going to jail. "You're the one person Huey seems to tolerate these days," her mother had said.

Abby smiled, thinking about the unique father-daughter bond they shared, a bond that had been tested over the years but remained strong because of weekly phone calls and genuine concern. But now, Abby had to admit her dad needed something more from her than a supportive, long-distance relationship. He needed to start behaving like a grown-up.

So, taking into account the month of personal days and

vacation time she'd accumulated, Abby made a difficult decision. After turning over a mountain of paperwork to a colleague, and explaining her situation to the most vulnerable of her cases, she'd arranged for a leave from her job so she could stay in Key West through Christmas. Her involvement with the young women in her caseload didn't end just because she was away, of course. She'd made sure everyone who depended on her had her cell phone number.

Leaving Atlanta had been difficult, but Abby was convinced she was doing the right thing for her family. If anyone could help Huey out of the mess he'd gotten himself into, it was her, not an island cop who thought he could change her dad by intimidating him. She only wished she could avoid Reese throughout her stay, as she had in the past, though she doubted that would be possible. Key West was, and always had been, a small town.

Thanksgiving Day was nearly over when Abby drove up to her old house with a couple of take-out turkey dinners on the floor of her car. She hadn't told her father she was coming, for two reasons: she didn't want him to worry about her making the long drive, and she didn't want to answer questions about why she'd planned the trip.

As she pulled up the cracked cement driveway, she encountered debris that spread from the lawn into the street. Much of it was charred and unrecognizable—and an indication that things were as bad as her mother had said. Abby parked, got out of her car and wrinkled her nose at the foul odor from the garbage.

Then she gazed up at the two-and-a-half-story house she'd grown up in. At one time she'd been proud that the 1857 mansion had been built by her great-great-great-grandfather Armand Vernay, a self-made millionaire during the island's infamous shipwrecking days. Today, eleven months since her last visit, Abby only sensed decay and desperation around her, emphasizing even more the painful memories of the choices she'd made thirteen years ago, and the consequences she'd been forced to live with.

Scraggly oleander bushes, once brilliant with pink blossoms, now reached heights of more than ten feet and invaded the wraparound porch. Bare limbs chafed the delicate rippled glass in the ancient windows. The wide brick pathway, where once two people could walk arm in arm to the front door, barely allowed one person to climb the three steps without risk of scratching ankles on unkempt brambles. Most of the windows were shuttered, giving the house a sad, deserted feel.

Clutching the turkey dinners, she picked her way toward the porch, half expecting Huey to burst through the door. He always seemed to have a special radar where she was concerned, somehow knowing when she was around. Disappointed, she walked in the door, which was never locked, and called his name.

Silence. She stared into the parlor, noting the disarray. Mail, mostly flyers, littered Huey's desk. Dust lay thick on the old mahogany pieces she used to polish with such care. She progressed down the hall, again calling for her father. Once in the kitchen, she set the turkey dinners on the table and peered out the window. Maybe he was in the backyard. She glanced at the overgrown bushes and a large, darkened patch of dirt that looked as though it had been burned— confirmation of Huey's run-in with Reese.

Abby shook her head and returned to the hall. Maybe Poppy was napping. She'd go upstairs and awaken him, she decided, just before her cell phone rang. She pulled the phone from her jeans pocket, read the digital display and answered. "Mom?"

"Hi, honey. Have you arrived at Huey's yet?"

"Yes, I just got here."

"Good. I didn't want to call and upset you while you were still on the road. I was afraid you'd drive too fast to get here."

Abby sat heavily on the bottom step of the staircase. "Mom, what's happened? Poppy's not here."

"I know." Loretta paused. "Now, don't think the worst, but he's in the hospital."

"The hospital?" Abby rose and hurried to the front door. "Why? What's wrong with him?"

"He fell, Abby. He'll be okay, but he's got a few bruises and a concussion. The doctors want to keep him overnight for observation."

"My God. Poor Poppy." She picked up her purse, which she'd dropped on the hall stand, and went outside. "I'll head right over. Are you coming, too?"

"I went when I first heard, but once I knew Huey was okay, I came to work. You can call here at the Shack if you need me."

"Okay. But wait, Mom, don't hang up. How did it happen? Why did Poppy fall?"

Loretta breathed deeply. "You won't like hearing this, Ab."

"Mom…"

"Huey says Reese Burkett attacked him."

ABBY'S HANDS SHOOK on the steering wheel as she drove the mile to the island hospital. She tried to picture Reese Burkett with her fingers wrapped around his neck. But instead of popping veins on his forehead, and broken blood vessels in his eyes, all that came to mind was a youthful, cocky smile and heavily lashed green eyes full of confidence and invincibility. That was Reese then. She had no idea what he looked like now, only that she would experience an admittedly selfish gratification in discovering he'd packed forty pounds onto his athletic frame and lost most of his thick dark hair. How dare he manhandle her father? She'd meet him in court, facing an abuse charge!

The sun was setting as she parked in the hospital lot and entered the lobby. Mechanically, she showed the required identification, had her picture taken and patted the ID sticker onto her blouse. She was used to hospital security regulations. In the course of her job, she visited many hospitals in the Atlanta area.

Huey was on the second floor. Abby exited the elevator, quickly scanned the directional signs for his room number and headed to the end of the hall. She heard Alex Trebek read an answer on *Jeopardy,* then recognized her dad's voice giving the proper response before the contestants could buzz in.

Huey snapped his fingers as she entered the room. He'd gotten the *Jeopardy* question right.

Abby hurried to his bedside, then stopped short when she saw the bruise around his closed right eye. "Poppy!"

He turned to her, and a huge grin spread across his face. "Well, I'll be. Baby girl! What are you doing here? You found out I was in this joint?"

"Not until I got into town, about thirty minutes ago. Mom phoned and told me you'd been admitted."

He stared at her with his good eye. "So what are you doing here? It isn't Christmas yet."

"No, but I came early, to spend more time with you."

"What? You're staying through December?"

"That's the plan."

"That's not like you, Abigail—taking off work so long."

"It's fine, Poppy. Everything's covered."

"But you never stay more than a couple of days."

"I know, but this is different." She pulled up a chair. "Anyway, I don't want to talk about me. I want to know what happened to you. How are you feeling?" She lifted the tube leading into his arm. "And what's this for?"

He lowered the TV volume with his remote. "It's nothing," he said. "Everybody gets a drip of some kind, they tell me. That's just sugar water or something." He tapped the side of his head. "It's the old noggin that's giving me trouble. But they gave me something that makes Alex Trebek look like Loni Anderson."

Abby leaned close. "What about your eye?"

"Oh, yeah, that. Haven't had a shiner in years."

She rested her hand on his arm. "Poppy, what happened? Tell me how you ended up in here."

He snorted. "You need to ask your old beau about it, Abigail."

"Don't call him that. He was never my beau, and you know it. If Reese did this to you, I want to hear the details."

"He did it, all right. Knocked me flatter than an IHOP pancake in my own front yard." Huey suddenly sat up straight. He stared over Abby's shoulder and gazed cantankerously at the doorway. "And there's the abuser now. Come to try and put the cuffs on me again, Reese?"

Abby spun around, the chair legs scraping on the speckled linoleum. Her heart pounded. There he was, well built, still with a full head of hair. *Damn you, Reese,* she thought, hating that her chest clenched with resentment and heartache and other emotions that, if she analyzed them, might scare her to death.

She stood up and placed her hand over her stomach in an effort to calm the trembling inside. She hadn't seen Reese in thirteen years. He'd matured, but he hadn't really changed. At twenty-one, he'd given lots of girls reason to hope he would ask them out, her included, though at barely eighteen, she hadn't sparked his interest. Until... She shook her head, banishing the image of that one night she'd tried so hard to forget, a night he obviously had.

As he walked toward her, Reese stared, obviously searching for her in the recesses of his mind. His lips twitched, as if he almost wanted to smile but figured it was inappropriate. He wiped his hand down the side of his jeans and held it out to her. "I can't believe it. Is it really you, Abby?"

She refused his handshake—a small act of defiance to let him know she was aware of his role in this travesty of justice tonight. "It is," she said, her voice harsh. "And I've arrived just in time, it seems."

"Come to finish me off, did ya, Burkett?" Huey muttered. He tugged on Abby's arm, getting her full attention. "Don't leave the room, Abigail. I'm going to need a witness."

"That won't be necessary, Huey," Reese said, twisting a ball cap in his hands. "I just stopped by to see how you're doing."

"How do you think I'm doing?" Huey said. "You roughed me up pretty good, *Captain* Burkett." He pointed to his eye. "I may lose my vision in this one."

Abby gasped. "Poppy, is that true?"

Reese frowned. "It's not true. I've talked to the doctor. Your dad's going to be fine."

"Lucky for you," Abby said. "If Poppy suffers any permanent injury because of what you did…"

Reese scratched the back of his head. "Abby, can I talk to you in the hallway?"

She glared at him with all the bravado she could muster. "I don't think that's necessary."

"Give me five minutes, Abby, please."

She looked at her dad, who reached for the TV remote and punched up the volume a couple of notches. "Go ahead," he said. "But don't believe a word he says. He tried to arrest me today and it got ugly. That's the truth of it."

Reese shook his head. "I'm sorry, Huey. I apologized to you earlier, and I'm apologizing again. I didn't want you getting hurt. You can't think that I did."

"Don't ask me what was going on in your head, I just know what I felt when you attacked me. And I got the bruises to prove it."

Reese stretched out his arm. "Abby?"

"Five minutes." She stepped ahead of him, then walked a few feet down the hall.

"Can we find a place to sit and talk?" he asked.

She stayed where she was. "This is okay. I don't want to be too far away in case Poppy calls me."

"Fine." Reese tucked the ball cap under his arm and ran his fingers through his hair. Strands fell onto his forehead, and Abby locked her gaze on the nurses' station rather than stare at him. "I know how this must look to you," he began.

"No, you don't," she said, focusing on his face again. "Because if you did, you wouldn't be here. You'd be out trying to hire a lawyer."

"I don't need a lawyer, Abby. What happened was unfortunate, but there was no physical abuse."

She didn't respond, letting him squirm. "Since you're here, I assume Loretta called you."

She nodded. "Thank goodness."

"Right. Anyway, then she told you that Huey's been starting fires on his property, which is an escalation of his other irritating antics."

"And I'm sure that, as a representative of the police force, you did your duty and warned him to stop."

"I did. Several times."

"And he cooperated?"

"For now, yes. But it's only been a few days. I also told him to get rid of a pile of burned, potentially toxic substances that remained from his last bonfire. The stuff is offensive to his neighbors. It stinks."

Abby remained silent. She couldn't very well argue the point. She'd experienced the foul odor herself.

"Anyway, responding to a complaint call from another resident of Southard Street, I went back to Huey's place today and discovered that he had dumped the mess at the edge of his yard, with most of it spilling onto the street. That's illegal dumping, violation of code number—"

"Never mind," she interrupted. "I'm not arguing with you about minor infractions my father may have committed. I want to know why you manhandled a senior citizen, a man at least thirty years older than you."

"I'm getting to that."

She glanced at her wristwatch. "You'd better hurry. You've only got two minutes left."

When he glared at her, she backed up a step. Perhaps she was hitting too hard.

"I told Huey I was going to arrest him. He deserved it, and damn it, Abby, I could *still* arrest him."

"If you think you're intimidating me with your threats, Reese, you're wrong. I'm not the teenage girl who left this island years ago. I've experienced a few things—"

He held up his hand. "I don't think for a minute you're that same girl, Abby. I'm hoping you're ready to hear a *reasonable* explanation for what happened."

Reasonable? Abby quickly tamped down her anger by mentally counting to ten. Was he insinuating that her behavior thirteen years ago hadn't been reasonable?

"In typical Huey fashion," Reese continued, "your father refused to get in the car and come down to the station."

Abby had no defense for that charge. She knew her father too well.

"He stood there over that trash like he was king of his self-made mountain, and wouldn't budge. In fact, he even said that if I wanted him in the patrol car, I'd have to drag him into it."

Abby could almost hear her dad's voice.

"That did it, Abby. After I'd warned him time and again about breaking the laws in Key West, I'd reached my limit. I stepped around the trash heap, grabbed his arm and started to pull—gently, mind you—pull him to the car."

"And what happened?"

"He yanked free, stumbled, slipped on something gooey at the edge of the yard and fell. Unfortunately, his head hit the mailbox, and that's how he got the black eye. The other bruises and the concussion? Collateral damage, I suspect."

She waited a moment, tapped her toe against the floor and said, "That's the story you're sticking with?"

Reese raised his hands. "Abby, that's the story. Period. I called an ambulance, and the rest you know."

She would definitely confirm this version with her

father. In the meantime, she made a great show of checking her watch again. "We're done here," she said.

Reese reached out as if to touch her arm. She stepped away and he dropped his hand. "I'm sorry it happened," he said. "That's why I'm here tonight—to make sure Huey's all right."

"And you have," she said. "You're free to go and celebrate Thanksgiving."

"Celebrating is the last thing on my mind," he said. "But I will go."

He walked to the elevator. Once inside, he pulled on the baseball cap and stared at her from under the bill. Then the doors closed, and Abby drew the first normal breath she'd taken in more than five minutes. But at least the worst was over. She'd seen Reese again and she hadn't melted or fainted or even babbled. She'd stood her ground pretty well. Now, though, as she went back to her dad's room, she realized that nearly every limb of her body was trembling. She'd have to work on controlling that reaction.

Jeopardy had ended. The TV was silent. "Buzz the nurse, Abby," Huey said. "Earlier they told me I could go home if I had somebody to observe me through the night. I guess you've got a good enough pair of eyes, so I want out of this place."

"Okay, Poppy. I'll see if I can arrange for your discharge."

He swung his legs over the side of the bed. "So what'd you think of Burkett after all these years?" he asked. "He's a piece of work, isn't he? Officious son of—"

"Let's not talk about that now," she said. "Let's just get you home. Those two turkey dinners I brought might still be edible."

CHAPTER THREE

ON FRIDAY MORNING, Abby raked dried leaves and twigs into a large pile. Somewhere under this mess that used to be her front yard, grass had to exist. And if it didn't, she'd plant seeds, fertilize and hope for the best.

After scooping part of the pile onto her rake, she dumped the refuse into a garbage can. Thank goodness the trash collector she'd phoned earlier had removed the burned debris from Southard Street. Abby considered the money well spent, since Reese wouldn't have anything to complain about for a while. She wondered why her father hadn't called the trash man himself. Did Poppy not have thirty dollars?

She'd just resumed her raking when the window to the second-story master bedroom opened and her father stepped onto the balcony, a cup of coffee in hand. She'd checked on him several times during the night, and he'd slept well, almost as if he hadn't a care in the world.

"Good morning, Poppy," Abby called up to him. "How are you feeling?"

He rested his elbows on the railing and gave her a robust smile. "Fine, but what are you doing down there? It's barely eight o'clock, way too early for you to be making all this racket."

She glanced at what she'd accomplished in the past hour. "This yard won't rake itself."

"But I don't get up this early. I have to work today."

She leaned on the rake handle and reined in her impatience. Unless his routine had changed, and she doubted it had, hours would pass before he pulled his vendor's cart from the side of the old theater building where he stored it, and set up his souvenir business in Mallory Square. "We'll decide about you going to the square later. It'll depend on how you're feeling then. Besides, you don't work until sundown, and the festivities are over by nine o'clock."

"That doesn't mean I want my daughter disturbing my rest before I'm ready to get up."

"Funny, but I was thinking that if you're feeling better, you could help out." She pointed to the veranda, where she'd stacked assorted lawn tools. "I brought two rakes from the carriage house."

"I'd help you, but I've got this bad eye. Keeps me a bit off-kilter, if you know what I mean. I hope someone comes along to give you a hand, though, baby girl." He pointed a shaky finger. "Only, not *that* someone."

A blue-striped Key West patrol car rounded the corner of Duval and Southard Streets. Abby couldn't see the identity of the driver, but her heart leaped to her throat just the same. When the car stopped directly behind her Mazda, Huey let loose a few choice words and disappeared into the house, leaving Abby to face Reese, who was stepping out of the cruiser.

Dressed in a standard police uniform, he walked toward her. "I hear Huey came home last night. How's he doing?"

"He's okay."

Reese gave her a lopsided smile. "Then you're not going to sue me or the department?"

Once she'd had a chance to consider Reese's explanation, Abby had reached the conclusion that his story was probably closer to the truth than her father's. Huey's version had included such colorful phrases as "rough-necked bully" and "power-hungry tyrant," while he referred to himself as "innocent victim." But not knowing Reese's reason for showing up this morning, she simply said, "I'm keeping my options open."

Reese smiled again and glanced around the yard. "I see the trash has been removed."

She gave him a smug look. "Of course. We're law-abiding residents of Key West, Reese. Ones who should not have to be fearful of being arrested."

He nodded. "Nope. Not anymore. Not about this, at least."

"Gee, it's nice that the police department is sending out one of its finest to follow up with surveillance of some of the most dangerous citizens."

"That's not why I'm here—exactly," he said.

"Oh?"

He held out his hand. "You wouldn't shake with me last night. I thought I'd try again." When she didn't move, he added, "It's been years, Abby."

She relented, clasped his hand and stared at the long fingers wrapped around hers. Bits of twigs and soil stuck to their joined palms. She pulled her hand back and wiped it against her jeans. He did the same. "Cleaning the yard, I see."

She swiped her rake across the dirt. "You cops don't miss a clue, do you?"

Reese folded his arms over his chest. "So how have you been?"

How have I been? Abby marveled at how absurdly casual his question was in light of what her life had been like since she'd last seen him. But of course, Reese never thought of that night. He'd had thirteen years to forget. She'd had thirteen years to remember. And regret.

She answered blandly, though her heartbeat pounded in her ears, nearly deafening her. "Fine." Ironically, in spite of the churning in her stomach now, that was mostly true— or should be. She had a fulfilling job, many friends and nice neighbors. And past relationships that didn't linger over-long in her mind when they ended. She had offers for dates that she sometimes accepted. In fact, her life was so busy she didn't allow herself to think about what was missing in it or what had gone wrong.

He looked toward the house, his features indicating a sort of benign acceptance. "I know Loretta called you. I'm sorry for putting both of you in the middle of this problem with your father."

Abby's back immediately stiffened—an involuntary reaction she experienced when dealing with anyone who even hinted that something might be wrong with Huey. "There's no problem. Poppy seems okay to me. But if it makes you feel any better about interfering in people's lives, I can tell you that we're working on a few things."

"I don't want this situation to get blown out of proportion, Abby. I have a job to do. You know that, don't you?"

She pretended to concentrate on her work. "I wonder how many acts of aggression have been committed under the guise of that excuse."

He started to respond, but she added, "It's okay, Reese. You have to protect the people of Key West from the threatening presence of a confused senior citizen. It must be a mammoth responsibility."

He rubbed his thumb over his clean-shaven chin and stared at her a moment, as though trying to decide if her sarcasm was for real. After a moment, he said, "I can't imagine why we haven't run into each other in the seven years since I've been back."

"I don't return to the island often," she said. *At least, I haven't in the past seven years.*

"How long you planning to stay this visit?"

She glared at him determinedly. "As long as it takes to get the authorities off my father's case."

His lips curled into a genuine grin. "It's a great time of year to be here. Decorations are going up on Duval Street and Mallory Square today. Plans are under way for the Christmas boat parade. You'll see a lot you remember about the holidays, plus some new additions."

"Can't wait," she said. How nice for Reese to chat about holiday decorations as if he weren't on a one-man mission to pester Huey into having the worst Christmas ever.

Deciding they'd had enough small talk, Abby was about to release Reese from this obligatory visit when her father shouted, "Scram!" A single word delivered from the veranda with enough force to approximate a shot from a rifle.

Startled, Abby spun around. Reese, seemingly uncon-cerned, took a slow step toward the porch. "'Morning, Huey," he said.

"Get off my property, Burkett!"

Huey filled the front entrance. His old shotgun rested against his right elbow, the barrel pointed toward the porch floor.

Abby rushed to him. "Poppy, what are you doing?"

He had the good sense to set the weapon against the door frame. "Reminding certain people that this is Vernay property."

She grabbed the gun and put it out of his reach. "Do you always greet visitors by threatening them with firepower?"

"Mostly just pain-in-the-ass police captains." He stared at her, obviously noting her shocked expression. "It's not loaded, Abby. I keep it for show."

She opened the breech of the shotgun he'd taught her to use years ago, and looked down the barrel. To her relief, he was being truthful. It was empty. "Someone could see you with this thing and get the wrong impression."

"No, they wouldn't," Huey said, his good eye narrowed at Reese. "They'd get just the impression I want them to have."

Huey appeared determined to make her efforts on his behalf impossibly difficult. She took the gun inside the house and came back to the porch. "Reese, I didn't know about this."

He shrugged. "Don't worry about it. He's got the proper paperwork for that old thing, and everybody's aware that he doesn't have shells for it."

"That you flatfoots know about, anyway," Huey said. "Just because you sent Loretta over here to search doesn't mean she found every bit of contraband." When Abby started to protest, he waved off her concern and whispered, "Keep your cool, Abigail. If I even have bullets, I don't remember where they are."

Reese looked down at the sidewalk and shook his head. Abby couldn't help sympathizing with his plight for just that moment. Huey didn't make keeping the peace on Southard Street easy.

"You folks have a nice morning," Reese said, heading

back to his squad car. "You need anything, just call the station."

"That'll be the day," Huey couldn't resist replying.

STILL SHAKING FROM a tumult of emotions she'd hoped not to experience, Abby sat on the porch steps and dropped her head in her hands. "For heaven's sake, Poppy, that whole thing with the shotgun was embarrassing."

Huey leaned against a support pole and looked down at her. "Don't be embarrassed by anything having to do with Reese Burkett. That man ruined your life."

She sighed. "He didn't ruin anything. My life is perfectly fine." *As long as I don't allow my thoughts to go back more than twelve years.*

"Well, he ruined mine, and I'd hate to think you were having any romantic notions about him."

She turned her head to give her father a cold stare. "Don't be ridiculous."

"He's the wrong guy for you to be fantasizing about."

"I am not fantasizing about Reese. For you to even suggest such a thing is insulting and demeaning." Abby wasn't sure how Huey's suggestion was either one of those things. Nor was she completely honest when she said she didn't fantasize about Reese. When a woman went to the lengths she had over the past years to avoid a man, it was a safe bet that she fantasized about him plenty. Just maybe not in a good way.

Huey pulled a wicker chair close to the edge of the porch and sat. "Ab, while we're being so truthful…"

Were they?

"I'm still wondering why you're here so much before Christmas. You're not having trouble at work, are you?"

"No. Everything is fine at work. I left a few of my teen pregnancy cases in limbo, but the girls can call me or any of the other counselors anytime. They know that."

Huey nodded, seeming to accept that explanation. "And why are you staying so long?"

She turned on the step to see him clearly. "You're almost giving me the impression that you don't want me here for a full month."

He raised his hand. "Nope. That's not it. If it was up to me, I'd have you move back here permanently. We have babies who need good families in the Keys, too. I'm just thinking that your mother might have called you with some cock-and-bull story about me having some problems with Reese."

"Poppy…"

"I can handle Reese. I can take care of anybody who comes on this property."

She thought of the shotgun. "A few minutes ago I saw how you treat trespassers."

"You're damn right, baby girl. This half acre is Vernay land. Always will be. Your mother had no business involving you."

"She's worried about you."

"The hell she is." He lit a cigarette and took a long drag. "I'm glad you're here, Abigail, but I'm starting to believe that you've bought into your mother's hysteria about the way things are with me."

Abby leaned toward him. "I'm not so sure it's hysteria, Poppy. Your confrontation with Reese yesterday convinced me that there are problems. I'm here to help, and if that means both of us standing up to Reese, then I'm with you all the way."

He frowned. "So *now* you're ready to square off with Reese?"

"Yes, now. And if this is some veiled accusation about how I handled the past, I've warned you before not to bring it up."

He shrugged. "Consider it forgotten. For now."

Abby stood. "I'll make you some breakfast."

She felt the press of familiar feelings of guilt as she went into the house. She knew the blame for what had happened thirteen years ago lay mostly on her shoulders. She was the one who had made the crucial decision.

REESE CALLED THE STATION and told the sergeant on duty that he'd be a few minutes late. The previous half hour with Abby had left him shaken. He'd gone over to see if he could make things right between the Vernays and himself. After all, Huey had been hurt on Reese's watch, and he could just imagine how Abby viewed the incident. Fortunately, Huey's injuries were minor, but they wouldn't have happened at all if Reese hadn't shown up and tried to force the guy into the patrol car. Cops often made tough decisions that they either had to rationalize or learn to live with later.

He headed north on Route 1 toward Burkett's Paradise Marina. If anyone understood the pressures a cop lived under, it was Frank Burkett. Though he'd given up the job years ago, he still felt a strong kinship with the guys on the force.

Reese parked in the marina lot next to his father's beefed-up Ford pickup, which was used for hauling boats. He got out of the patrol car and walked into the pristine blue-and-white metal building that combined a full-service mechanics area with a sales department that stocked every imaginable device for the avid boater, fisherman or recreational water enthusiast.

Ellen Burkett was behind the cash register, cashing out a customer who'd loaded up on prerigged trolling lines and plastic lures. Frank sat at the end of the counter, a cup of coffee steaming in front of him. "Hey, son," he called out. "What's going on in town? Rounding up any bad guys?"

Frank started every conversation with a question about Reese's job as a cop. He never began by saying how many boats he'd rented out, or if the billfish were running. Reese knew why his father had quit the force. Ellen had wanted him to. She'd claimed the stress was getting to her and she was tired of worrying about him every time he put on his uniform and left the house. Deep down, Reese knew his mother had always hoped her husband would be more than a patrol cop. She'd got her wish. Now he was the owner of the biggest marina on the island. And he spent every morning sitting and drinking coffee.

Reese ambled up to the counter. "Haven't run into any bad guys today," he said, "unless you count Huey Vernay. I was just at his place."

Ellen spared a glance in Reese's direction before returning her attention to the customer.

Frank stirred his coffee. "How's Huey doing? I heard on my scanner yesterday that the paramedics were called out to his house."

Frank listened to his home scanner to keep up with what happened on the island. Reese frowned. No doubt about it. His dad had been a good cop, and a happier man when he was on the force. In fact, Reese had been disappointed in him when he'd given in to Ellen's demands. Even as a kid, Reese had known that a man shouldn't stop doing what he was put on earth to do, just to please somebody else.

Reese had ignored his mother's pleas and become a cop

himself. Public service ran in his and his dad's veins. Reese, however, wouldn't give up his place in the department for anything. Especially now that he'd earned the position of captain of the Patrol Operations Bureau. He hoped to be chief someday.

"Reese?" his dad said. "Is Huey okay?"

"Oh, yeah. He just took a tumble in his front yard and got a black eye."

Frank shook his head. "Poor guy. It never gets any easier for him."

Ellen finished her transaction and came up to them. "Don't waste your sympathy on Huey Vernay," she said. "Have you forgotten that he's the one who told the police about Reese's involvement with those immigrants?"

"No, we haven't, Mom," Reese said. "But let it go. It happened years ago."

She sniffed. "I'm afraid I'm not so forgiving. Huey's motives when he turned you in had more to do with getting even with the Burketts than doing his civic duty. Besides, he brings all his misfortune on himself."

Frank conceded her point with a nod. "I suppose, but it's still a shame. He's likable enough if you peel away that crusty exterior."

Ellen busied herself clearing away Frank's coffee cup and wiping nonexistent stains from the counter. "Actually, we may not have to worry about Huey much longer," she said.

Reese stared at her. "What do you mean?"

"I heard something at city hall the other day. If Huey doesn't pay his back taxes, they're going to auction off his house. If we're lucky, maybe he'll move away."

Reese stopped her by placing his hand over hers. "Are you serious?"

"Absolutely. He owes a small fortune."

"And you just found out about this?"

"I had heard rumors," she said. "But now it's the year end. The county always does property appraisals about this time. Huey's taxes have shot up like everybody else's. And he still owes last year's payment and some from the year before."

Her husband stood. "Ellen, you didn't tell me any of this."

"Well, now you know, Frank. I say it's good news. That old house of Huey's is an eyesore, and the Community Improvement Board can't get him to do anything. This is what he deserves. Besides, we should worry about ourselves. Our taxes are going up, as well. Yours, too, Reese. Wait till you get the bill."

Reese rubbed his forehead. "Abby's not going to be happy when she hears this."

Ellen looked at him. "Abby? What's she got to do with this? Is she here?"

"Yep. I just left her in the front yard, raking up stuff from last summer's storms."

His mother's eyes widened. "I didn't know Abby was coming to town."

"Loretta called her to help out with Huey."

Ellen crossed her arms. "She's got quite a job there. I hope you don't get mixed up with that bunch, Reese. The whole lot of them are trouble. Loretta taking up with Huey's brother, Huey acting like a crazy man… How long is Abby staying?"

"I didn't ask her. But if what you say is true, she's got more worries with Huey than just his code violations."

Leaving the marina, Reese wondered if Abby had heard about the taxes. She probably hadn't, since Ellen knew everything on the island before anyone else found out, and he figured Huey wouldn't have told her.

Reese pictured Abby's reaction when she learned the news, and he decided to check his mother's facts on his own. Then he'd take an even bigger step. He'd tell Abby himself. She already resented his interference in Huey's life, but she had to believe she could trust him. He wasn't that wild guy she'd known years ago. He was a cop now, not a crusader who ignored the law.

He sat in his truck a minute, looking over the water, hoping the panorama of a glass-smooth Gulf would calm him. Not today. Not when Abby's troubles were on his mind. She'd stood right up to him this morning, staunchly denying that Huey had any problems.

He remembered that proud stubbornness from when she'd been in high school. She always kept herself apart from everyone. Apart and above. He'd never once heard of Abigail Vernay breaking the rules or getting into trouble. She'd been a straight-A student and always seemed to possess a fierce determination to succeed despite not having a lot of support from home. When Abby was just a kid, Loretta had tried to be a good mother to her, stretching limited dollars every way she could. But Huey had always managed to screw up.

Reese recalled Loretta's saying that Abby worked in social services in Atlanta. He figured she'd be tops at whatever she did.

He cranked up the engine on the patrol car and smiled. In his youth, he'd pulled a lot of stunts he wasn't proud of. Some of them he would arrest himself for now. And a couple of them, including that one brief encounter with Abby, came back to haunt him sometimes. But he'd bet that Abby didn't have much in her past to be ashamed of.

CHAPTER FOUR

FORTY-FIVE MINUTES AFTER Reese's unexpected visit, Abby stacked the breakfast dishes in the drainer and tried, unsuccessfully, not to think about him. She'd heard of some significant events in Reese's life over the years. Her mother had told her when he'd married, and then when he'd divorced, seven years ago. Abby didn't know the details, just as she didn't know if he was involved with anyone now. One thing she told herself. If Reese was in a serious relationship, she shouldn't care.

She hung the dishrag over the sink and looked out the window. Why in heaven's name was she wasting even a moment of thought on a man she'd sworn she'd gotten over completely? Unless she hadn't.

If only she'd been smarter all those years ago! She wouldn't be wasting brain cells on him now.

Grateful when her cell phone rang, she went to the kitchen table, where she'd left it. She recognized the caller's name and pressed the connect button as her concern mounted. "Alicia?"

"Miss Vernay? I'm sorry to call you…." The teen's thin voice trembled.

"Don't be. I gave you my number so you could use it if you needed to. Is something wrong? Is everything okay with the baby?"

"Yes, the baby's growing fine."

"Then are you rethinking your decision about the adoption?"

"I have to. Things have changed."

Abby sat in the closest chair and imagined the anguish on Alicia's pale face, the sadness in her big brown eyes. "But when I left, you'd made up your mind. You were going to keep the baby."

"That was when Cutter agreed to help me raise it."

Abby pressed her fingertips against her forehead. She'd heard this story too many times. "What happened, Alicia? Did he back out?" She hoped not. Alicia's boyfriend had been in trouble with the law a couple of times, but the prospect of becoming a dad seemed to be turning him around.

"No, ma'am." Alicia hiccupped—the prelude to what Abby knew would end in sobs. "He got arrested last night. He st-stole a car."

"Oh, no. That's not his first offense."

"It's his third. He's in jail right now. They aren't going to let him out." Alicia was crying. "I've got no choice, Miss Vernay. I've got to give up this baby. Otherwise my daddy's going to throw me out."

For just a moment, Abby considered that being thrown out of a ratty trailer sitting on cinder blocks on the outskirts of Atlanta might not be a bad thing. But she didn't say that. The single-wide was the only home Alicia Brown had ever known. And other than the group homes Abby sometimes sent girls to—an option Alicia had already rejected—Abby didn't have any other housing suggestions for her and her baby.

"Can you find me a family, Miss Vernay? A good family to take my baby?"

"You're at four months now, right?"

"Yes."

"We've got a little time. I want you to think about this very carefully. You need to use the best decision-making skills you have." Abby realized the near futility of what she was suggesting. When a vulnerable sixteen-year-old girl found out she was pregnant, her world fell apart. Yet that was when she had to make the most crucial decisions.

"I'm just a phone call away, Alicia," Abby said. "We can spend as much time as you want going over your options. I can try to locate a foster home for you. You can apply for work-study programs. I can guide you to some fine state-run child care facilities…."

"I've made up my mind. I don't want to do this without Cutter. And I want a closed adoption."

As many times as Abby had counseled young girls that giving up a baby was a personal and critical decision, as many times as she'd told them they had to make the decision based on their emotions, needs and expectations, she would never advise one of them to choose closed adoption. Even Abby, thirteen years ago, hadn't picked that option.

She approached the issue carefully now. "You know what that means, Alicia? You won't ever see your baby again. You won't know where he's gone. You'll never know what he looks like or what he becomes."

Alicia drew a trembling breath. "It's the way I've got to do this, Miss Vernay. I have to say goodbye to this baby and be done with it. I just need you to find a family. And I need it to be somebody who'll pay my doctor bills. With Cutter in jail…"

"Okay. That won't be a problem. I have more than forty families on my list at the moment."

"You think I'm being selfish, don't you?"

The desperation in the girl's voice almost brought Abby to tears. "No, honey, I don't. What you're doing is one of the most unselfish acts a mother can do for her child. I just want you to be sure." She waited until Alicia's sobs subsided. "I'll have one of the other counselors in the office begin the match for your child and the perfect parents today."

"Thanks."

"But there's time. If you change your mind—"

"I won't."

"Are you still going to school?"

"Yeah."

"Okay, good."

"Nobody can tell yet."

"Don't lose this number. You call anytime, day or night."

Alicia disconnected and Abby slid her phone into her pocket. She walked through the house to the front door. Huey had gone upstairs to rest. She should have appreciated the solitude, but the quiet only gave her more opportunity to think about the Alicias in the world.

Abby was getting better about accepting these stories as facts of life. And she was definitely grateful that she had the knowledge to help so many troubled teens through one of the most difficult times of their lives. She was relieved when she watched a birth mother come to terms with her future and take her baby home. She was equally happy when a birth mother agreed to a fair open-adoption plan with eager adoptive parents. Happy endings existed, and Abby considered herself lucky to be able to participate in them.

She hadn't felt so lucky thirteen years ago. And she hadn't experienced a happy ending.

Had she been in Atlanta, Abby would have started to

work immediately on Alicia's plan. In Key West, her home for years, she didn't know what to do, so she walked outside and looked for a diversion, something to take her mind off the place where it so often returned.

In a few minutes a 1965, canary-yellow Mustang convertible pulled in front of Vernay House. Abby ran down the steps to the car and popped open the passenger door. "Mom!"

Loretta jumped out and enclosed her in a fierce hug. Wrapped as tightly as a twisted ficus tree, the two women swayed together, giggling and sniffling and carrying on as if they hadn't spoken to each other in years, when in reality they'd talked twice last night. Through Abby, Loretta had gotten Reese's interpretation of Huey's injuries, and had in fact supported his theory.

Finally, she stepped back to get a mother's-eye view of her baby. "You look wonderful, sweetie…considering."

"Right. Sure I do."

Phil Vernay came around the front of the car and gave her a peck on the cheek. "How you doin', cupcake?"

She squeezed his hand. Phil was a good man. While she was growing up, he'd been a supportive and loving uncle. It had taken a few years, but Abby had slowly accepted Phil in Loretta's life, and now she appreciated how happy he made her mother. She couldn't resent Loretta's decision to leave Huey. Happiness was hard to find, and Loretta and Phil had made a life together. Unfortunately, Huey had never let the past go.

"I'm doing okay, Uncle Phil," she said. "How's everything over at the Pirate Shack?"

"Same as always," he said. "Thank the Lord."

Loretta jutted her thumb toward the house. "Has the bear wakened yet?"

"Oh, yeah. We've already had a close encounter of the Reese kind this morning."

Loretta grabbed Abby's arms and looked deep into her eyes. "Oh, honey, running into Reese can't be easy for you."

"It's not so bad," she said. "In fact, it was probably good that he showed up at the hospital last night. At least this morning I'd already gotten over the initial shock of seeing him. I didn't fall apart, and a few minutes ago Poppy didn't shoot him."

Loretta pointed to the porch. "Speak of the devil."

"For Pete's sake," Huey hollered. "Can this day get any worse?" He stomped down the steps and stood with his fists on his hips. "Doesn't the *good brother* have some kegs to tap and fritters to fry?"

Abby winced. She knew Uncle Phil was here to please her mother. This reaction from Poppy would only antagonize Phil.

"Nice shiner, Huey," Loretta said.

Phil, a younger, softer, beardless version of his brother, leaned on the hood of the car he cherished, and glared. "It's not ten o'clock yet, Huey. Even the worst of the worst on this island don't start drinking this early."

"Then get off my land and go irritate somebody else until it's time to fire up that week-old grease."

Phil shook his head, walked around the front of the car and got in. "Come on, Loretta. We're leaving." He smiled at Abby sympathetically. "Sorry, cupcake. I'll see you later—someplace where the air's a little easier to breathe."

Loretta tugged Abby toward the car. Before getting in, Loretta whispered, "So what did you think of Reese? How did he look to you after all this time?"

"Don't ask, Mom. I'm just glad I'm not stupid and eighteen again."

Loretta glanced up at Huey, who was tapping his foot impatiently. "Oh, sweetheart, even when we grow up, we can still be stupid."

AN HOUR BEFORE SUNDOWN, the migration toward Mallory Square began. Cars, bicycles, motor scooters and pedestrians headed along the narrow streets of Old Town toward the harbor to enjoy the decades-old celebration of sunset in Key West. And Huey roused himself from the ancient wicker rocker on the veranda and went inside to get his keys.

"I'm going with you," Abby said, grabbing a ball cap from the hook by the front door.

"You don't have to. I feel fine, and I'll only be two or three hours, depending on the crowd. I'll call when I'm through, and you can meet me at the Bilge Bucket for supper. My treat."

"The Bilge Bucket idea is fine, but I'm still going with you. I just brought you home from the hospital last night."

"I don't need any help. I've been selling the same crap for years. Having you alongside me won't change the profits any."

Abby wanted to argue that point. Considering Huey's usual personality, she thought a friendly smile at his vendor's cart might increase revenues. He soon had to pay the fines for starting the fires, and she suspected he didn't have the money for it. "I'm not taking no for an answer," she said, holding the front door open. "After you."

To save time, they took Whitehead Street instead of tourist-packed Duval, and pulled into a small private lot next to the old Customs House, where Huey had enjoyed free parking for years. Thank goodness the Vernay name still drew some perks. There were probably days when Huey's entire profit from sales would barely cover the fee at the public lot.

They walked the short block to the local theater building and located his mobile cart. With its large pair of wooden wheels and center post for stability, the sturdily built conveyance resembled a gypsy's wagon. Years earlier, Huey had skillfully painted the sides with bright, tropical colors meant to look like waves crashing along the shore. Now the designs were barely recognizable and the paint had faded to muted blues, yellows and pinks. The sign in the center of the whimsical peaked roof was still legible, however: Tropical Delights of the Conch Republic.

Huey released the padlock securing the cart to a fence post and hung the chain on a hook at the back of the cart. Then he lifted the twin posts on the front, one in each hand, and, rickshaw-style, strutted briskly toward the square, with Abby keeping pace. His inventory, secured behind locked side panels, rattled and clanked as he moved.

The harbor area teemed with activity as they approached. Crowds gathered in semicircles along the wide paved dock, where street performers with animal acts, comic routines and acrobatic skills vied for the attention of tourists with fat wallets. The entertainment was free, but each performer had baskets set up around his designated "stage," clearly indicating that tips were appreciated.

Reese had been right. Town maintenance crews had turned the square into a holiday wonderland. Streetlamps, curved at the top, had been wrapped with red and white ribbons to resemble candy canes. Lights decorated all the hotels, and fences and patio umbrellas displayed a riot of traditional Christmas colors. Nothing about Key West at this time of year even hinted of understatement. During the holidays every public building twinkled with multicolored bulbs and flashing signs that screamed, in case anyone should doubt it, This is Key West, and We're Making Merry.

Huey set his cart in his usual spot, back from the performers where mobile vendors like himself offered everything from Key West lemonade to handcrafted jewelry. He unlocked the panels of his wagon, exposing merchandise on both sides. Then he dropped the wooden boards, creating a level surface where more items could be displayed.

As her father sorted through chipped goods and threw them in a trash bin, Abby arranged the varied and colorful assortment of "stuff" that Huey offered for sale. Hanging from the roof on one side of the cart were dozens of fuzzy coconut heads, painted to resemble scowling, one-eyed pirates. Each was marked Made in China and priced from three dollars to five, depending on the detailing. Shell wind chimes hung from the other side, their hollow-sounding clackety-clack drawing attention in the breeze.

The rest of Huey's inventory was equally garish and also entirely foreign-made. He set up brightly painted ceramic blowfish, ocean-theme salt and pepper shakers, stuffed flamingos, palm tree mugs and conch-shell bells. Six-inch ceramic figures of chubby beachgoers carrying umbrellas and sand buckets added to the eclectic inventory.

Nothing on Huey's cart was priced higher than five dollars. Abby's hopes of improving her father's bottom line plummeted. But when families with children actually stopped and examined his goods, she became encouraged. Perhaps a market for Huey's goodies existed among young parents, who could only afford inexpensive souvenirs.

Unfortunately, her hopes were dashed again when Huey took a rickety folding chair and a pair of binoculars from the back of the cart. He opened the chair, plopped himself in it and held the binoculars up to his face.

"What do you need those for?" Abby asked.

"I use them every night," he said. "I keep thinking something interesting might happen. Hasn't yet, but you never know." He hung the binoculars around his neck and popped up a hat shaped like an umbrella, which he jammed onto his forehead, virtually hiding his eyes. Taking a deep, relaxing breath, he snapped open a newspaper. So much for watching the world. And so much for salesmanship.

Abby walked around the cart, stared down at her father and attempted to be diplomatic. "Ah, Poppy, don't you think you'd sell more if you showed more enthusiasm?"

He glanced up at her. "They'll ask if they want something."

All around them, merchants were hawking their goods, performers were drawing crowds and food vendors were offering free samples. Mallory Square at sunset was an entrepreneur's playground. Yet Huey sat, uninspired and totally uninvolved. Abby frowned. No wonder…

There were more ways to finish that thought than she cared to contemplate.

She tried to fill in the obvious gap in her father's merchandising technique. When browsers approached the cart, she offered to show them individual items. She even sold one little girl a flamingo—a sale that wouldn't have happened had Abby not placed the furry creature in the child's hands. Meanwhile, Huey read the newspaper.

A tense moment occurred when a boy no older than four came up to the cart and tugged on Huey's shirtsleeve. With bright, inquisitive eyes, he pointed to Huey's white beard and asked, "Are you Santa Claus?"

Anticipating a brusque reply, Abby prepared to soothe the child's hurt feelings. Her dad, however, merely dropped the paper to his lap, leaned forward and said, "You think every man with a beard is Santa Claus?"

The little boy smiled and said, "Yes. But why does Santa have a sore eye?"

Huey grunted. "Good question, kid. Reese, the Red-nosed Reindeer, punched me."

The boy giggled. "I thought his name was Rudolph."

Huey gently jabbed the boy in the center of the cartoon on his T-shirt. "Haven't you ever heard of anyone changing his name to protect the guilty?"

"No. What does that mean?"

"Don't worry about it." Huey grabbed a coconut head from a hook and handed it to the boy. "Here. Merry Christmas."

His mother nudged him forward a couple of inches. "What do you say, Trevor?"

"Thanks, Santa." Mother and son headed off toward a performer putting his trained cats through their paces.

Abby stared at Huey for several seconds before saying, "You know something, Poppy?"

He picked up the newspaper again. "Don't go getting all sentimental on me," he warned.

She kissed his cheek. "Okay, but your soft spot is showing."

He placed his hand where her lips had been. "Is not."

She smiled and stuck another head on the empty hook. And then she saw a patrol car slowly pull up to the edge of the harbor. Enough sunlight was left for her to determine that Reese Burkett sat behind the wheel. And he wasn't alone. Someone was in the passenger seat.

A shiver of anticipation, or dread, or maybe even disappointment, worked its way down her spine, and Abby stepped around the side of the cart to be out of sight. But she knew Reese had seen her. She sensed him watching Huey and her, felt his attention by an involuntary curling of her toes in her sandals.

"What are you hiding back there for?" her dad asked.

"I'm not hiding." She pointed. "Isn't that Reese?"

Huey turned in the chair just enough to glance over his shoulder. "Yep. Probably hassling citizens for fun. He ordinarily doesn't work at night, and never at the sunset ritual."

Abby feigned an interest in fuzzy stuffed dolphins and peeked at the car. "Who's with him? It looks like someone with long blond hair."

"You need glasses, Abigail," Huey said. "Long blond ears is more like it."

Abby couldn't resist; she came around the cart for a closer look. Reese was out of the car and coming toward them. A big yellow dog on a short leash trotted obediently beside him.

The twosome stopped at the cart and Reese smiled at Abby. "I thought you might be here with Huey," he said.

Huey made a show of rustling the newspaper. "You're an investigative genius, Burkett," he said. "No wonder you're captain of this illustrious police department."

Reese scowled down at him. "I see you're feeling better."

"You want me to really feel better?"

Reese seemed to think about it before saying, "Sure."

"Tear up your copies of those worthless citations. Then I'll know you mean it."

When Abby nudged the back of his chair, Huey mumbled something she was glad she couldn't hear.

Reese turned his attention to her. "How's business?"

"Fine. Great," she lied. "You were looking for us?"

Reese patted the animal's head, and the dog gazed up at him with huge, adoring eyes. "Just doing rounds."

She couldn't help smiling. The dog was overgrown and clumsy-looking, a definite hug magnet. "Is he yours?"

"Yep."

"What kind is he?"

"A Lab mostly. Name's Rooster."

"Rooster?"

"Yeah. I found him outside one of the restaurants in town. He was chasing after some of the chickens that run over the island. All that squawking and barking was upsetting the business owners."

"That's what I've always said about you," Huey muttered.

Abby shook her head. "Seems like a nice dog."

"He is."

"Well, see you," she said, with a wave of her hand. Only Reese didn't leave.

"Tomorrow's Saturday," he stated. "I'm off on weekends. Would it be okay if I stopped by your place in the morning?"

"Why would you do that?"

"I'd like to talk to you about something."

"What's wrong with right now?"

He glanced down at Huey, who was arguing with a few customers over the price of a plastic beach ball. The pregnant woman and her two kids seemed to be winning.

"We should keep this between the two of us."

Abby shrugged with an indifference she didn't feel. What

could Reese possibly have to say that concerned the two of them? Masking her curiosity behind a flip remark, she said, "I guess this means you're not canceling Poppy's fines."

Reese smiled again, this time an indulgent pull of his lips. "I'll see you tomorrow."

"Make it early," she said. "I've got errands to run."

He tugged on the leash. "No problem. I'm an early riser."

The yellow dog padded alongside him back to the patrol car, jumped in and took his seat as the passenger. Abby watched them leave the parking lot. She was a long way from admitting to herself that she was relieved that Reese's "date" had long blond ears.

CHAPTER FIVE

AT NINE O'CLOCK SATURDAY morning, a black Ford pickup turned onto Southard and stopped in front of the house. Abby increased her efforts to sand the decorative wrought-iron fence at the sidewalk. She was aware when Reese got out of the truck, but she decided not to acknowledge him right away. Big deal. He'd shown up. He obviously had an ulterior motive.

He strode up to her. "Hey."

She glanced up and continued working. "Hey, yourself."

He held out a tall mug and a plastic pack of accessories. "I brought coffee."

Noticing the trademark *M*, she took the mug and stirred in two sugars. "Martha's. Thanks."

He leaned against the fence. In tan cargo shorts and a green-and-orange University of Miami T-shirt, he was decidedly uncoplike and more like the young college grad who'd brought his reckless behavior and invincible attitude back to the island. The same young man who'd suddenly joined the navy and left Key West without telling her he was going. Not that he'd felt he owed her an explanation back then. He'd made that clear by not calling her after she'd met him on the beach for the encounter that changed her life. After two weeks, she'd given up hoping he would.

"You planning to paint that?" he asked, gesturing at the fence.

"You think it needs it?"

He smiled. "It has for the seven years I've been back."

"Actually, I thought I could talk Poppy into painting." She wrapped sandpaper around a pole and scraped. "I told him I'd rough it up first."

Reese stared at the front door of the house. "So I should expect him to come out any minute and start yelling at me?"

"Nope. He went for doughnuts." She sipped her coffee. "If you have something to say, you'd better get to it."

"Can you stop working on that fence for a minute?"

She stood up, dusted her hands on her shorts. "I'm all yours. Is this going to take longer than the five minutes I gave you at the hospital?"

He crossed his arms. "Great. I'm on the clock again."

She managed a small smile. "Let's sit on the stairs."

They settled side by side on the top step. After a few moments of silence, Reese said, "Abby, I discovered something yesterday—"

She held up her hand, interrupting him, and looked toward the corner. "What's that noise?"

He nodded, indicating he was familiar with the chug of an engine and the now-amplified chirpy voice that filtered through a speaker. "It's the Conch Tour Train," he said. "You remember that."

The Conch Tour Train, famous as *the* way for visitors to see the island and hear its history, rolled onto Southard. The engine, a cross between a kids' amusement ride and an old steam locomotive, pulled five passenger cars down the narrow street. A Christmas wreath blinked from the decorative smokestack. Each open-air tram, trimmed with colorful awnings, was packed with tourists pointing and waving and ignoring the driver's warning to keep their hands safely inside the vehicle.

"A cruise ship docked at Mallory Square this morning," Reese explained. "The tour trains will be steady all day until the passengers reboard."

"What are they doing on this street? We're not part of the tour, are we?"

Reese shrugged. "I really don't know. The guides pick the sites. They drive around to all the spots they think are important because of local color or historical significance." He gazed up at the house. "This *was* the home of Armand Vernay. Your ancestor had quite a reputation during the island's shipwrecking days."

Not this again. While she'd lived in Key West, Abby had struggled to live down the horror stories about her ancestor's misdeeds. And when she wasn't defending the family name for her great-great-great-grandfather, she was defending Huey's reputation as the island's ambitionless eccentric. She cringed when the tour guide spoke.

"Ladies and gentlemen, I urge your attention to your left, to the faded Classic Revival residence nearly hidden behind that pair of old banyan trees. This is Vernay House, built in 1857 by the infamous Armand Vernay. The house, with its interesting and colorful history, has remained in the hands of his descendants since that time."

Enough, Abby thought, mentally waving the guide on. It wasn't to be.

"Armand Vernay was a notorious salvager who braved Atlantic storms to aid vessels that became grounded on the treacherous reefs that border our island. In the 1850s, when

Key West was the richest city per capita in the United States, salvaging was our most profitable industry. The rules were simple. The first wrecker to reach a foundering ship had rights to its cargo, which could be anything from gold, to porcelain, to the finest European leather goods."

Abby's stomach clenched. She stood. *Here we go. More talk about Armand's wicked ways.*

"I didn't know your place was on the tour, Abby," Reese said. "But I'm not surprised. The legend of Vernay House is a good story."

The tram guide waved to him. "'Morning, Officer." He droned on as the train crept by the house like a lazy caterpillar, its passengers staring avidly. "Most of the wreckers were honest men who abided by the laws of salvaging at the time." He chuckled. "Unfortunately, that cannot be said of old Armand."

Abby took a determined step toward the little locomotive. Reese pulled her back.

"Let me go!" she said.

He didn't. "Just cool it a minute. They'll be gone soon."

"A wrecker's first obligation was to save passengers," the guide explained. "Recorded history tells us that the original Vernay was more concerned about rescuing the riches from the hold. He died with the blood of many hapless people on his hands."

Abby seethed with anger but remained in Reese's grasp.

The guide's voice faded as the tram continued down Southard, but she heard the last of his spiel. "They say Armand died a tortured soul in this very house, haunted by the spirits of those he condemned to a watery grave. If you look real close at the windows on the first floor, you might see Armand's great-great-grandson, Hugo Percival Vernay, who lives to this day in a house many people claim is still home to the very first Vernay male."

Abby was thankful Poppy wasn't here. Yet he had to have heard this embellished tale countless times.

The train turned onto Whitehead Street. "Next stop Hemmingway House, home of our most famous former resident…"

Abby drew several deep breaths, but wasn't successful at easing her anger. "I'm surprised Poppy hasn't pointed that stupid shotgun at the tour guides," she said to Reese. "Even *you* wouldn't arrest him for defending his reputation."

Reese grinned. "Well…"

"Don't these guides care about people's feelings?"

"In all honesty, Abby," he said, "I don't think the guide had Huey's feelings in mind. And I doubt he realized you're a relative."

"Still, it seems these tour companies are only interested in making a fast buck."

"Money's a definite motivation," Reese agreed. "But I have to tell you, I've heard that story about Armand's wrecking business since I was a kid. I'm not sure it doesn't have a basis in fact."

"That's ridiculous! What sort of man would let people die while he filled his pockets with booty? Why, Armand would have to have been heartless, thoughtless, selfish…."

Reese's lips quirked. "Yeah. It's hard to imagine a Vernay with those traits."

Abby bit her tongue to keep from calling him a smart-ass. She could understand a lot of Huey's resentment. He had lost his wife to his own brother, a man people on the island liked and respected. He had failed at several jobs. And he lived alone now, wandering around a big old house that, according to legend, was inhabited by ghosts. Not that she believed in spirits, but the idea was a creepy one. "Poor Poppy," she said, giving Reese a pointed glance. "Between the cops bugging him and his poor sales at Mallory Square, he's really gotten himself into a mess."

Reese didn't say anything, but his expression suddenly became almost grave.

"Why are you staring at me like that?" she asked.

"Abby, we need to get back to that talk—now, while Huey's away."

Her instincts warned her that whatever he had to say, she wasn't going to like it. "Okay. Guess there's no avoiding this."

He walked her back to the porch steps. She sat rigidly. "So, out with it."

Reese settled stiffly beside her. "I found out something disturbing. My mother told me she'd heard it, but then I checked the facts for myself."

Abby threaded her fingers together. "What facts?"

"Your father owes back property taxes for last year. Part of the total was paid, but what's left amounts to quite a bit of money. Taxes in Key West have been steadily rising."

Abby knew Huey had no mortgage responsibility for Vernay House. He'd inherited the deed free and clear when his father had died, while Phil got the land where the Pirate Shack stood. But of course, there were other expenses related to owning property. "How much?" she asked, and held her breath, waiting for the answer.

"He owes close to four thousand for last year and the year before, and he'll probably owe a little more than eight thousand for the one coming up. That's a total of—"

"Twelve thousand dollars!" She looked over her shoulder. "For *this* house?"

Reese nodded. "I admit it doesn't seem like much in its present condition. But besides the historical significance of the house, the property it sits on is a valuable piece of real estate." He gazed down the tree-lined street. "Anything in Old Town is worth a lot of money."

Abby immediately began scraping together piles of cash in her head. She had about twelve hundred in her savings account. Uncle Phil probably had a few bucks…. Yet he would never give any of it to Huey, and she couldn't remember one true friend Huey still had in Key West who might offer a loan. "Is Poppy aware of this?" she asked Reese.

"He should be. Several statements were sent to him about his failure to pay the debt. And he should have received a notice about the current amount, due the first of the year. But truthfully, Abby, I suspect Huey lives in a state of altered reality. I don't think he believes anyone would actually take his house away."

"Are you saying he's crazy?" Her antagonism against Reese flared. Just saying those words hurt.

"No, not the way you're imagining. He's competent enough day by day. I just think he refuses to admit that his problems have escalated to this extent. If he doesn't acknowledge the basic facts, then maybe they don't exist."

Abby recalled the stacks of papers, bills, circulars, all sorts of junk mail she'd seen scattered on nearly every piece of furniture inside. Many of the envelopes had never been opened. "Tell me exactly what will happen if he can't pay," she said.

Reese looked at his hands, clasped between his knees. "He'll lose the house. He could have had it taken away by now, but a chunk of the amount owing—a few thousand dollars—was paid in May, and some citizens petitioned the county revenue collector to give him more time." Reese shifted his attention to Abby's face. "The Vernay name still means something around here," he said. "Huey's right about his family's historic connection to the island. But eventually—"

She held up her hand. "I know. I get it."

"Look, Abby, I hate being the one to have told you this. But someone had to."

"Sure. You're just the innocent breaker of bad news."

"Something like that. And there's something else."

Oh, wonderful. "What?"

"There's a committee in town, the Community Improvement Board. They've been urging Huey to fix this place up."

"Urging? I'll bet."

"They even offered to buy the house from him and put it in the hands of the board. The folks on the committee want to restore the place before it's too late, open it to the public."

About this Abby was certain. "Huey would never sell to them."

Reese acknowledged that truth with a nod. "And that's part of the problem. He's not creating a lot of goodwill."

She stood again, her frustration too great for her to remain seated. "For heaven's sake, Reese. This is his home! No one has the right to drive him away from it."

Reese cast his eyes around the yard. "If he doesn't keep up his obligations, then that's not true, Abby."

She paced back and forth in front of the house. Didn't it just figure that Reese Burkett would be the one to deliver this blow?

Mechanically, instinctively, she placed her palm over her flat stomach, as she'd done many times in the past thirteen years. Reese didn't know he had fathered a child.

He hadn't cared enough about her to even call her after that night. He'd never said goodbye. Once he'd left for his tour of duty in the navy, once that one night had been nothing more than a fleeting memory of a drunken binge…

Abby rolled her shoulders, releasing familiar tension. That night had turned out to be Reese's way of dealing with the aftermath of smuggling refugees into Key West. He probably never thought of Abigail Vernay again, except perhaps as she related to her troublesome father.

She'd tried to tell Reese she was pregnant. That her life should be interrupted while he followed his plans, blindly ignorant, wasn't fair. Besides, she'd thought he ought to know. And she'd desperately wanted him to care. But when she went to his house, he was already gone.

What did the Burketts know of adversity, of pain and loss? The Burketts with their successful business, their status in a town that had always accepted and respected them. True, Reese had gone through a divorce, but did that compare with giving up a child? Abby didn't think so. Every day of her life she experienced the anguish of that decision. Every time she received a photo of Jamie from his adoptive parents, she relived the moment he'd been taken from her arms, hours after his birth, by a nurse, and whisked off to someplace in the hospital she'd been advised not to go. Now she didn't know if she believed what adoption counselors like her were urged to tell birth mothers—that it was better to at least say hello before you said goodbye.

She flinched when a pair of hands clasped her shoulders, stopping her from wearing a path in what little vegetation grew in the front yard. Shrugging out of Reese's hold, she spun around to face him. Maybe he wasn't responsible for her father's current problems, but he was at least guilty of harassing him. And he sure as hell wasn't blameless for the heartache in her past.

She stared up into his face. "You told me what you came to say, Reese. Your duty is done. You can go now."

"Look, Abby, if you need to talk, if I can help you clear this up—"

"I don't want your sympathy. I'll handle it," she said.

Abby squared her shoulders when she saw Huey's truck round the corner. She waited for Reese to take his cue and leave. After an uncomfortable moment, he got in his own truck and drove away, passing Huey.

Abby suppressed a sob. *Damn it, Reese,* she thought. *Will I ever get over what happened between us? More to the point, will I ever get over you?*

She picked up the sandpaper and went back to work, determined not to think about him. She had to figure out a way to save this house. Waving to her dad as he pulled into the drive, she muttered, "Merry Christmas, Poppy." The words disappeared into the rasp of sandpaper on metal.

REESE HEADED TO HIS favorite convenience store, on Truman Avenue. He intended to buy a six-pack, run his truck through the car wash so it was clean for his date tonight, then maybe treat Rooster to a romp at the beach. Once he'd established a plan for the rest of the day, he let his mind wander back to the half hour he'd just spent with Abby.

He especially wondered how he could have softened the blow he'd given her. "How do you tell someone they have to cough up twelve thousand dollars or lose their house?" he said to himself.

He didn't really blame her for resenting the messenger. He and Abby had a history, though Reese didn't know how much she remembered about that night. But he figured that the time they'd spent on the beach couldn't have been any girl's dream of a romantic encounter. He regretted what had happened between them, more so now that he'd seen her again. Despite the obvious chip on her shoulder, he liked her. She had the same innocent appeal of the girl he'd watched change through high school, plus the maturity and sensuality of a woman. Little Abby had definitely gotten better with age.

He pulled into the convenience store parking lot, and had just cut his engine when an island patrol car whizzed past, its light bar flashing. The siren wasn't going, so a major emergency wasn't in progress. Probably one of those incidents that were typically Key West. Reese looked at the store entrance and back at the speeding car.

He cranked over his engine again. He wasn't in uniform, and no doubt the officer could handle the problem, but what the heck? Reese wasn't feeling particularly good about the way his meeting with Abby had gone. He could use a diversion. So he left the lot and followed.

The fast-traveling patrol car soon outdistanced him, but when he observed it turn onto South Roosevelt, Reese figured it was headed to Smathers Beach. Minutes later he saw the cruiser parked alongside the beach road, its lights still flashing. He pulled in behind, got out and caught up to the officer trudging through the sand. "What's up, Mark?" he asked.

The officer slowed down, acknowledging Reese's presence. "Creative volleyball," he said.

"Oh." Reese understood. "Clothing optional."

Mark Groves smiled. "It's your day off. Why are you here?"

"Nosy, I guess," Reese said. "I saw you go by, and you know how it is. I hate to miss out on something this exciting." As they approached the volleyball net set up at the far end of the beach, eight young men stopped playing and stared at them. "I think we've been spotted," Reese murmured.

"Yep, here come the killjoys."

A ten-year veteran on the force, Mark followed procedure. He introduced himself first and then Captain Burkett.

"You fellas know how to read, right?" Reese said.

"Sure."

"Then you must have missed that sign over there." Reese pointed to the very legible list of rules for Smathers Beach that stood by the road. "Check out the rule that says, 'No Nude Bathing.'" He stared down at a cooler outside the volleyball court boundary. "It's right under the regulation that prohibits alcohol."

"That's just orange juice," one of the boys said.

"Sure it is. I think I'll have some."

The boy didn't offer. "Come on, officers," he said. "This is Key West, man. Cut us some slack."

"Yes, it is Key West, man. But rules are rules, and you guys are in violation of public decency regulation number…" Reese spouted off something official sounding, since he didn't have any idea what the exact numbers were. "This is a family beach," he added.

"It's early, man," the spokesman said. "And we're way at the end. You see any kids out here?"

Reese didn't. But he did notice a few senior citizens' attention had shifted from health regimens to sightseeing. "Game over, boys," he said. "Get your clothes on and get that cooler off the beach. If I catch you guys down here again, you'd better be sporting some wild Hawaiian knee-length trunks and be chugging smoothies."

"Okay, okay," the young man said. "But what about now? Are you going to ticket us?"

"We'll let it go this time," Reese finally said. "But I'm warning you…"

The boys scrambled for their clothes and cooler. "No problem," one said. "You won't have any more trouble from us."

"Good. Now get going."

Within a minute, every trace of the Florida Keys Nude Volleyball Team had vanished. Reese and Mark headed back to their vehicles. "I'd have ticketed them," Mark said. "Easiest revenue we get in this town other than from parking tags."

"I know, but I can't help comparing these guys with the kind of kid I was way back when." He smiled. "Don't get me wrong. I didn't run around the island shooting moons."

Mark tossed his clipboard onto the passenger seat of the patrol car. "The guys say you're a softy when it comes to our weekend rowdies. They say it's because of the trouble you used to get into."

"The guys would be right. Just ask my dad. He bailed me out a couple of times. Me, the son of a former cop."

"Isn't that always the case?" Mark said.

"Yeah, cops' kids are notoriously rebellious." Reese rested his elbow on the top of his truck. "But I think the reason I got in so many scrapes was that my dad *quit* being a cop when I was thirteen."

"I heard he was a good one," Mark said.

"The best. And he loved it. Wore the uniform with pride." Reese paused, shook his head and then got in his truck. He stopped just short of admitting that he'd never really gotten over his father knuckling under to Ellen's demands. When Frank stopped being a cop, he'd also stopped being the man Reese looked up to unconditionally. Reese loved his dad. And there were a lot of qualities to admire about Frank Burkett. But sticking to his principles, leading the life he wanted, wasn't one of them.

Reese went back to Truman Avenue, picked up that six-pack and drove through the quickie car wash. A few minutes later, he walked into his kitchen and popped the tab on the first beer. Taking it outside, he let Rooster sniff around familiar backyard territory and pick his spot. Then Reese punched in Belinda's phone number at the chamber of commerce office. "Hey, we still on for tonight?"

"I'm planning on it."

They discussed possible destinations and finalized the time. "Oh, one more thing," Reese said. "As a chamber member, you should have been out at Smathers Beach this morning. As a woman, you probably would have appreciated the view. It was definitely a photo-op moment."

"Sounds interesting. Details later, okay? I've got an office full of tourists."

He disconnected and thought about Belinda. Theirs wasn't a serious relationship, but she was fun. And happily independent, just as he was. He'd taken the marriage route once in his life and vowed to be very careful about following the same path again. When a marriage was working, it was great. But when it ended badly, two people were left with lifetime scars. And a blame game that never really had a winner.

He was on his sofa and in the middle of his second beer when he realized that sometime in the past few minutes his mind had switched gears, and he was back to thinking about Abby and that one night they'd spent at the beach. He drank the rest of the beer and tried to recall the details of that encounter. But even two weeks after it had happened, when his life had changed so quickly and decisively—when he sat in the marina van as his father drove him to the Key West airport to catch his flight to Pensacola—his brain had been foggy.

Now, since seeing Abby again, he recalled more than he had then. He remembered that she'd looked unbelievably sexy, with her blond hair waving below her shoulders, sort of the way it did now, only longer. She'd been wearing a cropped blouse that showed a slice of soft pink skin above the hip-hugging waistband of her cutoffs.

She'd been too cute for her own good, and far too sexy for his. He recalled how she'd leaned into him, shyly at first, then with a boldness he'd never have imagined. He'd been wasted, but he knew he'd asked her if she was on the Pill. And he'd asked her age. She told him she'd just had her eighteenth birthday. He'd been relieved. Considering the trouble he was already in, he didn't need to add morality charges to his crimes.

She'd been so willing. Reese had never forced a woman to do anything she didn't want to. And Abby had seemed to want to do it. She'd been sweet-smelling, warm and pliant in his arms. So unlike the girl who'd always come across as cool, aloof, too brainy to associate with mere mortals like the crowd Reese hung out with. It was almost as though she'd been driven to get away from Key West and people like him.

More than a decade had passed since he'd seen Abby. Maybe her resentment to him the past couple of days was due in part to her hatred of him for what they'd done that night. But he sure as hell didn't feel any resentment to her. In fact, if they hadn't gotten off on such bad footing with these problems with Huey…

"What?" He posed the question aloud. "You'd apologize for something that happened years ago?" He scoffed at his own foolishness. "It's way too late for that. She'd see right through a lame attempt to make things right now."

Reese went into the kitchen, set his can on the counter and reached around the back door where he kept Rooster's leash on a hook. "Let's go, boy," he said. "I find myself needing to walk off some frustration all of a sudden, so I hope you can keep up."

CHAPTER SIX

ABBY WAS SHOWERED and dressed by five o'clock, the time Huey had told her he'd be ready to leave for Mallory Square. Saturday was the biggest tourist night of the week. She thought it best not to distract him from making sales by telling him Reese's news about the taxes.

They'd just left the driveway in Huey's truck when Abby's cell phone rang. Since she'd spoken to Alicia earlier in the day and given her the name of the counselor assigned to her case, Abby didn't think this call would be from her. But it could be from any of the other pregnant teens who'd phoned since she'd been in Key West.

Relieved to see she wouldn't be involved in a lengthy counseling session, she connected. "Mom, what's up?"

"Abby, I need you to get over here to the Pirate Shack right away."

"Why? What's going on?"

"Are you with Huey?"

Abby glanced over at him. He was concentrating on his driving and swearing about the traffic. "Yeah."

"Then I can't talk now. Just get over here."

"But we're on our way to Mallory Square."

"I don't care if you're on a mission to the moon. You need to stop at the Pirate Shack. Alone."

That wouldn't be a problem. Huey never stepped over the threshold of his brother's business. "Okay. I'll have Poppy drop me off.

"That was Mom," Abby said after she'd clicked her phone shut.

"What'd she want?"

"She's asked me to stop at the Shack. I'll just be a few minutes, and then I'll walk the rest of the way to the square."

He drove the block off Duval and pulled up in front of the restaurant. "Do you want me to get you something to eat?" Abby asked.

He gripped the steering wheel and stared straight ahead, as if even looking at the establishment would cause him indigestion. "Not unless Phil's giving something away free. I won't put any of my money in his pockets."

She climbed out of the truck. "Suit yourself. We'll eat later."

He left and she went inside. The Shack was nearly empty—not unusual, since the dinner rush hadn't started. In a few hours the restaurant would be packed with mostly locals out for a good time.

Loretta came over immediately and took Abby to a back booth.

Abby sat. "Good grief, Mom, what is this all about?"

"No one will bother us here. Not even Phil. I told him we were discussing girl topics. I've never known a man who didn't cringe at the thought." She motioned to Nick, the bartender. "Can I get you a drink? A beer?"

Suddenly, that sounded like a great idea. "Sure. Whatever's on tap."

Loretta ordered in code by putting up two fingers. Nick

brought two tall frosted mugs. Abby took a long swallow from hers. "Okay, spill," she said.

"I got some bad news about Huey today," Loretta told her. "And guess where the rumor started."

Since Abby knew only a handful of Key West residents these days, and since she herself had heard disturbing news from one of them, she politely offered her suggestion. "Reese, maybe?"

Loretta looked shocked that such an idea could pop into Abby's head. "No. Of course not. Reese would never spread gossip. But you're close. The news came from that bitch who calls herself his mother."

"Oh. Ellen."

"Mrs. My-husband-owns-the-biggest-marina Snoot Nose," Loretta said.

Already sensing the answer, Abby asked, "What did she tell you?"

"*She* didn't tell me anything. Ellen Burkett wouldn't tell me if my clothes were burning."

Obviously, the animosity between the two women hadn't diminished much in thirteen years. "I get the picture," Abby said. "So someone who heard from Ellen told you this news."

"Right." She waved a hand dismissively. "Doesn't matter who. What matters is what."

"And that is…?"

"Your father's going to lose that damn house."

When Abby's expression didn't change, Loretta leaned over the table and studied her eyes. "You know already!"

"Yes. I heard from the saintly Reese, who never gossips."

"If Reese told you, then he was only trying to help."

Abby conceded that point. "He was giving me a heads-up on possible outcomes for Poppy's future."

"Did he tell you how much Huey owes in back taxes?"

Abby nodded, took another swallow of beer.

"Something like twenty-five thousand dollars?"

Abby nearly choked. "Good heavens, no! Now, *that* is gossip. He owes around twelve thousand. Bad enough, but not that bad."

"And I'm guessing Huey hasn't talked with you about this."

"No."

"Is he even aware of the problem? I mean, Huey's always been stubborn about pretending bad news doesn't exist."

"Hmm…your analysis of Poppy is strangely similar to Reese's," Abby said. "I would bet that Poppy doesn't know how bad the situation is. According to Reese, he should have received notices, but Poppy's record-keeping is… well, let's just say his filing system could use a major revamp. I'd bet he hasn't even opened the envelopes."

"Still, Ab, he has to know taxes are due. He's lived in that place his entire life. He must have made payments all along."

"I'm sure he did, when the bills were less. And apparently, one payment was made last May. But his business isn't going well. He's just making living expenses."

"Do you have any idea how much he has in the bank to apply to that bill?"

Abby gave a sarcastic chuckle. "It's my opinion that Poppy is flat broke." She blinked when tears started to form.

Loretta patted her hand. "It's a shame that you're here just when this news breaks," she said. "Even I feel sympathetic to Huey about this one. And I've always maintained that he's a big boy and should solve his own problems." Loretta looked sad, as if she was remembering the past. "Only, he never did," she added.

"Does he have any resources we don't know about?" Abby asked.

"I can't recall any hidden gold mines." Loretta sat back in the booth and blew out a breath. She tapped her fingernail against her mug. After a moment, her eyes widened and she said, "The hell I can't."

"What do you mean?"

"Huey's living with his resources. He's sitting on them, stacking useless junk on them and letting them collect dust."

Abby waited for her to explain.

"That mausoleum is crammed with resources." Loretta grinned. "All we have to do is convince him to part with some of them."

Abby was beginning to follow her mother's line of thought. "You mean sell his belongings?"

"Absolutely. Some of those pieces could be worth a small fortune to the antique dealers who have settled in this town recently. And who knows what's moldering away in the attic."

Instantly absorbed in the plan, Abby smiled. "This is a great idea, Mom. But will Poppy go for it?"

"Not if I suggest it. If you do, though, we've got a shot."

"Okay, I'll do it."

"I can't help you with this, Ab. I've got to work, and Phil would have a fit if he knew I was doing anything that would benefit Huey. But I was thinking, if you need a hand moving things around, Reese would probably be willing—"

"Stop right there, Mom. Forget it. I'm not asking Reese to help with anything. Poppy wouldn't like it, and I don't want to owe Reese any favors."

Loretta sighed. "You know, honey, you've got a bitter side to you that isn't very pleasant."

"What? Mom, this is Reese we're talking about."

"Yes, and I still regret that he didn't handle things differently back then. But he's a good man, Abby. He cares about this island. He's fair and honest—"

"Oh, please." Abby turned on the bench and stared across the empty Pirate Shack. She couldn't believe her mother was listing Reese's virtues.

But Loretta wasn't about to let up. "And I regret that you and I didn't try harder to reach him. We did what we thought was best at the time, and God knows, Jamie has a happy life…."

"Enough, Mom. I am not going to go over this territory again."

"I know you don't want to. You've lived your life pushing this incident to the back of your mind, but, honey, you have to admit that it won't stay there. It comes into your thoughts all the time. I don't want to make you feel bad, but since you're going to be in Key West for a while anyway, I think you should consider telling Reese the truth."

Abby reconnected with her mother's soft blue eyes. "What? Thirteen years have passed. Jamie is twelve years old, and you believe I should tell Reese about him *now?*"

Loretta was resolute. This wasn't the first time she'd thought about this. "Yes, I do. For your sake more than Reese's."

"Are you crazy?"

Her mom smiled. "Some people might argue that I am, but no, I'm not. Consider this from Reese's perspective first. He never had a say in the decision to give Jamie up for adoption."

"I tried…."

"Yes, you did. But Reese was a victim of his mother at

the time. She's never happy unless she's controlling the lives of the men in her family. She would have built a moat around that house of theirs to keep her precious son from hooking up with a Vernay."

Abby scowled at her. "I'm not going over this again. It was my decision. I had plans back then, plans that didn't include a baby. I wanted to go to college, to make something of myself away from this island."

"Of course you did, and I don't blame you. I'm proud of what you've accomplished."

Somewhat mollified, Abby tried to relax. How many times, and how carefully, had she gone over her decision to give up her baby? Now her mother was acting as if that decision hadn't torn her heart in two. "I wasn't in any position to raise a baby," Abby said. "And, Mom, neither were you."

Loretta nodded. "I considered keeping him. I really did. But things had started to sour between Huey and me years before. Ours wouldn't have been a healthy situation to bring an innocent child into."

Abby agreed. "And besides, people on this island would have looked down their noses, saying, 'How like a Vernay to get knocked up. Even the brainy Abigail, who always thought she was better than her family, better than everyone, found her level.'" Loretta's features softened. "I knew, Mom," Abby said. "I knew what people said about me back then."

"Words don't mean a damn thing, Ab. I would have pushed that baby in his stroller down Duval Street as if he were my own, if I could have brought him into a house of love. And I would have paraded him in front of Ellen Burkett's fine stilt home until she closed every expensive drapery in the house."

Wow. There was some bitterness in Loretta, as well.

"But that brings us back to Reese, and you telling him," Loretta said. "I'm not suggesting this for Reese's benefit, although I think he has a right to know the truth. This is for your benefit, so you can cleanse the past of the pain and the guilt." She held up her hand when Abby started to protest. "I understand your guilt, sweetheart. It's been eating you up for years, and it's time to rid yourself of this burden."

Abby swiped at a tear that fell onto her cheek. "No."

"Abby, what do you tell the teen girls you counsel?"

"I tell them that the future of their baby is their decision. Theirs! What matters is what they want and what's best for the baby."

"You mean you never advise them to tell the father?"

Loretta had her there. "Of course I do. Unfortunately, far too often the father doesn't want any part of fatherhood, so it's a moot point."

"But you tell them to involve the father, because then they know they have truly analyzed all the options honestly and openly, isn't that so?"

Abby remained silent. Her mother was right.

"You've learned a lot since you were faced with this decision yourself. You can't change what happened then. But you can certainly help yourself now, just like you're helping all those girls you counsel."

Abby finished her beer and stood. "I have to go. Poppy's waiting for me."

"Okay. You don't want to talk about this anymore. I can see that. But I still think—"

"I know what you think, Mom," Abby said. "Now, give me a chance to do some thinking of my own. As if I haven't been doing just that since I got back to Key West!"

Loretta smiled. "Anyway, you're going through with trying to sell some of Huey's things?"

"Yes. I'll call antique dealers."

"Fine." Loretta slid out of the booth and picked up both beer mugs. Then she kissed Abby's cheek. "I meant what I said. I really am proud of you."

Abby smiled. "In that case, I'll let you pay for my beer."

ABBY WALKED BRISKLY DOWN Duval Street, her thoughts on the past half hour. Was Loretta right? Her mother's instincts were often perfect. But how could Abby confess everything now? Maybe Reese was a decent man. Abby had seen evidence of that herself. But how would this "good man" react if she told him she'd given up his son for adoption?

With Mallory Square just ahead, Abby increased her pace. No. She couldn't tell him. She'd learned to live with the guilt over keeping this secret, and would continue to do so. Once these problems with Poppy were solved, she'd return to Atlanta, to her life, and try to forget that she'd seen Reese face-to-face. She'd push him to the back of her mind, where he belonged. Only, her mother was right about that, too. Reese refused to stay there.

Abby reached the last intersection before crossing over into the crowd gathering at the square. Satisfied for the moment with her decision, she waited at the crosswalk for the pedestrian sign to change. A familiar black pickup stopped beside her at the light. Reese was behind the wheel, and this time he definitely had a woman in the passenger seat.

Abby tried to look away before he noticed her, but it was no use. He focused on Abby and raised his hand from the steering wheel in a little wave. Abby nodded. The woman, an attractive brunette, checked her out. The light changed and Abby crossed the street.

She imagined Reese continuing on his way, smiling and talking, his attention back on his date. And why shouldn't it be? He lived here. That meant he had friends, a social life with people who didn't ask him to get off their property. Abby had Huey, and at the moment he was her priority. She walked toward his cart, determined to forget Reese and concentrate on selling ceramic trinkets.

ABBY AND HUEY STOPPED FOR take-out chicken dinners on the way home from the sunset celebration. The bill was under ten dollars and he paid. "Pretty good night," he said, sitting across the kitchen table from her. Chicken Hut sacks stood between them. "Sold nearly eighty dollars' worth."

That, along with the thirty dollars he'd brought in the night before, gave him a one-hundred-plus two-day total. Enough, if he didn't blow any of it, to pay his illegal-fire fines. Since they'd just discussed money, Abby figured now was as good a time as any to bring up the subject of the property taxes.

"Of course I knew about it," he said after she'd told him what she'd learned from Reese. "But I don't appreciate Burkett or any other government employee butting his nose into my business."

"Does that mean you have a way to pay the bill?" Abby asked.

"I've started saving up," Huey said. "I've put away a little from each social security check the past six months."

"How much is 'a little'?"

"I couldn't tell you off the top of my head."

"Estimate."

He frowned at her. "I've got maybe three hundred fifty saved."

Abby's dinner threatened a revolt. The amount was about what she'd expected, but certainly not what she'd hoped. "After the first of the year, the bill could be nearly twelve thousand, Poppy. And it's only because some of these bureaucrats you hate so much showed some consideration that the house hasn't been seized already." She gave him her most serious look. "But time's up. You've got to pay."

He sat silently for a moment, then rose and carried their take-out sacks to the waste can. "We have ice cream for dessert."

She stood and followed him. "I talked to Mom today. We have an idea that could save the house."

He frowned. "I'm not deeding the place over to Phil."

"No one's asking you to."

He glared over his shoulder. "Good thing, because I'd burn it first."

"That would accomplish a lot."

He snorted, then began rinsing the dishes.

"Tomorrow you and I are going through the things stored in the attic and the carriage house. I'm hoping we find enough of value to sell to one of the antique dealers."

He stopped rinsing. "You're suggesting we sell everything?"

"Not everything, but enough to get you out of this current jam."

He shook his head decisively. "No. I won't sell anything to the robbers in this town."

She sighed. "I don't see any other way."

He stacked a glass in the drainer. Then he stared out the window toward the faded brick outbuilding that used to be

Armand Vernay's summer kitchen. "I guess I could let some of it go," he finally said. "For the right price."

Abby went to the refrigerator. "Good decision. Now, can I get you a couple of scoops of Rocky Road?"

CHAPTER SEVEN

HUEY BLEW THE DUST OFF a top hat he'd just found in a steamer trunk he and Abby had carried from the attic. "I can't sell this," he said. "It belonged to my great-great-grandfather. Came all the way from France."

Abby took the hat and set it on top of his head. "It's dashing, Poppy. You should keep it. But we need to air it out."

She was pleased with their progress. So far, just from one trunk, they'd accumulated several interesting artifacts. Huey had been persuaded to sell old tools, a collection of liquor bottles and flasks, grooming supplies and clothing, as well as jewelry and lacy handkerchiefs. Studying each item, Abby learned that Vernay men had chosen fashionable ladies for their brides.

Huey had also agreed to sell several pieces of furniture, including small cabinets, a wine rack, a pair of intricately carved étagères, even a spool-leg William and Mary buffet with Armand Vernay's initials carved in the back—a detail that Abby hoped would add to the piece's value.

"What do you know about Armand, Poppy?" she asked later, when she and Huey were having sandwiches on the back patio. "It's not true what the tour guide said about him, is it?"

Huey only grunted and took a swallow of iced tea.

"Well? Is it true or not?"

"I can't say for sure," he said. "Could be, I suppose. There were a lot of disreputable wreckers in those days, especially before Congress sent federal judges to control their behavior."

Huey sat forward in an old wrought-iron chair and stared out at the overgrown yard. "I can tell you that Armand was the richest of the Vernays. He built this house from Honduran mahogany. The original draperies came from Belgium. The chandeliers are Austrian crystal." He jutted his thumb at the old carriage house. "You remember that buggy in the shed?"

A decrepit conveyance of some sort had been stored there for as long as Abby could remember. She never paid much attention to it, since the upholstery was covered in bird droppings and the fittings were badly tarnished. "Yes, I know the one you mean."

"It's called a French dog cart, small but elaborate in decoration. Armand had it made in Paris and shipped over here. Quite an extravagance, if you ask me. On an island less than six miles square, what need does a man have for a horse and carriage? But Armand would hitch his Arabian stallion to the cart on a Sunday afternoon and trot about town, showing off his good fortune."

"Apparently, he didn't have much humility."

Huey chuckled. "Right. As to whether he was strictly honest, let me just say that if a man could amass all these possessions by never bending the rules, I might have gone straight years ago." He held up one finger. "But I will admit this, Abigail. I never saw a ghost or a spook in this house. So if Armand died a tortured soul like those guides say, the ghosts went with him to the Great Beyond."

Abby laughed. "That's good."

She followed her dad into the house. Dusk had settled, and the interior was gloomy—which was fitting, considering their last conversation. Abby wandered into the parlor, where the items for the antique dealers sat in the shadows, and she suddenly experienced an overwhelming melancholy being amid all the mementos of the Vernays. Selling her heritage was proving almost as difficult for her as it was for Huey. But necessary, she reminded herself.

Maybe she would walk down Duval Street and spend a few minutes among the tourists remaining on a Sunday night. She could listen to music coming from one of the local bars. She certainly wouldn't think about Reese and the woman in his truck last night. Abby would focus on the sounds, the sights, the lights….

The lights? Abby's gaze was drawn to the front window, where a white glow flickered near the base of the balustrade. She walked over. Tiny lights jerked crazily, as if controlled by an unseen hand. "Poppy," she called. "Come here. Something weird is going on."

He stepped into the room, saw the strange phenomenon and rushed out the door. "Oh, for Pete's sake, it's Burkett," he hollered back to her. "What the hell are you doing now, Reese?"

Abby scurried after him to find Reese, looking up at them with a wide grin on his face and a string of Christmas lights dangling from his hand.

"It's the holidays, Huey, and this old monstrosity of a house is about as Christmas-y as the hull of a clipper ship on the floor of the ocean." He stretched the string across a portion of the veranda railing and fixed it in place with a staple gun. "Surely even you can't object to a little Christmas cheer."

REESE DECIDED THAT adding holiday spirit to Vernay House, and seeing Abby's face while he did it, was a lot more satisfying than stringing decorations across the front of his own place. He paused in his work and took a moment to appreciate the surprised expression on her face. "'Evening, Abby."

Her mouth opened, but a few seconds passed before she said, "Reese, why are you doing this?"

He resumed decorating. "I figured you wouldn't ask me to leave if I was making your house merry." He held up his hand to stop her from protesting. "I'm aware you don't need my help, but I had a few extra lights, and Dad had some things in his shed, so why not put them to good use?"

"It does look good," she said.

Huey stomped down the steps. "What's all this crap going to do to my light bill?"

Abby followed him into the yard and stared back at the house. "It'll add a few bucks. But you shouldn't care. It's worth it."

A bark erupted from the black truck parked at the curb. "You brought your dog," Abby said.

"Yeah." Reese nodded toward the cargo bed. "Do you mind? He's kind of excited about Christmas."

"I don't mind."

Reese whistled and Rooster bounded out of the truck, his big feet scrambling for purchase on the lawn. He ran first to Reese, then galloped over to Abby.

"Tell that beast not to leave any presents in my front yard," Huey said.

Reese snapped his fingers and Rooster squatted in front of him on his haunches. "You heard the man, Roos. He doesn't want any presents this Christmas."

"I found an outlet, son," Reese's dad yelled from the side of the house. "I'm plugging in."

Three small wire deer outlined in white lights began bobbing their mechanical heads at the side of the yard.

Huey squawked. "Oh, Lord, it's Frank. One Burkett isn't enough? You tell your father—"

Reese smiled at Abby. "I know. Dad, Huey doesn't want you to leave him any presents."

Frank strode to the middle of the yard. "What's that?"

Abby walked over to him. "Never mind, Mr. Burkett. It's nice to see you again." She extended her hand as if she truly meant the sentiment. Reese wasn't surprised. Frank was nice to everyone, and he and Phil Vernay had been friends for years.

"You, too, Abigail," Frank said. "Hope you don't mind us livening the place up. Reese called and asked me to give him a hand."

Abby glanced up at the house, a smile on her face. "It's amazing what a few lights will do."

Finished, Reese handed the stapler to his dad. "Do you want them to twinkle or stay on permanently, Abby?"

"Twinkle," she said. "Just the way they are now."

"This house looks almost good enough to give Mrs. Howell a run for the ribbon," Frank said, nodding toward the neighbor's immaculately preserved century home. "And she's gotten awards from the Home and Garden Club for her decorating."

Abby hadn't bothered to walk by Mrs. Howell's place, but now she stepped around the shrubbery to get a look. Reese followed her. The neighbor's yard was filled with lit palm trees and an animated flashing train. Huge stars blinked from her porch eaves, and a giant snow globe sat in the center of it all, with Mickey Mouse riding a dolphin amid a flurry of plastic flakes.

"Edna will get the ribbon," she said over her shoulder to Reese. "But our house is understated yet elegant."

"Maybe the tour guides will forget about haunted spirits when they drive by," he mused.

"This was nice of you, Reese," she said. "I've been so caught up in Poppy's problems that I'd just about forgotten Christmas is on its way."

"Don't mention it. I haven't made things easy for Huey…." He paused before adding, "Or vice versa. But I never intended for him to get hurt the other day."

She sighed. "Unfortunately, you probably shouldn't expect Poppy to thank you for doing this."

"That's all right. I did it as much for you as for him."

"You did? Why?"

"Because things haven't been easy for you, either, since you returned."

She shrugged noncommittally. "I didn't expect this to be an easy trip," she admitted.

Reese hollered to his father. "Will you take Rooster home for me, Dad?"

Once he'd agreed, Reese said, "Abby, you and I are going to have a talk, one we should have had a lot of years ago."

Her eyes widened with what he hoped was eagerness, but he wasn't certain until she said, "It's probably not a good idea for us to go over—"

"A half-hour walk downtown," he interrupted, checking his watch. "I'll have you back by nine-thirty." He waited a moment, then added, "It's just a walk."

Right.

He pointed his index finger at her. "You're coming. No

arguments." Softening the order with a smile, he stated, "It's time to clean the slate."

He had no idea how dirty that slate was.

Apparently assuming her silence was agreement, Reese went to his father's truck, opened the door and whistled, and Rooster jumped in. Man and dog drove off, Frank waving out his window. "Merry Christmas, Huey."

Huey's answering wave was more a "good riddance" flip of the hand.

Abby came up beside him. "I'm going for a walk with Reese," she said.

"What for?"

"Because he invited me, and since he just strung all these lights…"

"You don't owe him for that. No one asked him to do it, and besides, I'll probably have to take them down."

Abby struggled to control her temper at her father's behavior. She glanced over at Reese to see if he'd heard what Poppy had said. If he had, his expression reflected unbelievable patience. "I'll only be a short while," she said to her dad, then joined Reese on the sidewalk.

Her nerves were on edge. Neither of these men understood the pressure she was feeling. Reese didn't know why she was feeling it, and Poppy didn't care that his resentment of the Burketts made her uneasy.

She started walking. "Do you have a destination in mind?"

"What do you say to Celia's Wine Bar?" Reese suggested. "The place shouldn't be too busy, and it's a nice night to sit outside."

They turned the corner and entered an island-style winter wonderland. Lights twinkled from every store window. Artificial trees decorated with everything from clam shells to pirate hats framed doorways. Reindeer peered down from rooftops. Even a twelve-foot stuffed marlin over the entryway to the Big Catch Saloon sparkled with blue lights.

Abby looked up at Reese and asked the question that had her heart pounding. "So what are we going to talk about?"

He steered her to an empty table on the restaurant patio. "Old times," he said with an easy smile.

She felt the first grip of panic squeeze her chest. Maybe she could steer the conversation away from that night on the beach. Or maybe he had another topic in mind, although she couldn't think of anything else about the past that they could possibly discuss. After all, despite what they'd done, they were practically strangers now— although, ironically, connected in the most profound way.

SENSING ABBY'S ANXIETY, Reese ordered a carafe of wine and poured them each a glass. Abby sipped hers, then ran her tongue over her upper lip. He fixated on the moisture glistening there and tried to remember how those pink lips had felt against his when he'd kissed her. He'd bet they'd felt darn good.

Damn. This was an awkward situation, and Reese didn't do awkward very well. He was direct, open. Most cops were. There were definite lines a cop wouldn't cross. They saw things as good and bad. Legal and not. Even when he'd gotten his divorce, the final decision to end his faulty marriage had boiled down to a basic lifestyle choice. After his wife had had two miscarriages, and blamed both on him, he'd still wanted kids. She hadn't. He'd come to the only conclusion that was sensible, though not without a boatload of regret about lost love, misplaced trust, wounded pride.

And Reese had other regrets, as well. About his past, the laws he'd broken by falsely believing in his own invincibility. About the path his father had taken and the fact that Reese hadn't even tried to talk to him about it. And about Abby. Regrets that had recently begun niggling at his conscience again.

He liked her, admired her stubbornness, her loyalty to Huey. He wanted to know more about the woman she'd become. Even though he hadn't thought about her too often in the years since they'd both left Key West, he'd been thinking about her plenty since she'd returned. He wanted to make things right between them, maybe alter some of those notions she still held about the kind of guy he used to be. He couldn't change anything about his past, but he could try to change Abby's opinion of him in the present.

He swallowed some wine and studied her across the table. She was lovely. The glow from the candle in the center of the table caught the sunlight color of her hair, the pink in her cheeks. She still had that fresh, natural beauty he remembered, but now those tomboyish teen angles had smoothed into sensuous curves.

Reese smiled to himself as he realized that the young woman who'd tempted him at the beach still appealed to his most elemental instincts. If they were at the beach now…

"What made you become a police officer?" she asked.

He blinked away the image of him and Abby alone in the moonlight, a scene that, until the past few days, he'd nearly forgotten. Only they were doing it right this time….

"My career choice must seem like a stretch, considering that much of my past was spent avoiding the cops," Reese said with a chuckle.

"Well, there were rumors about you."

"I wish I could tell you that most of the stories weren't true, but you know better."

She smiled. "So?"

"I guess I followed in my father's footsteps." There was no need to tell her that he'd joined the force hoping to be even half the man his father was before Ellen changed him.

Abby seemed surprised. "Oh, that's right. I remember Frank was a policeman before he opened the marina." She drank more of her wine. "He's done well there. At the marina, I mean. Did he ever regret giving up law enforcement?"

Only every day of his life. Reese answered vaguely. "I don't suppose any of us make important decisions that don't involve some regret."

She held her glass in the air and looked at him over the rim. Her eyes were vividly blue in the soft light. "I suppose not," she said.

"And what about you? I hear you're doing social work." Recalling what Loretta had told him a while back, he added, "Working at an adoption agency, right?"

She nodded, set down her wine.

"Why did you choose that career?" he asked.

She stared into the glass. "It just seemed right for me at the time. Placing kids with adoptive parents is rewarding."

"I'm sure it would be," he said. "It's a situation where a person in your position can guarantee that everybody wins."

She blinked several times. "I don't know about guarantees," she said. "Life doesn't come wrapped up in a big red bow."

"No, it doesn't." Reese sensed he'd somehow made her uncomfortable. He changed the subject—not that this one would make her more relaxed. "Abby, how much do you remember about that night?"

For a moment, he thought she hadn't heard his question, but then she looked up and said, "Not much. It was so long ago."

"Yeah, but I sense this connection between us because of it." He smiled, trying to put her at ease. "Maybe resentment is more like it. At least on your part."

"Don't assume anything, Reese. We met that night. Things got out of hand. That's pretty much all there was to it."

He smiled. "I find that hard to believe. If it makes you feel any better, what memories I have are all good."

She glanced up at the sky. "Reese, as I said before, I don't know that we'll accomplish anything by rehashing what happened years ago."

"This isn't *re*hashing, Abby. This is first-time hashing. And now seems like the perfect opportunity. There's a lot going on with you. I'd really like to see Huey stay in his house…." He smiled again. "And out of jail. I believe that getting things out in the open is the way to go. Don't you feel the same?"

She shook her head, as if the concept was somehow confusing. "Well, sure," she said after a moment. "Generally speaking. But there can always be extenuating circumstances."

"Not in this case, I don't think. If what occurred that night is standing between us, and we can clear it up with a conversation…"

"We can't."

She said the words so quickly he sat back. "Why not?"

Her gaze unwavering, she stated, "The time to discuss this was thirteen years ago."

"No doubt. But I left soon after."

Her lips pulled down at the corners—not despair exactly, but definitely an expression of sadness. "You certainly did. You'd just come out of college, and you signed up for the navy." She traced a line along the base of her glass with her fingertip. "That was a rather sudden decision."

"It was. I enlisted at the recruiting office at the naval yard the same day you and I…got together, and I went for basic training in Pensacola two weeks later."

"I remember," she said. "I heard you'd gone."

"Yeah, I was in trouble. That decision to smuggle those Cuban immigrants onto the island wasn't the smartest choice I ever made in my life. Which might explain why I wasn't exactly myself the night I met you at the beach. I had some pretty serious consequences hanging over my head, and I was using a bottle to forget for a while."

She closed her eyes and released a quick breath of air— a seemingly subtle reaction, but he realized how his words might have hurt her. "I didn't mean that the way it must have sounded. I don't want you to believe that what I did, what *we* did, was just me being crazy."

"No, we were both being crazy."

"Maybe, but I never intended for you to be part of the madness."

"You weren't solely responsible for what happened."

He felt that he was. She'd been a sweet, innocent kid, barely eighteen. He was a twenty-one-year-old man who'd gotten himself into more fixes than he cared to remember.

But when she'd padded across the sand in her bare feet and sat beside him, she hadn't seemed like the untouchable Abigail Vernay. When she'd rested her cheek against his shoulder and curled her hand over his thigh, he'd lost his head. When she'd let him kiss her, when his hand had snaked along that tempting slash of skin above the delicate dip of her naval...when she'd leaned in, pressed her breasts against him, he'd forgotten all sense of right and wrong. He shouldn't have, but "shouldn't have" had been the mantra of his life for a lot of years.

She took a long sip of wine now and fixed him with a gaze so penetrating he felt it in the pit of his stomach. "I heard you were at the beach that night," she said. "I looked for you. I wanted to find you."

He inhaled a long, slow breath to give his brain a chance to process what she'd just said. Did she mean what he thought she did? This was the last thing he'd expected to hear from her. Abby Vernay, the girl who always held herself to a higher standard, had intended to seduce him, the bad boy of Key West.

She gave him a tentative smile. "You're surprised."

"A little." He should have gagged on the understatement.

"I wanted you to kiss me, to find me attractive."

Oh, he'd found her attractive. And if the number of times she'd entered his head in the past few days indicated anything, he still did. He couldn't tell her that. He wasn't drunk. He'd changed and she had, too, in ways he still didn't know, which was why anything he could say now would sound lame and insincere.

So he said something that was at least true about what had happened after that night. "I thought about you. If I'd stayed in town, I would have called." He smiled. "I figured you would have hung up on me."

Her eyes clouded with something he couldn't identify. Regret? Suspicion? "But you didn't call...in those two weeks, or ever."

"Once I left here, I got caught up in the whole military

thing." He paused, realizing that what he'd just told her probably sounded like a flimsy excuse. "I couldn't come back here. The details of my enlistment were all over town. It was a deal my parents and I made with the judge to keep me out of jail."

"I heard someone spotted you the night you picked up the immigrants, and turned your name in to the police."

Right. Huey Vernay, to be exact. But Reese wasn't going to tell her that. He held up the carafe. She shook her head and he poured the last few drops into his glass. "We aren't the people we were back then." He drained his glass and called the waiter over. "That's a good thing in my case."

"You've become Mr. Responsible," she said. "My mother says you're admired by everyone on the island."

He slipped a few bills to the waiter and stood. "I don't know about that. I'm still trying to impress the Vernays. Huey doesn't admire me. And I've only started working on you."

"IT'S STILL EARLY," Reese said when they left the restaurant. "Care to walk off that wine?"

She should decline. His conclusions about her job, his admission of regrets had left her anxious, her stomach feeling as if the wine had turned to vinegar. She could almost convince herself that he knew her secret and his comments were aimed directly at her heart, that part of her that had carried the guilt for so long.

"For a few minutes, I guess," she heard herself say, and realized at that moment she would never be over Reese. Once again, she refused to play it safe and just go home.

They strolled down a side street. He took her elbow whenever they stepped off a curb or hit a patch of uneven sidewalk. He was almost gallant. She was practically giddy. And she hated herself for it. Especially when her mind wandered, as it so often did, to that night.

When she'd seen him at the beach, something inside her had snapped. She'd experienced a need so strong it had frightened her even as it gave her courage she hadn't known she had. She'd just left a graduation party, where she'd had too much to drink. She'd parted from her friends and headed to the beach, thinking, hoping, to find him. She told herself later that the beer was responsible. It had unleashed a bold, spontaneous side of her personality that refused to be denied.

The truth was she'd had a crush on Reese for years. He'd filled her thoughts and invaded her dreams, and was the stuff of all her fantasies. Older, confident, popular, he'd been nice to everyone, even a quiet, proper girl three years younger than him. And there he was that night, sitting alone and apart from his buddies, gazing at the ocean as if waiting for something. Taking a totally unfounded leap of faith, Abby had convinced herself he'd been waiting for her.

But in the next two weeks she'd discovered that he hadn't been.

Reese pointed down the street to where a crowd had gathered in front of an old theater. A tall man in a black cape and tricornered hat seemed to be in charge of the group. "How do you like his outfit?"

"Is he supposed to be a ghoul or a pirate?" she asked, grateful Reese had brought her back from the past.

"A little of both, I imagine."

Abby remembered one of the tourist activities the island was famous for. "Is he conducting one of the ghost walks?"

"Yep. He calls himself The Undertaker."

The man gestured toward the theater and spoke about its supposedly haunted past. Cameras flashed. The Undertaker turned, caught sight of Reese, took off his hat and bowed. "'Evening, Captain Burkett," he said. "We're being law-abiding ghost hunters."

Reese gave him a little salute, and the crowd moved on.

"I see the ghost tours are still popular," Abby said.

"You bet. This island has a few ghoulish tales to offer up for the price of a few bucks."

Abby smiled. "So I heard. One of them involves Poppy's house."

They continued down the block until they stood where the paying customers had been, across the street from the theater, which was illuminated by a single light beside its double doors and another in its upper story. "How long since a business has operated here?" Abby asked.

"Years. Maybe the building's not inhabited by ghosts—although anything's possible, I guess—but the fire that destroyed the interior was real enough, and people did die. And no business has made a go of it since then. It's like the place is jinxed."

Abby sighed. "I remember hearing about that fire."

Reese wrapped his hands around her arms. "I didn't mean to make you sad." He smiled. "It's the holidays and you're in paradise."

Key West hadn't been a paradise to her for a long time. "Is that how you think of this island? That it's a paradise?"

"Absolutely."

She envied him. How nice to feel totally relaxed in an environment, to belong. "Why?"

He thought a moment. She figured he was going to give her the pat answers—sun, sand, moonlit sails, margaritas…the stuff that filled the tourist brochures. Instead, he tightened his grip on her arms and pulled her a fraction closer. Her heartbeat accelerated.

"What's not to like about a beautiful Sunday night in Key West, Abby?" he said at last. He glanced up and down the dark street. "I'm alone with a pretty girl, and for once her father isn't glaring down at me from his front porch. A guy would have to be nuts not to consider this paradise."

A ribbon of anxiety fluttered in her stomach. For a moment she thought, maybe even hoped, he was going to kiss her, though she couldn't let that happen. She looked away and concentrated on the building with the sad history. "Yeah, and a haunted theater makes for a perfect addition to your image of paradise."

He laughed. "Well, there is that." He brushed her hair from her shoulders and placed his hands on either side of her neck, bringing her attention back to his face. "But I'll protect you!"

The fluttering increased. Abby's breath hitched. "But what if I don't need protecting? I don't believe in ghosts."

"Doesn't matter. Haven't you heard? Men like to role-play."

He lowered his face. She leaned away from him, but not fast enough. His lips claimed hers for a quick, warm kiss. She backed up as if she'd caught fire. "Reese, we don't want to do this."

He still held her. "We don't? I do."

She said the first thing that came to her mind. "I saw you with a date last night."

"Oh. You got me there. But I'd probably be right if I assumed you had dates in Atlanta."

She didn't respond. Of course they both dated. And this

was just a kiss. Anything she would say would paint her as an uptight woman who placed more emphasis on a kiss than it deserved. Anything except the truth.

"I have to get back. Poppy's expecting me."

He waited, as if debating his options. After a moment, he dropped his hands and walked toward Duval Street. They were soon lost among the tourists still roaming from shop to shop, bar to bar. When they reached Southard, Reese stopped at her house and said, "What if you were my date? My official date? Would that make a difference?"

The porch light was burning, and Abby went toward it. When she'd put distance between them, she turned back. "I don't know."

He grinned. "That's the way we should handle this. I'm not going to let you hide out in that house this time."

CHAPTER EIGHT

ABBY WAS IN BED BY eleven, but a long way from falling asleep. When her cell phone rang, she set down the book she wasn't reading, and connected. "Mom?"

"What were you doing strolling down Duval Street a while ago with Reese Burkett?"

"How did you know about that?"

"This is Key West. I work at the Pirate Shack."

Abby didn't resent her mother's interference this time. She wanted to tell her what had happened. "Mom, he kissed me."

"Hmm...nobody mentioned that part."

"I stopped him before it went too far."

"I'm sure you did. How was it?"

"The kiss?"

"Yeah."

"Inappropriate. Uninvited." Abby waited a moment before adding, "Spectacular. But Reese and I can't have that kind of relationship. We have a history. I'm here for Poppy, to make sure Reese doesn't take advantage of him, that's all."

"I realize it's complicated, Abby."

"It's more than complicated. He has a son he doesn't know anything about."

Loretta exhaled. "Abby, if you're going to allow a relationship to develop…"

"I'm not. The kiss was wrong. It shouldn't have happened."

Loretta continued as if she hadn't spoken. "Then you have to tell him."

"I should stop seeing him. I managed to avoid him for thirteen years. I can do it again."

"What do you want me to say, Ab? Do you want me to agree with you so things will be easy? I won't do that. You made your decision back then based on your goals and your situation at the time. But now you're a grown woman. Your situation has changed. You need to make amends so you can get on with your life, and maybe, believe it or not, even find a place for Reese in it. Besides, I like him."

"So you've told me often enough."

"And I think you like him, too. You always hoped that if you ran into him you wouldn't, but you do. And you've never quite forgiven yourself for giving away his son."

This was the crux of the issue. In Atlanta she managed to block out reminders of what she'd done for hours at a time. But now, back at the scene of the haunting memories, she was forced to face the horrible consequences of her choice over again.

"Abby, back then we did what we thought was best for that baby, and for you," Loretta said. "We can't second-guess ourselves now. That doesn't help anyone."

"I know that, but…"

"You should tell him."

"But what if this kiss was just Reese acting in the moment?"

"What if it wasn't?"

"I saw him last night with a date."

"Redhead or brunette?" Loretta asked.

"He dates one of each?"

"He's a good-looking guy, Ab. And even with men out-numbering women on this island, he still does pretty well for himself."

"Obviously."

"Anyway, what difference does that make? You are never going to move past what happened until you tell him. Trust me. I know something about the cleansing power of truth."

Abby remained silent, contemplating her mother's analysis of a complicated problem. Loretta was right. She'd faced a powerful and difficult truth in her life, lived through it, and was happier now for revealing it. There could be no future with Reese unless she told him. But how could there be a future with him anyway? Abby was going back to Atlanta, where she helped girls who reminded her of herself—confused, uncertain. Reese would stay here, being admired and respected and dating redheads and brunettes. No. There couldn't be a future with him, even one that lasted only as long as Christmas.

"I'll think about it," she said, and disconnected.

BY WEDNESDAY AFTERNOON, Abby had avoided Reese both times he'd stopped by the house. She'd gotten Huey to par-ticipate in her white lies by telling Reese she was out shopping or down at the Pirate Shack. Loretta refused to lie for her, insisting that Abby was being childish. She was. And she was miserable. She was flattered by the at-tention Reese was paying her, and didn't enjoy denying herself the pleasure of being with him.

Huey looked over at her from the sink, where he was mixing a pitcher of iced tea. "How are you doing with rechecking that total, Abby?"

She concentrated on the stack of bills on the kitchen table and layered the twenties on top of the hundreds, counting as she went. "It's correct, Poppy. Six thousand five hundred. That's a great start toward paying the taxes."

He scowled down at the money. "It's a pittance for all that stuff. I expected twice that amount."

Abby could only marvel at his view of what she considered fair and honest offers by the dealers who'd bought the things up for sale. "Some of those pieces weren't in the best condition," she reminded him. "The roof leak in the attic from the last hurricane ruined a lot."

"Nothing that couldn't have been made like new again with a bit of effort."

What did he call effort? Abby's hands were sore from polishing and varnishing. Her skin was chafed from hours of hand-washing the linens they'd sold.

Oblivious to her feelings, Huey picked up the stack of money, folded it in half and stuck it in his pocket.

"What are you doing?" she asked him.

"Keeping it safe." He patted his pocket. "I'm not putting it in the bank. It's better right where it is."

"Poppy, you can't keep the money. You have to use it to pay your fines and your tax bill."

He shot her the coy grin she'd learned never to trust. "In due time, Abigail. In due time."

"No. Now. And that reminds me. I've been meaning to ask where you got the money you put down on last year's tax bill."

His brow furrowed. "What are you talking about?"

She scattered papers over the tabletop, looking for the

right one. When she found the statement, she handed it to him. "Three thousand was paid in May, apparently after you received a couple of overdue notices."

Huey studied the statement. "What the hell? I didn't pay this."

"But you must have."

He hooted. "Hot dog, Abigail, this is the first time the government has made a mistake in my favor."

She could only stare at him. "You don't really believe that."

"I didn't pay it. I believe *that*."

She reached for the statement. "Obviously, we have to check into this."

He crushed the paper to his chest. "Not on your life! I'm paying these greedy bureaucrats enough without doing their job for them. It's not my place to point out the mistake some fool bean counter made in record keeping. Besides, it's time fate gave me a break."

Abby couldn't understand the rationale in continuing this argument at the moment. "We'll talk about it later." She held out her hand. "For now, give me the cash from your pocket. We'll take it to city hall right away. This amount doesn't solve your problem, but it should stall them until we can come up with other ways to make money."

He reached in, withdrew the wad and made a great show of reluctantly putting it in her hand. "You're just like your mother. Domineering, bossy…"

Abby closed her fist over the money. "Don't forget *right*."

"Even a hopeless nag can get lucky once in a while."

She tucked the bills into her purse. "Are you coming with me to city hall?"

"Hell, no. You're a signer on my bank account. You deposit the money and write both checks. At least I can save myself that humiliation."

She smiled. "Okay. What are you going to do?"

"I'm heading down to the square in about an hour. See you there?"

"Yep. I'll be along." They hadn't been to the sunset celebration in a few days. Poppy participated only five days a week, Wednesday through the weekend. Since she believed she was helping increase his sales, Abby didn't want to abandon him now, even if being in public meant she might see Reese. Besides, she was through acting like a child.

As if reading her mind, Huey said, "I appreciate your help, Abby, but what if you run into Captain Buttinski down there?"

"Don't worry about it. I'll handle Reese if he shows up."

"I'll bet. About like you handled him thirteen years ago. I should have taken care of Reese back then, for all the good you did."

Abby's jaw dropped. Huey had voiced the forbidden topic. Several times when Abby had visited Key West, her dad had reminded her that she should have let him handle the problem with Reese. She'd never once considered that an option. At first, she'd been forced to listen to Huey's vitriolic tirade about Reese leaving squarely on her shoulders the situation he'd created. Even after Abby had repeatedly reminded him that Reese didn't know she was pregnant, Poppy hadn't let up. Finally, she'd threatened never to come back to Key West again if he didn't promise to drop the subject.

He'd abided by her wishes for the most part, only referring to Reese in generally unpleasant terms, never zeroing in on the specific incident that had changed all their lives.

Apparently, he had decided today that he could no longer maintain his silence.

"Don't bring that up, Poppy," she said, not even trying to mask her anger.

"Why not? You talk to your mother about what happened, don't you?"

"That's different."

"Why?"

"Because she doesn't harbor an irrational hatred against the Burketts."

His eyebrows came together. "She damn well should. They ruined her life, too."

"Nobody's life was ruined—at least not by the Burketts."

"The hell. Your mother wouldn't have left me for Phil...."

"The Burketts aren't to blame for your failed marriage."

"You wouldn't have fled the island in disgrace...."

This pointless game of verbal ping-pong had suddenly gotten wicked. Abby squared her shoulders. "Poppy, you don't want to continue this conversation."

But obviously, he did. "I told you to have an abortion. It was the only thing that made sense once Reese took off. I said I'd drive you off the island to a clinic in Miami. But no, you insisted that you were going to have the baby."

"And I've never once regretted that decision." *Though I've suffered in countless ways because of it,* she silently acknowledged. But she knew she would do the exact same thing again.

"You let Reese Burkett drive you away," Huey said. "I lost you all those years ago because he didn't live up to his responsibility."

"He wasn't aware he had a responsibility, Poppy. You know that."

"You should have told him, or let me go over to that fancy house they live in. I'd have made those Burketts do the right thing by you."

"It was my choice and I made it," she said. "I couldn't ruin Reese's life. Or mine. I'd been working for years to go to college."

"Here in Key West at the community college."

"To start, yes, but I would have eventually gone on to a university. That was always my plan, and I didn't want to give that up." She sat heavily on the nearest kitchen chair. "I've never once been sorry I got that education."

She and Huey had avoided talking about this issue for so long Abby had convinced herself that the two of them had come to a sort of truce. A strained one, maybe, but at least a silent acceptance of the events of the past. Apparently, that wasn't the case anymore.

There was no question now that her father still felt a great deal of resentment. The truth was Abby *had* left the island to cover up her pregnancy. And to protect Reese from leaving his basic training and ending up in jail. Ultimately the education she'd received at the University of Central Florida was the fulfillment of her goal, one she might not have achieved had she not left Key West. Not all the consequences of that one foolish act had been bad.

Loretta had gone with her to Orlando to wait for the baby's birth. In a way, Huey was right. He'd lost both of the women in his life after that night on the beach. Abby hadn't returned, and when Loretta had, she'd stayed with him only a few months. She'd decided she couldn't live with Huey's constant accusations, both silent and spoken. And she'd turned to Phil, the man who claimed to have loved her for years.

Abby looked into her father's eyes now, fully expecting her anger to boil over. Huey had done the unthinkable and opened the Pandora's box that he'd sworn to leave closed. But the sadness in his eyes told her he truly loved her, and in his mind he'd lost her. She reminded herself that she'd come back to Key West to help him. She couldn't make his misery worse.

She stood and walked over to him. "Poppy, you never lost me. And you never will. My life is in Atlanta now, but part of my heart will always be in this house with you."

He looked her square in the eyes. "Having part of your heart is good, Abigail. I'm grateful for that, and Lord knows your heart's big enough to go around. But I want more."

She clutched his hand. "You've got to accept things the way they are, because I won't live here again."

He opened his mouth as if he might argue the finality of her statement. But instead, he pulled his hand free and headed toward the parlor.

She called to him. "Poppy?"

He stopped, his back to her.

"You've always kept your word," she said. "You never told Reese about the baby. I need to know that you will still honor that vow."

He rolled his shoulders, straightened his spine with the stubbornness that defined him. "I won't tell him. My word to you is more important than anything Reese Burkett has ever done or will ever do." Huey took a step forward, then turned back to her. "But if you want me to threaten him with the shotgun, I'm ready and willing."

She smiled. "I'll remember that."

He strode to the door. "Meet you at the square."

THE MONEY TRANSACTIONS went smoothly. Abby deposited the cash into Huey's account at the bank, walked the block to city hall, paid his fines and then proceeded to the tax collector's office. Her former high school civics teacher was behind the counter.

"Mr. Haskins," she said. "Are you collecting taxes these days?"

"Well, I'll be. Abigail Vernay. How are you?"

"I'm fine. Surprised to see you here."

The man explained that he'd retired early from teaching and discovered he didn't have enough to do to keep busy or to prevent his wife from complaining that he was around too much. So he'd applied for this job, and was now happily employed as a public servant. He took the check Abby slid across the counter. "I'll bet this is about Huey's tax bill," he said.

"Yes, it is. I guess everybody on the island knows about my father's debt."

"It's pretty much common knowledge now, Abby. But we're all pulling for him."

"Thanks." She waited for Mr. Haskins to read the amount on the check. "What do you think? Will that buy him a little time?"

"Oh, you bet. But just remind him that the rest of the money will be due after the first of the year."

"I will." Abby said goodbye and proceeded down the hallway to the front entrance of the building. At the reception desk, she noticed a signboard listing upcoming town business meetings. One in particular caught her eye—the meeting of the Community Improvement Board that very evening. The board members were mentioned at the end of the announcement. Abby walked closer and read the names. And gulped back her surprise and anger. "How could he?"

"Hey," a voice called from over her shoulder. "There you are."

She spun around to face Reese in uniform.

"I've been looking for you," he said. His easy grin faded as he studied her face. "What's the matter?"

She pointed a trembling finger at the board. "And there *you* are," she said.

He leaned in close. "What are you talking about?"

"Your name! You're on that stupid Community Improvement Board that bugs my father every other day."

He peered. "Impossible. I'm not a member."

She steadied her hand and tapped the glass.

His eyes widened. "What the hell? How did my name get there?"

She dropped her arm and glared at him. "Oh, I don't know. This is small-town politics. Maybe you paid to have the honor. Maybe you tore up a couple of tickets for somebody. Maybe you wrote a letter to the editor about putting a poor old man out on the sidewalk. Anyway, there you are, right under your mother's name!"

WELL, THIS WAS embarrassing. Reese raked his hand through his hair. "Honestly, Abby, I don't remember…."

He paused, thinking back, and recalled a quick meeting with the chief of police at least a year and a half ago. It wasn't even a meeting. It was more a two-sentence edict delivered in the hallway of the police station. Ray Fitzpatrick had said the town wanted someone from the force on the CIB. Reese had asked how that affected him, exactly, and Ray had stated, "I've decided you're it."

Recalling those words now, Reese wished he'd have fought harder to get out of that stupid assignment. But Ray had pointed out that since Reese's mom was on the board, it only made sense for Reese to be the representative from the force. "Besides," the chief had told him, "you won't have to go to any meetings."

And he hadn't. Once he'd told his mother the next day that he was a member in name only, he'd forgotten about it.

Reese tried to explain all that to Abby now. She listened alertly, as if evaluating every word.

"I know how this must look to you," he finally said.

"Really? It seems like you're a two-faced liar. With one breath you say you don't want to see Huey thrown out of his house. With the next you admit you're part of the Key West vigilantes who send him notices all the time that he should clean up his place before you sic the authorities on him."

Reese tried not to smile, but felt his lips twitch. "Vigilantes, Abby? Isn't that a little strong?"

She held her ground. "No. I wouldn't be surprised if your pals somehow increased his taxes to this ridiculous level so he'd have to move out."

"We're a powerful force in this town," Reese said, unable to conceal his sarcasm. "But I don't think even the CIB can control property taxes. However, if it makes you less inclined to hate me, I'll resign my post just as soon as they can find a replacement." He smiled. "Believe me, I won't be missed."

She stared at him as if judging his sincerity. Then she tucked a strand of hair behind her ear and said, "Fine, let me know when you've done that." She turned abruptly and started for the exit.

"Hey, wait a minute." He caught up to her on the steps. "Aren't you curious about why I've been searching for you?"

She stopped, gave him a look that was part curiosity and part exasperation. "Okay. Why?"

"I wanted to ask you out. On that date I threatened you with the other night." He pointed to the photographic representation of Georgia's Stone Mountain on the front of her T-shirt, and back at his own chest. "Just you and me."

"A date?" she squeaked, as if the idea had come from the musings of a lunatic.

"Yes. For the annual Christmas parade this weekend. What do you say?"

She thought much too long for his comfort. "This isn't an invitation to bungee jump," he said. "It only requires a simple yes or no."

"I might go," she said.

"Great. I might pick you up Saturday at six forty-five then."

"Fine." She headed down the steps.

"I could see you later," he called after her. "I'm working a double shift today. Are you going to be at Mallory Square?"

"I am," she said. "So, you're right. You could see me."

She got into her compact car and drove off.

Reese smoothed his hair back and put on his cap. Then he shook his head. Who would have ever thought that damn committee would turn out to be a bullet he'd have to dodge months later? But at least he had dodged it. He hoped.

CHAPTER NINE

WHEN ABBY SHOWED UP at Mallory Square a few minutes later, Huey had set up his cart and was reading the newspaper. The sun was nearing the horizon. Street performers were beginning to draw crowds.

She placed her hand on Huey's shoulder. "I'm sorry we had words, Poppy. I don't want to argue with you."

He squeezed her fingers. "Forget it."

She rearranged a few of the items on his cart to look more appealing. "You're running low on these beach baby ceramics," she said. "And I was thinking you might add some turtles. I imagine the Friday-night turtle race over at Turtle Kraals is still as popular as always."

He nodded. "Oh, yeah, folks are still blowing their hard-earned dollars on which damn reptile will reach the finish line first. But turtles might be a good idea for my cart. I have to run up to Miami next week to restock at the wholesaler. I'll see if he has any."

Hoping to attract attention, Abby smiled at customers as they walked by. She even sold a few things.

An hour or so later, Reese showed up. He'd changed into blue shorts and a white knit shirt with the police department's logo on front. He was on a bicycle, so obviously whoever he was filling in for was a bike patrolman.

Reese stopped next to the cart, looking all tanned and pressed and gorgeous. "How's it going?"

"Not bad," Abby said.

Huey stared up at him. "I haven't seen you at the sunset celebration twice in seven years, and now, all a sudden, you're haunting the place."

He grinned at Huey. "I just need to make sure that honest businessmen like you aren't hassled by petty thieves."

Huey grunted, picked up the binoculars he always brought with him and stared through them. "Fine. I feel safer just having you hovering over us." After a moment, he said, "As long as you're here anyway, you can watch my stuff while I focus on the real troublemakers."

Reese leaned over him. "Is something out there?"

"One of those damn go-fast boats. There ought to be a no-wake policy this close to shore."

Reese squinted into the setting sun. "It's not that close. The driver's not breaking any law that I can see."

Huey jumped up from his chair. "You might want to rethink that, Captain Courageous. He just dumped something off the side of his vessel."

Reese reached for the binoculars, tugging the strap at Huey's neck. "Let me see."

"It's too late now. Whatever he threw off is already in the drink. It might have been a body."

Abby peered out to sea. "What?"

Reese fiddled with the lens adjusters. "Are you sure, Huey?"

"I can certainly tell if something as big as a duffel bag is tossed overboard, Reese."

"There *is* something floundering around out there," Reese said.

Abby grabbed his arm. "What are you going to do?"

He dropped the binoculars onto Huey's chest with a thud, then hit a button on his shoulder mic. "This is Reese. Send a patrol boat to Mallory Square." A short pause followed, during which Abby tried to understand the muffled response. "Yes, immediately. I'll be at the seawall. And tell whoever's driving to make sure the lifesaving equipment is easily accessible."

He reached for the strap at Huey's throat. "I need to borrow those binocs."

"Be my guest."

Reese took off at a sprint toward the dock. "Be careful," Abby called after him.

In less than a minute, she saw the flashing blue lights of the Key West police boat. Reese jumped on board, and the *Whaler* headed toward open water, leaving a trim, foamy wake in its path.

HIS HEART POUNDING, Reese gestured toward a channel marker he'd pinpointed next to the site where the object had been jettisoned from the cigarette boat. He was happy to see Chuck Lewis commanding the police craft. Chuck didn't mind putting the throttle full forward, and he was the best driver on the force.

"What's out there?" Chuck asked above the roar of the twin, two hundred horse Mercury outboards.

"I don't know. Huey Vernay said something was thrown off a passing boat." The go-fast was already lost on the horizon, and Reese knew catching it would be impossible. All they could do now was try to save whatever might be struggling to survive in the Gulf.

Reese shielded his eyes against the sun sinking rapidly

toward the blue water. What was left of the famous Key West sunset was the one chance they had of spotting whatever might be floating out there. Once night fell, it would be too dark to see.

"Over there!" Reese said. Something was definitely moving, creating ripples on the otherwise smooth surface.

Chuck steered closer. Reese hung over the side of the boat. They were in time. It was paddling, struggling to stay above water…. Reese spotted a tinge of auburn in the shadowy Gulf. A person with red hair, perhaps. "Hang on," he shouted. "We'll get you."

Chuck cut the engines, drifted the last few feet. The sun was almost down. Reese braced himself and extended an arm into the dark sea. He made a few passes with his hand, hoping to grab something solid.

A growl came from the murky waters. Reese almost withdrew his hand when his fingers connected with something coarse, like the bristles of a brush. It certainly wasn't skin or clothing. "What the…?"

"Whatever it is, it's not human," Chuck said. "Don't let it bite you."

Reese darted a glance at his friend. "Thanks for the advice. That makes me feel great." He grabbed hold of something thin and bony. The creature writhed in his grip, trying to get free. "Stay still, damn it," he said.

Chuck shone a light off the side, and Reese finally saw the object of their frantic rescue attempt. His gaze connected with a pair of round golden eyes, wide and frightened. A large mouth yawned, revealing sharp teeth. Canine teeth. "Holy shit," Reese said. "It's a dog."

He wrapped both arms around its torso and pulled the waterlogged animal into the boat. He ordered Chuck to head back to the dock, and then tried to assess the creature's condition. The poor dog wiggled around on the deck and made several valiant attempts to stand. Each time, exhaustion and slippery floorboards sent it sprawling again.

Reese spoke in his most soothing voice. "Take it easy, fella. We're here to help." Finally, the animal lay prone, his chest convulsing with the effort to breathe.

"He's not going to make it," Chuck said. "Must have swallowed gallons of salt water."

"Step on it," Reese replied. "We've come this far. I'll be damned if I'll just watch him die."

A crowd had gathered at the seawall. The performers had suspended their shows. An ambulance, lights flashing, waited to take the victim to the hospital.

Abby and Huey pushed through as the boat drew next to the embankment. Shouting that he'd been the one to witness the possible tragedy, Huey stationed himself at the edge of the dock and refused to be jostled away. He fired questions at Reese and Chuck. "What'd you see? Did you save him?"

"Get back, Huey," Reese hollered. He lifted the dog from the bottom of the boat. A collective gasp rose from the crowd.

"Who would do such a thing?" one woman asked.

Another person voiced the obvious. "It's a dog."

With Huey's help, Reese lay the now-unconscious animal on the concrete and jumped up beside it. A paramedic rushed over, looked down and simply stared.

Do something, you damn fool," Huey said. "You're in the business of saving lives, aren't you?"

The medic dropped to one knee and began pumping the dog's chest.

A wisecracker from the crowd commented, "He needs mouth-to-mouth."

"You're the dog lover," Huey said to Reese.

"I don't know how to revive a dog." Reese rubbed his hand over his dry mouth. "But I suppose I could try."

"Oh, hell." Huey pushed the medic out of the way and crouched beside the animal. He cupped one hand over the snout and opened the jaw with the other. Looking up at Reese, Huey said, "If he bites me, have us both tested for rabies."

Reese, his soaked shirt matted with dog hair, gawked in wonder along with a hundred tourists. All two-hundred-plus pounds of Huey Vernay covered the dog as the self-proclaimed descendant of French aristocracy locked lips with a mangy mongrel. For a full sixty seconds, Huey puffed, released, puffed again, blowing life into the animal.

Reese didn't believe in miracles, but he was pretty certain he witnessed one under the twinkling Christmas lights on Mallory Square when the dog began belching up seawater. Huey rolled the animal onto his side and stroked his wet fur. When the dog's breathing approached nor-malcy, Huey stared up at the crowd. "That's how it's done, folks," he said.

Abby knelt beside her father and hugged him. Reese patted his back. "Good job, Huey." Even the dog, too weak to do much more than flip his tail in gratitude, seemed to regard his savior with something almost like worship.

"What happens to him now?" Huey said.

"I'll call animal control to come get him," Reese said. "If he needs further medical attention, they'll take care of him at the vet's."

"And more than likely gas him," Huey said.

"Not necessarily so," Reese said. "He'll probably be adopted, especially once this story hits the newspapers."

He took in the large group of people snapping photographs. "Which is quite sure to happen."

"Still, let's not take the chance," Huey said.

Abby petted the dog's large head. "What are you saying, Poppy? Should we bring him with us?"

Huey grimaced. "I don't recall uttering those words, Abigail."

"You don't even like dogs."

Huey looked up at Reese. "Okay, dog expert. What kind is he?"

"I don't believe he's any specific kind," Reese said. "But I'd say he's got a lot of Irish setter in him."

"I don't care much for the Irish," Huey said. "They're basically a lazy lot. Don't like to work for a living."

Reese started to point out the obvious similarity to a certain Frenchman, when Abby shot him a warning glare. Instead, he said, "It's my belief that stereotypes don't necessarily apply to mixed-breed animals."

Huey considered. "I suppose you're right. I guess I could bring him home awhile, since nobody else appears to be on his side right now." He glanced at Abby. "Do you mind?"

"It's a wonderful idea."

"Okay. Just for a few days. I'll make sure he's okay, give him a bath and fatten him up some. Reese, lend me a hand getting him to my truck."

A couple of other police officers parted the crowd, and Huey and Reese, each supporting half of the weight, carried the soggy animal to Huey's vehicle and carefully set him in the cargo bed.

Huey looked from Abby to Reese. "You two stay with him while I close up my cart. Keep him quiet. Don't let anybody point any cameras at him. The flash might upset him."

As he walked away, Abby regarded Reese, who shrugged at the mysterious workings of the universe. "Who could have predicted that?" he said.

She grinned at him. "Yeah, and who would have thought that I'd be keeping company with two real-life heroes this evening?"

Reese looked away, suddenly struck with an unexpected rush of humility. That comment from Abby felt even better than the sandpapery lick a long canine tongue was applying to the back of his hand.

THE NEXT MORNING, Abby awoke to the ringing of a telephone. She glanced at her travel alarm and had a moment of panic. She should have been to work forty minutes ago! She'd already missed appointments…. And then she remembered where she was.

She hadn't slept this late in weeks. Maybe her old room, with its faded ivy wallpaper and tea rose curtains, was starting to feel like home.

The phone rang a third time. Abby scrambled out of bed. "Poppy, are you getting that?"

When he didn't answer, she began a mad search for the telephone on the top of every table in the wide hallway. No luck. "Poppy, where's the phone?"

"What's that?"

She ran to the open window at the end of the upstairs hall and looked out on Huey and the dog in the backyard. "Can't you hear the phone ringing?" she hollered down to him.

"Yeah. So?"

She rolled her eyes. "Where is it?"

"Under my nightstand, maybe."

She raced for his room, tripped over the threshold and

landed next to the bed on her fanny. But at least she was near the phone. Whoever was calling was persistent. She'd counted eight rings. She put the receiver to her ear, thinking this was the first time her father's phone had rung since she'd arrived a week ago. "Hello."

"Hi. You sound out of breath."

Well, I am now. "Reese. What do you want?"

"I called to see how the dog is after his big adventure last night."

Abby stood, massaged a slightly painful spot in her ankle and hobbled to the window. "He's—" *eating a doughnut?* "—fine. Having breakfast."

"Tell Huey not to give him too much at once. And use good sense with the menu. The salt water could still be affecting his stomach."

She watched Huey pull apart a cruller and feed a portion of it to his new pal. "You mean only give him dog food, right?"

"Well, sure. That's all dogs should eat, anyway."

Poor dog. Although upon inspection, Abby decided he looked quite satisfied with his unhealthy meal. Just like Huey. "I'll tell Poppy," she stated.

"Hope you have a nice day," Reese said.

"Thanks. You, too. I suppose Huey and I will be watching for what people throw off boats going by Mallory Square tonight."

"Hang on." Reese spoke to someone in his office—the dispatcher, Abby guessed. He ordered a unit to head to Roosevelt Boulevard. "I have to go, Abby. One of the school bus drivers just reported a guy weaving over U.S. 1 with a beer bottle to his lips."

"At this hour? And around kids?"

"No, the driver had already dropped them off. We've got the tag number and a description of the car."

"Be careful."

"I'll be fine." She heard labored breathing as he rushed to his car. "In fact, I already have an idea who it is. He's a night watchman who claims he only has a few drinks when he gets off work. Unfortunately, his clock doesn't coincide with most of the others on the island! I may have to give him a stronger reminder now."

A car door slammed. "Till Saturday," Reese said, and disconnected.

Experiencing a totally unexpected, and certainly unwanted, euphoria, she returned to her room and dressed for the day. Reese had called just to chat—something couples did when they were establishing a relationship. Something married couples did. "Don't be ridiculous," she said to herself as she went down the stairs. She met her dad and the dog at the back door. "Hey, fellas," she said. "How's the patient?"

Huey beamed down at his companion. "Show her how you are, sport." He held up a finger and commanded the dog to sit. The animal stared up at him with unabashed adulation, and did nothing. "That's what I like about this dog, Abigail. Got a mind of his own. Doesn't dance to any tune but the one in his head."

Abby leaned against the counter and reached for the pot of coffee and a mug. "I can't imagine why you'd find that such an appealing quality."

Ignoring her, Huey rubbed under the dog's jaw. "I might even take him down to Fort Zachary Taylor Park today so he can show off his independent streak in front of the other animals."

Abby was about to comment that the dog would like that, when she heard the familiar rumble of the Conch Tour Train turning onto Southard. "Great. The stupid tour again," she said to Huey.

They went to the front entrance and stood just inside the door. The guide's voice carried across the yard. "On your right, folks, is one of the oldest houses on the island, the home of four generations of Vernays—"

"Blah, blah," Huey said. "Here we go again."

"Shh, Poppy. Listen." Abby sensed the speech was different today.

"Key West's latest hero lives in this house, Hugo Percival Vernay, the man who just last night saved a poor old dog that had been cruelly tossed into the sea. The way I hear it, Hugo used mouth-to-mouth on that animal right on Mallory Square, bringing the near-dead creature back to life."

Abby spun around to her father. "Do you hear that, Poppy? I'm not the only one who thinks you're a hero."

This time Huey shushed her. "He's still talking, Abby."

"…claim this house has a supernatural history," the tour guide said. "I don't doubt it. Some of the locals have decided to call the miracle dog Snowflake because Christmas is almost here, and last night that animal had about a snowflake's chance in Key West of surviving his ordeal. If you look sharp, you might see ol' Hugo and Snowflake in the window, sharing what can only be called an unearthly bond."

The train chugged by, leaving Abby and Huey speechless. After a moment, she said, "They want to see you, Poppy, for a good reason this time."

He tugged on his beard. "Damned if they don't. I might give them a peek one of these days. But I don't like that name."

"What? Snowflake?"

"It's a sissy's name. That dog's no sissy."

She smiled at him. "Just call him Flake. Somehow it seems fitting for any creature who'd live in this old haunted place."

Huey laughed. "I'll have you know, Abby, four generations of Vernays are taking exception to that little comment...." He looked down at the dog, who'd appeared at his side. "I might have to keep this animal, Abby. I think I'll repaint the cart, add a whole new island theme to the side of it. Instead of Tropical Delights of the Conch Republic, I'll change it to Hugo and Flake's Tropical Delights. Now that we're famous," he added.

Abby smiled. It was a fitting Key West name.

CHAPTER TEN

EVERY COUPLE OF MONTHS Reese forced himself to review the department-mandated materials in the trunk of the patrol car. Late Friday afternoon, after he got off work, he dressed in shorts and a T-shirt and released Rooster to the fenced backyard. Then he popped a beer and opened the trunk. Talking to himself, he checked off items according to a printed list provided by the department. "Flares, blankets, first-aid kit, ballistic shield…" He smiled. He'd never once used that awkward thing and prayed he never would. "Stun gun, ammo, crime scene tape…"

He was down to the spare tire when he heard a car pull into his drive. The burgundy Chevy Impala stopped a few feet behind the patrol vehicle.

Reese walked to the driver's door. "Hi, Mom. What are you doing here?"

Ellen Burkett, looking crisp and cool in white shorts and a blouse embroidered with martini glasses and beach umbrellas, got out of her car. She leaned in for Reese's peck on her cheek, before removing a baking dish from the backseat. "I thought you might be hungry for my chicken Alfredo. You never eat right."

Reese lifted the aluminum foil and sniffed appreciatively. "Smells great. Thanks."

"I'll just pop this in the fridge." She went into his kitchen and returned a few seconds later. "Did I catch you in the middle of something?"

"Nothing important, unless you ask Ray Fitzpatrick. You want a drink?"

"A glass of wine would be nice."

He got himself another beer, handed the wine to his mother and sat next to her on a lawn chair.

"I had a call from Belinda," she said.

"Oh?"

"She said you weren't taking her to the parade tomorrow."

Reese had spoken to her yesterday and told her he was escorting an out-of-town visitor to the event. She hadn't seemed upset. "That's right. I'm not," he said.

"Do you have plans for tonight?"

"Yeah. My softball league has games scheduled."

"That's all you're doing? Playing softball?"

"I imagine we'll go out for a few beers later. We always do."

"So, are you going to the parade alone?"

He stared at her quizzically. Other than a few occasional questions about his social life, his mother rarely insinuated herself into his personal matters. "Why do you ask?" he said.

She sipped her wine and smiled. "Reese, honey, if you're cooling off on Belinda, that's fine with me. As you know, I have my reservations about her."

Now that he thought about it, he recalled his mother saying a few negative things. He'd ignored them at the time. Who he dated wasn't his mother's business.

"Have you met the new woman just hired at Bremerton Art Gallery?" Ellen asked.

Suspecting where this conversation was headed, Reese shook his head. "No, can't say that I have."

"I met her at the garden club. She's delightful. A year older than you, but she looks much younger than her age—not that thirty-five is old."

Reese shrugged.

"She's cultured, dresses well, comes from a good family in Connecticut...."

"Mom, are you trying to fix me up?"

"Would it be so bad if I was? You haven't settled down since that disastrous marriage. You're alone every night. That's not good for a man. I worry about you."

He sighed audibly. "In the first place, you don't know what I do every night, so drawing the conclusion that I'm alone is based on guesswork, not investigation. At least, I hope you're not investigating me."

"Don't be silly."

"And second, I can meet women on my own. I have done so quite a few times with a certain measure of success."

Her back stiffened. "Surely you're not opposed to a suggestion from someone who only has your best interests at heart."

Ignoring that comment, he continued. "And third, I already have a date for the parade."

That perked her interest. "You do? Who?"

"Abby Vernay is going with me."

Her glass stopped halfway to her dropped jaw. "Not really?"

"Yes."

"Why her?"

"Why *not* her?"

"Because I just told you a week ago that you should avoid getting mixed up with that family."

"Yes, I remember that you did. And your point now is?"

Her voice hitched. "Don't be flip with me, Reese Burkett. I'm watching out for you. You don't need to make another mistake."

"I'm not asking Abby to marry me, Mom. I'm only taking her to the parade. Besides, what do you have against Abby? She's a nice girl."

"How would you know that? She's been gone for years."

"I remember her from before. She was sweet and smart. And I thought she was cute."

"I know darn well why you remember her, Reese. And it doesn't have anything to do with cuteness."

Reese nearly spat out his last gulp of beer. "What are you talking about?"

Ellen rolled her eyes. "Don't be naive, Reese. A mother hears things."

"Unfortunately. Things that are none of her business. Anything that may or may not have happened between Abby and me is none of your concern."

"That's easy for you to say now, Reese. Your life's on track, sort of. But back when you were in trouble, you were happy to let your father and me intervene with the judge on your behalf. We used our influence to save you from a jail sentence."

He couldn't argue that. But what he found disturbing after all this time was that his mother was bringing it up now. Was she that determined to keep him away from Abby? Surely she was aware that Abigail Vernay had made a success of her life. His mother's old prejudices didn't make sense anymore. In fact, they never had.

He stood up, reached for her glass. "Are you finished?"

She reluctantly handed it over.

"This conversation has ended," he said. "What I do and with whom is off-limits to you. I'm grateful for what you and Dad did for me thirteen years ago when I screwed up big-time, but it's history. And for your information, I'm not proud of myself for helping Manny that night, but I'm not sorry, either."

"False nobility isn't a good trait," Ellen said. "Especially when you seem to conveniently forget that Huey Vernay was the person who turned you in to the police."

"I remember. But no point dwelling on it now. He was doing his civic duty."

Ellen chuckled with poorly concealed bitterness. "Civic duty? Hardly. You have no idea of the consequences of your poor judgment in helping smuggle those immigrants."

Reese sucked in a breath. "First of all, I don't regret helping those people to freedom. And we all know the consequences. Manny spent a year in jail. Half the immigrants got sent back to Cuba. And I got off scot-free by cutting a deal with the judge and joining the navy. It worked out pretty well for me compared with the rest of the people involved." He stared at her. "So what other consequences were there? And what does any of this have to do with Abby?"

"Not Abby," she said. "But you're forcing my hand, Reese. You're forcing me to tell you…"

"Tell me what?"

"Huey Vernay only turned you in to the police when his attempt to blackmail your father didn't work."

"Huey blackmailed Dad?"

"He tried to. He asked Frank for two thousand dollars

to keep quiet about what he saw. Your father wanted to give it to him. I wouldn't allow it. If we'd handed over the money, he would have only asked for more."

"And when you didn't pay up, Huey told," Reese murmured.

Ellen nodded. "That's why I don't like him, and why I don't want you to have anything to do with that family."

Reese was certain Abby didn't have a clue that her father had been the eyewitness to the crime that night. But all at once, this animosity between his mother and the Vernay family was making sense. Could the fact that Huey had asked the Burketts for money explain his longtime resentment? Was he ashamed now because he had asked? Or because he had followed through on his threat to turn Reese in? But the thing Reese found most puzzling was his father's lack of resentment toward Huey, now or at any time that Reese could remember.

"Why doesn't Dad feel the same as you do about Huey?" he asked his mother. "Dad doesn't hate him. He even tries to make friends."

"There's something you should know about your father," Ellen said. "He's not a strong man."

Oh, Reese knew that. Ellen had stripped her husband of his pride and now Frank was stuck in a business he didn't even enjoy.

"I've always been the one to make the tough decisions in our family," Ellen explained. "And look at how successful Frank is today." She walked around Reese and headed to her car. "You'd do well to heed my advice about Abigail."

He stopped her. "I have a little advice for you, Mom."

She turned around. "Well?"

"I don't believe Abby's aware of all this history between you guys and Huey, but I advise you never to tell her."

Ellen smiled with a cunning he found irritating. "Don't worry, Reese. I don't expect to be having much interaction with Abby anytime soon." She placed her hand on his cheek. "I'm only thinking about you."

Ellen got in her car and left. If she'd intended to cool her son's interest in Abby, she'd failed miserably.

ON SATURDAY EVENING, Abby dressed in the only outfit she'd brought from Atlanta that might be considered festive—a short-sleeved red sweater and white jeans. A date. She was going on a date with Reese Burkett. After all these years, after they'd had a child, she was dating him. She looked at her flushed face in the mirror. "You must be nuts. This will change everything."

As if the image talked back, she told herself, "One date could lead to more, and then you're in a relationship, and then…" She added a swipe of blush she didn't need, her skin was so heated. "Who knows where this will lead? Certainly to the truth."

When she heard Reese's pickup, she went to a front window and watched him approach the porch. He appeared coolly civilian in dark green chino shorts and a splashy island print shirt. From the thick dark hair falling onto his forehead to the distressed leather of his boat shoes, he resembled a native—bronzed, relaxed and entirely too sexy. And Abby experienced an instant replay of all those overwhelming girlish emotions she'd felt about him years earlier.

She blotted her lipstick, smoothed her damp palms over her jeans and met him at the door.

"Wow, you look great!" he said.

"Thanks." He held the screen door for her. "I guess this is sort of my coming-out night," she said. "Probably no one remembers me from before, but we'll find out soon enough. This is the first time I've been with a local crowd. You don't see anyone but tourists at Mallory Square, and the only other places I've been are the Pirate Shack a time or two, and city hall."

"I heard you made a payment on Huey's taxes," he said.

She laughed. "This town and its grapevine. But yes, I did. I think the officials were more relieved to see a payment than I was."

"Trust me, Abby, no one wants to have Huey punished for owing money."

Tonight she believed Reese.

He walked beside her down the sidewalk to his truck. "So, how many people will recognize you from high school?"

"My best guess? None. Do many of our classmates still live here?"

"Oh, sure. This island's full of dedicated Fighting Conchs. You'd be surprised. And all of them will be at the festivities tonight."

She wasn't certain if that was good news or not.

Once they were in the truck, Reese crossed Duval, where authorities were setting up barriers for the parade. He took Simonton Street a couple of blocks to historic Eaton and turned into the driveway of a charming white cottage with blue trim. Potted plants decorated the small but lush front yard. A single carriage light glowed next to the centrally located entry door. A wide porch supported by six square columns and framed with a Victorian spool balustrade made the unassuming home appear warm and inviting.

"Who lives here?" Abby asked when Reese shut off the truck engine.

"Rooster and I do."

Whoa. She didn't know what she'd expected, but not this lovingly restored piece of island history. "It's nice. Did you do the renovations yourself?"

"Mostly. When I came back seven years ago, I had some time on my hands, and I got a pretty good deal on this place before the real estate values went up." He regarded the cottage with unmasked affection. "It looks a whole lot different now than when I bought it." He got out of the truck and went around to open her door. "We're barely more than two short blocks from Duval here, so I thought you might not mind walking." He grabbed two lightweight chairs from his side yard. "I'll carry these."

"Great. It's a beautiful night. I'd enjoy the walk."

They soon became part of the crowd migrating down Eaton to Duval. When they reached the old hotel in the center of town, Reese set up the chairs just outside the double-door entrance. Abby noticed a poster on the front window. "This is where the Ghost Walk Tour originates," she said.

"Yep. You can buy tickets in the lobby just after dark. And then The Undertaker, or one of the other guides, leads the group down the dark alleys and even darker history of this island."

"It must make for a fun evening."

"I imagine so." He pointed up Duval. "Just like this one will be. I see the start of the parade."

Abby was thinking how nice it was to view the traditional holiday event again. So far, she hadn't seen anyone she knew, no old classmates who might bring up her abrupt departure from the island.

Just when she was relaxed and enjoying her anonymity, a chirpy voice came from over her shoulder. "Oh, my God, Abby Vernay! Is that you?"

She turned and stared into the smiling face of Key West High School's pep squad leader from fourteen years ago. Only, now the woman was leading a squad of a different sort; she had three children hanging on to her.

"Mary Beth Comstock," Abby said. "You look terrific."

"Me? Heck, I've added three kids and thirty pounds since I last saw you. But you haven't changed a bit." She patted the side of Abby's head. "That gorgeous blond hair still with all those curls. I was always so jealous."

"Not on the frizzy days you weren't." Abby laughed.

Mary Beth grinned. "At least I'm a blond now, too. The bottle variety." She gave Reese a kiss on his cheek and glanced from him to Abby. "Are you guys together?"

"Just for tonight," Abby said.

"Yeah," Reese echoed.

Mary Beth smiled at both of them. "Whatever." She drew her children forward and introduced them, from the youngest, her four-year-old daughter, to the eldest, a son who was nine. "Who does he look like?" she challenged when the introductions were complete.

At a disadvantage, Abby stared at the boy and tried to associate his facial features with a celebrity. Harry Potter, perhaps, since all the kids these days wanted to look like him. "I'm not sure," she admitted.

"Eddie Reiser," Mary Beth said. "Everyone says little Peyton here is the spitting image of his father."

Abby attempted to picture her former classmate. Then, miraculously, she remembered him as a forward on the basketball team. Other than the ball player's six-foot-four-inch height, she couldn't come up with any identi-fying characteristics. "So you married Eddie?" she finally said.

"Big surprise, huh? We went together all through high school."

Abby glanced around. If Eddie Reiser was nearby, she didn't want to insult him by not recognizing him. Feeling secure that an especially tall guy wasn't in the vicinity, she asked, "Where is Eddie?"

"He's in the parade. Driving the mayor in our '68 LeMans convertible. Eddie's the chief maintenance officer for the island's official vehicles. You remember how he loved engines."

Abby nodded. She only remembered him loving basket-balls, and, now that she thought about it, hot dogs.

"He keeps everything running, from street cleaners to the police cars." She nudged Reese. "Isn't that right, Burkett?"

"Don't know what we'd do without Eddie." Reese stopped pretend-punching Peyton. "Abby, do you want something from the bar? The cops are pretty lenient about the open-container law on parade night."

"Sure. Whatever you're having is fine."

"I'm having a beer."

"Okay."

"Mary Beth? My treat?"

"No, thanks. She patted a backpack slung over her shoulder. "I've got fruit punch in here. That's what Eddie and I mostly drink these days."

Reese tickled both Reiser girls and asked if they were ready for Santa Claus. They squealed that they were. Mary Beth cupped her hand over her mouth and murmured, "I hope Christopher Biggs isn't dressed like Drag Santa this year. It's hard to explain to the girls why Santa's wearing a red hula skirt, a coconut bra and blue sequined eye shadow."

Reese smiled. "Sorry, but I saw him earlier when I went to pick up Abby. He's added a neon spangled wig under his red hat."

Mary Beth sighed. "I'll have to tell them again this year that he's a very merry elf." When Reese laughed and went inside the hotel, Mary Beth took his empty chair. She spoke to her son. "You watch your sisters. Mommy's talking." She leaned over to Abby and grinned. "So, you and Reese Burkett. How long has this been going on?"

"Nothing's going on, Mary Beth. I live in Atlanta. I'm just here to help out my father. Reese was kind enough to invite me to the parade."

Mary Beth was still smiling. "You sort of had a crush on him in high school, didn't you?"

Had it been that obvious? She and Mary Beth hadn't been close friends. Abby avoided a direct answer by chuckling. "What girl at Key West High didn't have a crush on Reese?"

"True," Mary Beth agreed. "But I'd definitely like to see him get lucky one of these days."

Get lucky? Did she mean that the way it sounded? "I wouldn't count on him getting lucky with me," Abby said.

Mary Beth shrugged. "You can never tell, huh? Reese deserves some happiness. That ex-wife of his—I met her, and she wasn't like all of us here on the island. She was snobbish. You know the type. She came from some *Mayflower* family in Richmond. That's where Reese met her, when he was stationed in Virginia. They only went together for about two months, and got married before he shipped off to somewhere in the Middle East." She lowered her voice. "I don't think Reese really knew her all that well. It's a shame."

Abby couldn't resist the opportunity to get information about Reese's ex-wife. "Did you hear why it didn't work out?"

"Well, sure. From a reliable source. His wife had two miscarriages. She blamed both of them on Reese."

"On Reese? Why?"

"She didn't approve when he re-upped for a second term in the navy. She said if she hadn't been so worried about him serving overseas, she wouldn't have lost the babies." Mary Beth snorted. "It's ridiculous, of course. A good wife doesn't put that kind of pressure on her husband, especially when he's serving his country."

Abby tried to be fair to the former Mrs. Burkett. She helped so many young women that she'd witnessed heartache in many of its forms. "Some women are more fragile than others," she said. "If she missed Reese, if she was concerned for his safety, that might have played a role."

"Whatever," Mary Beth said. "I just see how Reese is with my children. He loves kids. He'd be a great daddy. It's a shame he hasn't had any of his own."

CHAPTER ELEVEN

HEAT CREPT INTO Abby's cheeks. She focused on her lap as the sounds of people laughing and carols coming from businesses lining the street faded. In her heart, she knew Mary Beth's words were true. Reese would make a wonderful father.

He came out of the hotel and handed over a plastic glass. Abby took it without lifting her eyes.

"Hey, you okay?" he asked.

She blinked away blurry images of Christmas lights and raised her face. "Of course."

He pointed to her drink. "Sorry, no umbrella, so if it rains, your beer will get wet."

She smiled. "I'll manage."

Reese and Mary Beth argued over who should get the chair, with Mary Beth convincing him that mothers of young children didn't need chairs anyway, since they were always on their feet. "Besides, we're going up the street so we can be first in line when Eddie shows up." She beckoned her children to her. "Come on. Let's go see Daddy." Before she left, she spoke to Abby. "We have to get together while you're here. On a school day, of course."

"That would be fun," Abby said, and watched her move up Duval toward the head of the parade, which was making its way down the street. She and Reese sipped their drinks as pirates, mermaids and celebrity look-alikes from one of the nightclubs strutted in front of them. Color and glitz and holiday spirit, island style. They all contributed to helping Abby relax again.

"So, does this make you homesick?" Reese asked her after the Methodist Church choir strolled by, singing traditional carols.

"It's nice, and yes, in a way." She smiled. "I didn't know Elvis and Barbra Streisand would be here."

"They haven't missed a holiday parade since I've been back," Reese told her. "But at least we've got a little of everything." He turned his attention to a souped-up pickup pulling a silver-and-red speedboat on a shiny trailer. "Here comes Dad," he said. "He's got the Fighting Conch cheerleaders in elf costumes."

Abby waved at Frank before pointing to the vintage convertible behind. "There's Eddie."

Grinning and nodding along with the mayor, Eddie motored by at a leisurely pace. "I guess you can see that Mary Beth is a pretty good cook," Reese said.

Abby laughed. "Eddie looks less like a forward on the basketball team and more like a defensive lineman."

The last parade entry arrived in a candy-apple-red Cadillac convertible driven by a man with reindeer horns. "Thank goodness," Abby said, smiling at the jolly, whiskered man in the red suit sitting on the ledge of the backseat. "After seeing that fake Santa in the hula skirt, I was worried the real one wouldn't show."

"He always does," Reese said. "Although I usually feel a lot better when he arrives in traditional costume."

Santa threw candy canes and Mardi Gras–style beads

from a bag in his lap. When he drew alongside Abby, he reached in, took out a big handful and tossed them onto the sidewalk in front of her. "Merry Christmas, cupcake," he called, and winked at her.

She stood up, feeling almost as excited over seeing Santa as she had when she was a child. "That's Uncle Phil!"

Reese knelt to gather her booty and said, "Sure is. The holiday committee picked Phil to play Santa this year."

"I'll bet Poppy doesn't know."

"It's my guess he doesn't. No one would tell him for fear he'd come down here with a paintball gun and blast Santa's suit."

Abby couldn't argue. Huey definitely would do that— or worse. "Uncle Phil makes a great Santa."

"Yes, he does, but your dad would make a better one. Wouldn't need any padding."

Abby laughed. Imagine—Huey as Santa. Once the guest star had progressed the rest of the way down Duval Street, the crowd began to disperse. People walked by, many of them stopping to talk to Reese, a few even staring at Abby for a moment and then recognizing her. She chatted with the local beautician, who still did Loretta's hair, the owner of an ice cream stand where Abby had worked on weekends, and one gangly fellow who'd grown much more handsome since he'd been her lab partner in chemistry class.

By the time Reese folded the lawn chairs, Abby was more content than she'd been in days. Perhaps she could attribute this feeling to a couple of glasses of beer. Or perhaps to the people from her past who accepted her back on the island with grace, even enthusiasm. Or maybe the man smiling down at her was responsible.

Whatever it was, she almost said yes when he asked, "You want to go back to my house?"

She could picture them sitting together on a butter-soft leather sofa. Reese would have leather. He might even light a fire. She'd seen a white brick chimney sticking out of his tin roof. He would offer her something to drink, maybe suggest a movie. It was a perfect evening for two people in love, or even two people who considered the possibility. But certainly not for Abby Vernay and Reese Burkett. Such a scenario wouldn't work for the man Mary Beth had said would be a great father and the woman who could likely break his heart now with one confession.

She looked up at him. "Actually, I think I'm hungry."

She imagined a flash of disappointment in his eyes. Or perhaps it was only his way of reacting to a change in plans. "I could eat," he said. "How about the Pirate Shack? We'll avoid most of the tourists by going there."

The Shack was crowded with locals enjoying the festive atmosphere. Gold garlands hung above the bar. Lights shaped like chili peppers draped from the ceiling. And an eight-foot pine tree sparkling with large multicolored lights and decorated with all sorts of pirate paraphernalia stood in a corner.

Reese stopped to talk with friends. Abby spotted her mother across the dining room and hurried over to tell her she'd loved Phil as Santa Claus. Loretta had three strings of beads around her neck. Abby fingered one of them and smiled. "So Santa made a special stop here."

"No, I took off a few minutes and went to see him. He made an adorable Saint Nick, didn't he?"

"You bet. The kids loved him."

Loretta smiled at her daughter. "Is this an official date?"

"Reese is calling it that."

Loretta smiled. "I've always trusted his judgment."

Abby smirked. "Have you got a free table or not? We're famished."

She led Abby to a table for two near the bar, and waved at Reese. "Hurry up, honey, before someone grabs your seat."

He claimed the chair across from Abby.

"So what'll you have?" Loretta asked.

Reese ordered a grilled chicken sandwich, fries and a beer. Abby ordered a salad and iced tea. A half hour later, Reese popped the last fry into his mouth and washed it down with the remaining ounce of beer in his frosted mug. Abby's plate was still half filled with salad, but she knew she couldn't eat another bite.

Something about sitting across from him, watching the animated play of his features as he talked about his job, his dog, his experiences as a fishing guide, made her think less about food and more about the kind of man he was. Forget handsome. Reese was definitely that, and he always had been. But she was learning now that he was also interesting, adventurous, knowledgeable about many topics.

And Abby was beginning to worry about how she would put the emotional brakes on something that shouldn't be happening at this stage of their lives. Maybe he didn't feel the same about her. But what if he did? Their relationship was based on deception.

Loretta returned to their table. "You guys finished? You want coffee?"

Reese waited for Abby to decline, then called for their tab and laid bills on the table. Five minutes later, after asking Phil if he could leave the lawn chairs for a while, he escorted Abby to the door. "Again, it's close enough to walk to your house," he said as they stepped onto the sidewalk.

Groups of tourists still meandered down Duval, a block away. Many shops remained open after ten o'clock. *'Tis the season,* Abby thought. *Rake in the bucks while you can.* She couldn't blame the storekeepers. She'd seen the official population of the island on a promo poster at city hall. With only twenty-three thousand permanent residents, Key West businesses couldn't survive without tourist dollars.

She and Reese headed toward Southard Street. After a few steps, he casually draped his arm around her back, his fingers curled over her shoulder. She resisted the urge to lean against him, determined not to let herself become used to the feel of him, protective, caring…and most of all, she reminded herself, temporary.

They reached the house after about a ten-minute walk. Abby stopped at the wrought-iron fence she'd recently sanded, and commented that the outside Christmas lights were still on, as well as several interior lights. "Poppy's home," she said.

"I imagine," Reese stated. "It's nearly eleven."

She kept her attention on the house a moment before facing him. She felt as though she was on a first date again, poised at the front door. Should she duck inside, wait for a kiss, hope for more? "Thanks for suggesting the parade," she said. "I had a great time. It was nice running into old friends."

He held her elbows. "You know what they say—old friends are the best."

They stood like that, in a sort of tentative embrace, neither one moving, neither talking, until Abby said, "Well, good night."

Reese didn't let go. "I've changed my mind about the coffee."

"What?"

"I said I didn't want a cup, but now I do."

"That was back at the Pirate Shack."

"True, but I'm assuming the Shack isn't the only place a guy can get coffee."

She smiled. "No. We have coffee here. I can fix a cup and bring it to you in the backyard. How does that sound?"

"It sounds like what I wanted to hear."

"You go on. I'll meet you." She went in the house, looked for Huey and decided he must have turned in. Relieved, she prepared the coffee and carried it to the yard, where Reese was seated on a wrought-iron bench in the shadow of a thick bougainvillea. The garden was pleasant at night, with the breeze carrying tropical scents, and the darkness hiding Huey's now infamous fire pit.

Reese took the drink from her and slid over, giving her room to sit next to him. "You didn't want a cup?"

"No."

He set the mug down on a table by his side. "Me neither. I never drink coffee at night."

"But you said—"

He put his arm around her and pulled her to him. "I remember what I said. I was desperate."

"For what?"

"I think you know." He lowered his face and brushed his lips over hers.

Abby resisted, as she knew she should. A groan of protest came from her throat. She attempted to push him away. Reese would have none of it. He held her tighter, one hand on the small of her back, the other gently massaging her side under her rib cage. He deepened the kiss, sliding his tongue over her bottom lip.

And Abby felt as if she'd spent the day on the beach under the hot sun. Her skin warmed, her internal temperature spiked. The sensible voice in her head that had been telling her to stop suddenly became the reckless voice of the teenage girl who had hoped to find her dreams come true on a Key West beach. *Oh, hell, Abigail, you know you want this,* the voice now said. The inclination to argue fled as Abby wrapped her arm around Reese's neck, sighed against his mouth and opened to the thrusts of his tongue.

Reese made a sound that was a combination of a chuckle and a moan, purely male, dominant, playful…and effective. Abby's senses focused on his tongue, his lips, her own heartbeat and finally on the hand that strayed up her midriff until his thumb teased the bottom of her breast. She leaned into him, inviting him to explore every tingling inch of her mouth. He complied, running his tongue along the insides of her cheeks, the ridges of her teeth. He curled his fingers over the scooped neckline of her sweater, his blunt nails tantalizing her flesh.

She gasped, pulled away to catch a breath and allow logic to prevail. "Reese, we can't do this," she mumbled against his warm neck. "We're outside my father's house, for heaven's sake!"

He lowered the red fabric over her shoulder and pressed his mouth into the hollow of her collarbone. "We should have gone back to my house. Rooster minds his own business."

She sputtered, half laughing, half breathless. "What if Mrs. Howell—"

He interrupted, his lips still nuzzling her skin. "Edna

Howell may live alone now, but she has nine grandchildren. I think she'd understand."

Abby gently pressed her palms against his chest. The time wasn't right no matter how good his lips felt on hers. He sat back, his eyes intent on her face. "No, huh?"

"No."

"So what *should* we do?"

There was no kidding herself anymore. Abby was on the brink of a decision that would change Reese forever and permanently alter his opinion of her. The old excuses just didn't work. She liked him. Too much. And more, she admired him. And if she wanted to continue seeing him this way, she had a responsibility to tell the truth. If she didn't, then she had to say goodbye to him. It was the only thing to do, the moral thing to do. And she had avoided the moral thing for too long.

But there was still ground they hadn't covered, and it was time they did. Abby needed answers before she revealed everything. She needed to know Reese to the depths of his soul. It was the only way she could be sure that she could trust him as the guardian of information both intimate and life changing.

"Reese, I heard something tonight," she began.

His eyes widened. "Oh. For some reason this doesn't sound good."

She smiled. "Mary Beth told me a little about your marriage."

His expression sobered. "She shouldn't have. It's not that I have any dark secrets, but if anyone should be discussing that part of my life, it should be me."

"I can't argue that, but now I know, and it makes me curious."

"Okay. What do you want to ask me?"

"About your wife's miscarriages…"

He lowered his gaze to his lap. "Oh. That's not easy to talk about."

"I understand, and you're certainly not obligated to tell me anything. But I am in the baby business, in a way. And as you said the other night, we are connected. I'd like to understand what happened."

He remained silent for a long minute, until Abby began to worry he was shutting her out. Finally, he exhaled deeply and said, "She claimed it was stress. That she lost the babies because she was going through the pregnancies alone."

"Stress is often a major factor in pregnancy. An expectant mother has to consider a lot of things." Abby touched his arm. "Not all pregnancies are happy ones."

He shrugged. "Ours were," he said. "At least, I believed so. Back then I had a hard time accepting stress as the reason we lost the babies. I'm a guy, Abby. Guys deal with stress by swinging a bat harder or waxing their cars."

"I'm glad that works. But women are different. We tend to suffer more physical effects."

A muscle worked in his jaw. He clenched his hands together. "My mother used stress as an excuse once," he said. "She said my dad's career was affecting her health. My father did what he thought a good husband should do. He gave in to her demands." Reese stared over the yard. "I think he's regretted it ever since.

"Rachel didn't want me to reenlist. I did anyway. I wasn't ready to leave the navy. Maybe I was selfish. Maybe I was recalling what had happened to my dad."

Reese shifted on the bench and looked at Abby. "I would do it differently now. I would listen, try to understand. If I had known that both babies—" He stopped, blinked hard. "I think about them a lot. What sort of kids they would have become. If I thought I was responsible in any way…"

"Sometimes miscarriages just happen and we can't determine the cause," Abby said. "There can be abnormalities in the baby's chromosomes, hormonal problems, any number of reasons."

He didn't speak, but she could tell he was listening.

"Where is Rachel now?" Abby asked.

"Remarried. Happily, I guess."

"Children?"

"Not the last I heard. When she told me she would never endure another pregnancy again, I suppose she meant it." He frowned. "It was the major reason we broke up. I don't believe that Rachel was ever cut out for motherhood."

"And you wanted to be a father?" Abby asked.

His eyes softened. He smiled. "Still do."

Abby's heart squeezed. Her voice trembled when she said, "You'll make a great one."

"Thanks." He grasped her hand. "Need to find someone who'd make a good mother first, though."

"You will."

He leaned over and kissed her gently. "You know, Abby, I never talk about this. It's a part of my past, like a few others, that I always figure is best left hibernating somewhere in my brain. And I'm not a gut-spilling type of guy. But somehow with you, it seems right."

He brushed a strand of hair from her forehead. "Maybe it's the counselor in you." He stared at her a moment and then kissed her again, harder, needier. When he drew back, he said, "But that's not it. Something's going on between us. Do you feel it?"

She touched his face and her fingertips tingled. There was a bond; she couldn't deny it. But most of all she felt the connection in the familiar ache inside her, which had never gone away and was only stronger now. At the same time her heart was expanding every second, finding room for Reese in a whole new way. But to let him in, even if only until Christmas, she had to do what was right. "Yes," she said.

He took her into his arms and kissed her temple. "So, what'll we do tomorrow?"

He was making plans. A smile stretched her lips and she leaned against him. And then the light came on above the small service porch entrance.

"Abby, you out there?"

Reese laughed, withdrew his arm. "It's the curse of a guy's life," he said. "If it's not one damn porch light, it's another."

"I'll be in soon, Poppy," she called. "I guess we'd better call it a night," she said to Reese.

"Right." He got up, strode across the yard and stopped at the side of the house. "I'll see you tomorrow." Then he grinned at her. "But for the record, I'd call it *quite* a night."

CHAPTER TWELVE

SOMETIMES REESE'S neighbors irritated the heck out of him. Like this morning. It was Sunday, his day off. He'd gotten up at nine, walked Rooster, and then driven down to Martha's for coffee and doughnuts. When he returned, he'd phoned Abby and arranged to pick her up at eight. He was giving Rooster a snack when Bud Chambers called. If Huey Vernay was the most stubborn old-timer on the island, Bud was second. And Ralph Fresco was third.

Once, Reese had considered both Bud and Ralph his friends. Now, after two hours of negotiating hell, he didn't figure he was either man's friend any longer. And he wished he hadn't answered the phone.

"I'm not working today," he'd told the elderly man.

"But I need you over here. I don't want just anybody from the police department, Reese. I want you. You've got to arrest Ralph."

Since Reese had known Ralph for twenty years, he drove to Olivia Street to determine what all the fuss was about.

The evidence had been clear. A two-pound brick had broken the window of Bud's classic Victorian five-bedroom house. The damage hadn't stopped there. The brick had landed on an antique parlor table, turning a supposed five-hundred-dollar hurricane lamp into shards of milk glass.

The brick matched ones used in the garden wall of the property directly to the east, which was owned by Ralph, who'd complained for months about the annoying squawks of Bud's valuable Amazon parrot.

Now a damage claim was pending. Bud had threatened to file a civil law suit against Ralph because the brick had come to rest near the parrot's perch, and Bud claimed the creature's health and mental stability would never be the same. The bird hadn't uttered a sound since. Worst of all, Reese had been forced to take sides, aligning himself against the brick thrower.

After extracting promises from both men to behave themselves until he could at least file a report, Reese went home, mistakenly thinking his day might proceed more smoothly. And then his phone rang again. He checked the caller ID and connected. "Belinda, hi."

"Hi, yourself. Did you enjoy the parade last night?" Her voice was flat, the words clipped.

"It was a great parade," he replied. "A chamber of commerce triumph."

"How did your out-of-town visitor like it?"

Figuring there was no point dancing around the underlying issue, Reese said, "So what's really on your mind, Belinda?"

"That was no tour guide act, Reese. I doubt you would have had your arm around someone who just wanted to experience the island at Christmas."

Reese considered a smart-ass answer and passed. He and Belinda got along great, for the most part. She was fun and never placed demands on his time. But he could honestly say that any wounds to his pride would have healed pretty quickly if he'd noticed her on the arm of another guy. Obviously, she didn't feel the same way. "You're right," he said. "It was a date."

"With someone you've known for a long time," Belinda added, proving that she'd done some investigating before phoning him.

"I used to know her. We went to high school together, but I haven't seen her since before I went into the navy."

"Is it serious?"

"I can't answer that." *Though I hope it could be.* He smiled. That was the first time he'd admitted it, even to himself. "She's only been back a short while and she lives in Atlanta." This was the first time he'd faced that fact, as well. And he didn't like it.

"Look, Belinda, I'm sorry if I've upset you, but you and I have always had an understanding about dating other people."

"I thought the understanding had changed. I've been exclusive with you, Reese."

"I didn't know that." Maybe he was dense, but he'd heard of other guys asking Belinda out. He figured she probably accepted some of those invitations. Maybe he should have been paying more attention.

"Here's a new understanding, Reese," she said. "Don't call me. Have a good life."

When he heard only dead air, he stared at the phone as though it was an alien thing. "I'm just trying to have a good *day,*" he said. And he was counting on Abby to make that happen.

ABBY GOT UP Sunday morning with Reese on her mind and the awareness that she was falling in love with him. Not the wild ride of a teenage crush, but a real, last-forever, total-commitment kind of love. And loving him meant that she had to be completely honest about the past—tonight.

If she spent the day thinking about what she had to do later, she might chicken out, rationalize taking the easy route and keeping the secret she'd harbored for thirteen years. She had to keep busy until the moment arrived. So she decided to follow through on an idea she'd gotten after Huey redecorated his merchandise cart. Once the breakfast dishes were cleared away, and Huey was puttering around in the yard with Flake, Abby left to run an errand. She returned from the lumberyard a short while later and hauled the scraps she'd picked up to the back, where she set them on the porch.

Huey, with Flake, opened the door. "What's all this?" he asked, looking down at the stack of boards. "Did I forget to pay the electric bill? Are we cooking over an open fire tonight?"

She smiled. "No. You're going to paint." She pointed to the lumber, all shapes and sizes. "These are your canvases." She showed him an artist's supply box she'd left on a shelf. "And I found your oils in the back of your closet. You used to produce some pretty nice work."

If he was angry, she couldn't tell it. In fact, he seemed intrigued. "What makes you think I can paint anymore?"

"I saw what you did with the merchandise wagon. Very nice."

He smiled. "It is, isn't it?" He took the artist's box from her hand. "What subjects am I supposed to paint now?"

"This island. The gardens, the old buildings, the Hemingway six-toed cats, even the chickens that roam around downtown. Paint any nook and cranny that strikes your interest."

"So you believe I have talent?"

"Poppy, I believe you're a creative genius. And it's time everyone else around here discovered it. And paid for it."

"You think I can sell these?"

"I do. We're going to add a new board to the wagon." She made an arc with her hand. "Huey and Flake's Tropical Art Gallery."

He chuckled. "Got a ring to it."

She picked up a gallon of red paint she'd also bought, and held it out. "And while you're at it, I want you to think about painting the old dog cart in the carriage house."

"Why would I do that?"

"Because it needs it. We can repair the leather and polish the brass. Restored, that carriage would look great by the veranda."

He stared at the can of paint. "And you want this color?"

"I studied the cart. The side panels have traces of red. So why not? It's Christmas and—"

"Oh, swell." He mimicked a woman's voice. "It's Christmas. Let's all be jolly."

She laughed. "You can start your first painting whenever you want. You'll have the house to yourself tonight."

"Burkett again?"

She shrugged.

"You and Burkett. A dog in my life. My possessions gone to pay taxes. And pretty soon a shiny red dog cart in the yard. What's my world coming to?"

"A new beginning for a new year," she said, and headed for the back door. She stopped before going in, and grinned at him. "Don't forget to sign each painting. I consider these works of art my inheritance."

He leaned over and spoke to Flake. "Poor girl. A Vernay original and a dollar bill will get her a cup of joe at Martha's."

REESE WAS SUPPOSED to pick Abby up at eight. At seven-thirty she checked her appearance in her bedroom mirror. Hair shiny and falling in waves to her shoulders. Makeup light and natural. Splashy sundress hopefully just sexy enough to help her through the toughest night of her life. Brand-new sandals framing newly painted coral toenails. Satisfied she'd primped as well as she could, she went to her car and headed to Eaton Street to waylay her date before he left his house—the place she hoped he'd feel most comfortable.

She pulled into Reese's driveway, relieved to see his pickup still parked behind the patrol vehicle. When she got out of her car, excited barking came from the little house. She ran her hands down the sides of her dress and walked to the porch. She experienced a flash of panic, and even considered an escape plan. She'd wait until she was face-to-face with Reese. Maybe she didn't truly love him. Maybe she was in love with love and had chosen her old crush as a target for misplaced emotions. There was still time to back out of this supposed commitment she'd made to herself.

Reese opened the door before she had a chance to knock. All fickleness vanished. This was no renewed crush. Her stomach dropped; her heart pounded; her hands sweated. Simply put, this felt like love.

"You look fantastic," he said. Desire flared in his appreciative gaze.

She swallowed. *Back at ya, Reese.* He was dressed in a

silky Havana shirt, which hung loosely over dark slacks. His hair was damp. A few strands fell onto his forehead. His smile brightened his entire face. She muttered something that sounded like, "Thank you."

"I was supposed to come to your place, right?" he said, pulling the door wide.

"Yes, but I thought we might change our plans."

His expression was blatantly hopeful. "Really? How so?"

"Do you mind if we stay here and have a drink, and I'll treat you to dinner later?"

He followed her inside. "I'm game."

She stopped in the middle of the living room. He was there, near enough for her to touch, to smell, to feel the heat radiating from his skin. He cupped her chin, tilted her face up and kissed her. "My mind's running away with me, Abby. Does this mean what I hope it means?"

Her defenses crumbled. She wrapped her arms around his neck and returned the kiss. Her desire for him was almost desperate, a blend of her passion and her fear. His hands splayed across her back, and he pulled her to him, their bodies as close as they could get, her breasts pressed against him. The kiss went on forever, deep, hungry, committing them to more.

Somewhere in the back of Abby's mind, a voice broke through the delicious haze to tell her this was wrong. That it was backward. She was beginning where she'd planned to end. She had to talk first. Though she felt dizzy, alive, heavenly, she could no longer kid herself. She'd wanted this to happen since she'd first seen Reese in the yard at her house—and since that night thirteen years ago. But if they were going to make love, which Reese seemed to want as much as she did, she had to be honest first. She stepped back from him, brushed her fingertip over her moist lips. "Reese, we have to talk."

He blinked. "Not my first choice." His voice was thick, husky.

She took his hand and led him to the sofa by the fireplace. A small Christmas tree twinkled with colored lights in the window nearby. Rooster, his head on his front paws, lay on the soft braided rug covering the hardwood floor. Tears burned Abby's eyes. This was a scene of total contentment. The fulfillment of a dream.

They sat. She swiveled to face him, tucked one leg under herself and clasped her hands in her lap. Reese smiled. "If we're really going to talk," he said, "can I go first?"

Abby drew her bottom lip between her teeth. What was this? Was he going to say something that would change the course of this evening? Had she read the past minutes all wrong? Did he not care as much as she believed he did? Insecurity bombarded her. She tried to smile, but her lips trembled. "Sure, go ahead."

He clasped her hand and gently massaged her knuckles with his thumb. "I ran into Undertaker today. Remember him from the ghost walk tour?"

She nodded.

"We talked for a while. I asked him how business was. He said it was great, but he'd like to have more stops on his tour. When we went our separate ways, I suddenly had this idea that might help solve some of Huey's financial problems."

"You did?" She acknowledged the irony of them both thinking of ways to help Huey today. Of course it was natural for her to want to help her father. But Reese had no such obligation. "What's your idea?" she asked.

"What if Huey became part of the ghost walk tour?

Vernay House could be added to the list of places the group visits. He could wear a costume from the period and pose as the reincarnation of Armand." Reese grinned. "And get a cut of each ticket price."

Abby thought a moment. Would Poppy agree to such a public display of his family's history? She decided he might. She could easily picture him dressed as a prosperous nineteenth-century ship captain in waistcoat and breeches. He could wear Armand's top hat and carry the ebony cane they'd found in a trunk in the attic.

"Huey could stand on the front porch while the tours stopped," she said. "We could add some low lighting, special effects, background sounds. Poppy could moan and appear tortured by his past, repentant and frightened at the same time."

Reese chuckled. "Huey repentant? I'm not sure how that would work."

"He would love it. This would be perfect for him. I'll ask him. What would be the next step?"

"I'll talk to Undertaker. I'll bet he goes for the idea, too. On their brochures they could advertise that an actual descendant of Armand Vernay was portraying the old man. Seems like a win-win situation to me."

"Reese, this is fantastic. Finally, the history of Poppy's house could benefit him. I don't know how to thank you."

He kissed the tips of her fingers. "You don't? A few minutes ago you were already beginning to."

A few minutes ago, when everything was wonderful. Abby withdrew her hand and dropped it to her lap. She considered not going through with her plan. This evening had started out so well, so brimming with hope.

Reese lay his palm against her temple. "Hey, what's the matter?"

"I was just so wrong about you. When I first got here, I thought you wanted to put Poppy in jail. That you wanted to teach him a lesson. I know he can be difficult…"

"Abby, I can't tell you I wouldn't have arrested Huey had he deserved it. But I wouldn't have gotten any pleasure out of doing so."

"I realize that now."

"Then something else is wrong. What is it?"

She blinked, considering her words carefully. "Reese, what I came here to tell you tonight is important. And when you hear it, this relationship we've established in the past days will change."

His brow furrowed with concern. "Okay. Change can be good. Did I do something to upset you?"

"No. I'm afraid it's going to be the other way around." Her language didn't nearly convey the seriousness of what she had to say, or the difficulty of saying it. His gaze was warm and comforting but did little to ease her anxiety.

"Abby, is this about what happened all those years ago?"

She could only nod. Her throat burned with what had to be said.

He stroked her face with his thumb. "I've begun to see that maybe what we did wasn't just a couple of crazy kids together on a beach. That night meant something. And means even more after all this time." He smiled. "In case you can't tell, I'm pretty crazy about you."

She looked into his eyes. "Reese, why didn't you contact me in the two weeks after it happened?"

He glanced up at the ceiling, took a breath, then refocused on her. "I wanted to, thought about it plenty, but then I knew nothing could come of a relationship between us for a very long time. I was committed to two years of court-ordered military service. You were just out of high school. I'd heard you had a scholarship to the community college." He smiled. "You were so smart, Abby. You were going to make something of your life. I was in big trouble and searching for a way out of here. We were two lives crossing at the wrong moment." His eyes darkened. "I was not, in any way, the man a sweet girl like you deserved."

A sweet girl. Abby closed her eyes and moved away, putting space between them. "I tried contacting *you,*" she said.

"When was that?"

She looked up at him. "Two weeks after that night. I went to your house. Your mother told me you'd left that morning." Abby's voice shook. "I was…surprised."

"Yeah. My departure was sudden." His eyes narrowed. "Mom never mentioned that you'd come by the house."

"She said you would be difficult to reach, that the rules of basic training prohibited a lot of contact with the outside. I waited a couple of days and then I tracked you down in Pensacola. I got the phone number of your barracks."

His eyes widened under arched eyebrows. "You did?"

"The man who answered didn't know you. He said there were over two hundred new recruits. But I left a message for you to call me."

"I never got it." He paused, obviously struggling to remember details. "We had a large corkboard where all phone messages were posted. I'm not surprised that some of them got lost. It wasn't a very good system. What did you want to tell me?"

In his eyes, she saw only a profound regret for the missed communication. Her heart squeezed painfully. At the time, she'd almost experienced relief that he hadn't called back. His insensitivity had hurt, of course, but it also freed her to pursue her plans to go to college and build a new life away from the island.

The question he'd just asked hung in the air. She'd come this far, and had to answer. Otherwise there could be no future for them. But the admission might have the exact same consequences. She swallowed and said, "Reese, I was pregnant."

His lips moved as if he were trying to form words. At first, none came. He stared at her, until he filled his lungs and uttered, "You had a… *We* had a…"

She squeezed his hand. He let her, but there was no warmth flowing between them anymore. The connection had been lost. "There's so much to tell you."

His stern gaze remained on her face. "Did you have the baby?"

"Yes. A boy."

His shoulders sagged, erasing the stiffness of a moment earlier. "My God, Abby. We have a son."

"It's not that simple."

His hand jerked in hers. "Where is he? Is he all right? Healthy?"

"Yes, he's fine."

Reese's lips twitched, as if he might smile through his shock, but then realized he didn't have all the facts yet. She couldn't let him feel any joy in this admission. She raised her hand. "I put him up for adoption, Reese," she said. The decision that had made so much sense thirteen years ago sounded hollow and cold and self-serving tonight.

"You what?" His eyes narrowed. "You gave him away? Without contacting me?"

"I just told you. I tried to. I went to your mother. I left a message...."

"That's it? One conversation with my mother. One phone call."

Her mouth went dry. She swallowed. "Your mother said you couldn't come back here, that you would be arrested."

"Did she know why you needed to reach me?"

Abby shook her head. "I didn't tell her. I never told anyone outside my family. Weeks passed and I had to make a decision. Poppy wanted me to..." She paused. She hadn't considered abortion then, so why bring it up now? "I just needed to get off the island before my pregnancy became obvious. I had to be where I could think clearly."

He listened stoically, but his face was blank, like a stone mask.

"In the end, my mother went with me to Orlando, where we both got temporary jobs. I worked in an office until the baby came. I'd already signed the papers with an adoption agency, so on the day of the birth, my son...the *infant*...was taken away. I enrolled in the University of Central Florida in Orlando, and once my mother knew I was determined to stay there, she returned to Key West."

Abby paused, waiting for his reaction to a story told in a few simple sentences.

"That's all you have to say?" Reese's voice was practically a growl. "Unwanted pregnancy. Girl runs away, gives birth, hands baby over to strangers." He raked his fingers through his hair. "End of story?"

No, it wasn't the end. There was so much more.

"I was able to approve the selection of parents," she said.

"They were wonderful people in their late thirties. The baby was their only child. They'd been trying to conceive—"

He held his hand in front of her face. "Stop it, Abby. Do you honestly believe it makes any difference for you to spout the virtues of the people who took possession of my son? What do you want me to say? Thanks, Abby, for turning my child over to kind strangers instead of monsters?"

She looked away. His scorn cut deeply into wounds that had never healed. "No. I just thought you would like to know—"

"I'd like to know where my boy is." His voice was flat, toneless, frighteningly so. "I'd like to know what happened to my rights as a parent. And mostly, I want to know how I can get my son back."

Abby reached out to him, and he flinched. "Reese, please, just consider a minute—"

"How am I supposed to consider anything when all I can do right now is feel? And let me tell you how I feel. Betrayed. Swindled out of a child. That's what I'm feeling now. And when I do start thinking again, I'm going to try to figure out how to undo what you've done."

The first tears, hot with humiliation, fell to her cheeks. He hadn't had time to sort through the information, but she'd had thirteen long years. And now, added to her own countless regrets, thoughts of the other two children he'd lost filled her mind. Right now he probably didn't consider Abby much different from his wife who'd blamed him for the loss of their babies. But Abby reminded herself that she had felt compelled to be honest with him, so he knew where he stood. "Reese, there's nothing that will undo what's been done."

"The hell there isn't." He rose from the sofa and began pacing. He hurt physically. In the pit of his stomach, in his constricted lungs. He stalked from one side of the room to the other, but the area was too small. He clenched his hands, feeling the skin over his knuckles stretch taut. Something had to give. He was going to explode. Fifteen minutes ago he'd have sworn he loved Abby Vernay. Now he didn't even know who she was.

Her voice penetrated the buzzing in his brain. "Have you ever heard of Florida's putative father registry?"

He stopped, glared at her, trying to connect the image of her face with the one he'd been sleepless over for days. He was aware of the registry, but he'd never dreamed it could apply to him. The putative father registry required that any man who slept with a woman and believed a pregnancy could result must include his name in a statewide database of single fathers. Then he would be notified in case adoption proceedings were initiated.

That was all Reese knew about this ridiculous piece of legislation. As if every guy who slept with a woman would add his name to the database in the unlikely event a baby resulted from careless sex. He doubted one guy in ten would do that. But on the chance he might learn something, he said, "Yes, I've heard of it."

"Then you know that you would have had to register as the father of any child who could have resulted from the one night—"

"That's bull, Abby. The registry is useless."

"No, it isn't. It's designed to protect the anonymity of the mother."

"That and any law can be challenged," he said.

"Reese, thirteen years have passed. The child is twelve

years old. Other men have fought the system with regard to much younger children, without success."

"How do you know so damn much—?" he asked as an undeniable truth hit him with the force of a punch. "Of course," he said, his voice unbelievably controlled. "Your job. You work for an adoption agency. That's no coincidence, is it, Abby?"

She flinched.

"You took a job that would assuage your guilt over what you did. By placing other kids with homes, you tried to compensate for what you did to me."

She didn't speak, but he could see in her wide eyes that he'd hit a nerve, uncovered a truth that maybe she hadn't realized. Well, good. She'd played with his life, and no amount of self-examination would take the blame from her shoulders. "Does Huey know this?" he asked.

She nodded slowly.

Reese stared at the Christmas tree until the lights blurred into a garish concoction of colors. "No wonder he's hated me all these years. I knock up his daughter, take off for the navy and she leaves."

Abby sobbed. "No, no, it's not like that. Huey knows about the baby, but he's aware that I never told you. I swore him to secrecy. Like I said, no one knows except for my family."

"And now the father," Reese said bitterly.

He picked up her purse from the floor by the sofa and handed it to her. "I have to go somewhere and you're parked behind me."

She looked as if she might speak, but wisely didn't. He was in no state to hear anything else she might say. She tucked the purse under her arm and headed for the door.

"Wait a second," he said. "Maybe with all that adoption knowledge you have, you can tell me how to find my son."

Her face paled. "Reese, don't…"

"Well, do you know? Do you know where he is?"

She stood at the door, her eyes downcast, her hand on the knob.

Hell, yes, she knew. "So you won't tell me? You can't do that after what you've done?"

She twisted the knob. "No, I can't." She opened the door and stepped into the darkness.

As soon as Reese heard her car pull out of his drive, he grabbed his own keys and went to his truck. Next stop, the stilt house by Burkett's Paradise Marina. It was late. He didn't care. He had to find out who knew what about the child Abby was determined he would never see.

CHAPTER THIRTEEN

REESE CLENCHED the steering wheel until his knuckles ached. His nerves thrummed with anger and frustration. He needed someone to blame for how he felt. Someone besides Abby, because in spite of hearing the confession from her own lips, he still couldn't believe she'd done this awful thing.

Abby had gone to his mother back then, but she claimed she hadn't told Ellen why she'd wanted to contact him. That didn't mean that Ellen didn't know. Ellen Burkett had radar that defied logic.

The living room lights were on in his parents' Gulf-side home. Reese climbed the twelve steps leading to the front entrance, and knocked on the door.

His mother answered, wearing a pair of silk lounging pants and a knee-length robe. Her dark straight hair lay flat against her scalp, lacking the benefits of whatever product she used to style it. She seemed surprised to see him. "Reese, my goodness. Why didn't you use your key?"

She'd asked him that question countless times since he'd returned to Key West. He only used his key when checking on the place if his parents were on vacation. He maintained a separate address from them for many reasons, privacy being the main one, for them and for him.

"I forgot to get it from the kitchen drawer," he said, to avoid a pointless discussion.

She pulled the door wide. "Well, come in. It's ten o'clock. Is something wrong?"

"You could say that."

The volume on the television lowered and Frank called from the living room. "Who is it, Ellen?"

"It's Reese."

A few seconds later, his dad appeared in the hallway, wearing creased pajamas. Ellen Burkett was meticulous about everything, even ironing clothes no one but her husband would see. "Hello, son. Didn't expect you to drop by at this hour. Everything okay down at the station?"

"Yeah, fine, Dad." He explained that he wanted to speak to his mother, but there seemed no way Frank was going to retreat to the TV screen. "Let's go into the kitchen," his father suggested. "Ellen, you can put on a pot of coffee."

"No, thanks," Reese said. "This isn't a social call."

"Are you in trouble?" his mother inquired. It was a conclusion she'd jumped to often in his youth.

"Not that I know of," he replied.

They all went to the spacious kitchen, where Ellen started making coffee anyway. When the machine gurgled into action, she sat down at the table with the two men. "Tell us why you've stopped by, Reese. You have me worried."

"I've just been with Abby," he said.

His mother frowned. "Oh," she said flatly. "So you chose to ignore my advice."

He didn't respond to that. "She had some disturbing news."

"Has something happened to Huey?" Frank asked.

"No. Huey's fine. This has to do with what happened

thirteen years ago." He stared at his mother. Her lips were pursed. She was already thinking back, deciding whether what he was going to say would affect her.

"Mom," he began, "Abby told me she came to see you after I left for Pensacola."

She finally focused on his face. "Really? I don't recall. Of course, that was so long ago…."

Frank sent her a piercing look. "I remember," he said. "I'm surprised you could forget that visit, Ellen. We'd just taken Reese to the airport, and Abby and Loretta came by that evening. I asked later why they'd stopped by. You said it didn't concern me."

She glared at her husband. "I would think I'd remember that, Frank. Loretta and I weren't friends. We didn't seek out each other's company."

Reese shifted in his chair. "Abby said she asked you how to contact me."

Ellen appeared thoughtful. "Did she? That might have happened. I'm sure I didn't give it much importance at the time."

"So you do remember?"

"Vaguely." She got up, went to a cupboard and retrieved a sugar bowl. "Why does it matter?"

"Do you recall telling Abby that I couldn't be contacted?"

Ellen busied herself with getting cups from the china hutch. "I can't tell you what I did last week, much less thirteen years ago," she replied.

"Mom, you can remember what I wore the first day of kindergarten."

Frank chuckled. "He's got you there, Ellen."

She set a saucer in front of her husband with a clatter. "That's ridiculous."

"Come to think of it, Ellen, I don't know why you were so secretive about that night," he said.

"I don't tell you everything, Frank."

Frank's lips thinned. He sat back in his chair and stared at his wife.

Reese shifted his attention to his mother again. "Do you know why Abby came by that night?"

Ellen picked up the coffeepot and brought it to the table. "I honestly don't remember. My goodness, this sounds like an inquisition."

Frank lifted his cup so she could pour. "Reese is just asking a few simple questions, Ellen."

She glared down at her husband as she filled his cup. "Okay, fine. It's not surprising that I can't recall details about something that didn't seem important. That was an anxious time for your father and me, Reese. We had just moved mountains to get you out of trouble. I didn't see how anything Abby had to say would help your situation."

Reese considered that answer for a few seconds. "Let me add one more explanation," he said. "You didn't want me to have anything to do with Abby, then or now."

"All right, Reese. I won't deny that. But mostly I wanted to protect you. That's what parents do. I had suspected for some time that Abby had a crush on you, and if she wanted to reach you… There was that one night…"

Reese raised his hand. "Mom, don't."

"Fine, but if Abby wanted to reach you about some childish schoolgirl nonsense, I wanted to prevent it. I warned her what would happen if you came back to the island."

Reese tried to imagine how Abby must have felt that night, struggling with an unwanted pregnancy, getting no cooperation from his mother. Still, that didn't excuse her for the devastating choice she'd made.

"You should have told me that she was trying to get a hold of me," he said.

"For what purpose? The Vernays are opportunists. Always have been. It wasn't enough that Huey tried to blackmail your father—"

"Ellen!" Frank rose, hitting the edge of the table and spilling coffee over the side of his cup. "We agreed that Reese would never know—"

"*You* agreed," she said. "I never did. And the other day I told him. It was time he knew what the Vernays are capable of."

Frank cast pleading eyes on his son. "It wasn't a lot, Reese. Huey had lost another job and he was desperate. I would have given him the money if it meant he could put food on his family's table." He absently wiped up the coffee spill. Force of habit. "I wasn't happy when Huey went to the authorities about what you'd done," he added, "but you actually benefited from your time in the navy." He scowled at Ellen—something Reese had never seen him do. "I've all but forgotten about that incident," he said. "We all should forget about it. Makes no sense to dredge up the past."

Ellen sniffed, sat stiffly at the table again. "You're right about that," she said. Then she spoke to Reese. "Abby left soon after stopping by here. She got away from her family and made something of herself. You both went your own ways. You became a decorated naval officer. Abby had a life in Atlanta."

In his mind, Reese added, *All's well,* and nearly pounded the tabletop.

Ellen rolled her shoulders with an irritating smugness.

"At the time I couldn't imagine that any association you two might have had would be good for you. I assumed Abby was just suffering from a crush that would never have gone anywhere anyway."

Frank shook his head. "Ellen, you should have told Reese about Abby wanting to reach him. He was a grown man by then—"

"One who didn't know right from wrong," she said.

Reese stood, hoping to defuse what was happening between his parents. But he couldn't ignore a small burst of pride that his dad was standing up to Ellen for his sake. "It's okay, Dad. I've heard enough." He walked to the door.

"You can't leave like this," his mom said. "Sit and have your coffee. I have chocolate cake. Besides, you haven't told me what this is all about. Why the sudden interest in something that happened thirteen years ago?"

Convinced that his mother didn't know the truth behind Abby's visit, Reese stopped and shot her a glance over his shoulder. "Doesn't concern you, Mom."

"But…"

The last voice Reese heard was his father's. "Let him go, Ellen. If he wanted you to know, he'd tell you."

Reese gunned out of his parents' driveway. Without thinking, he detoured on his way home and drove down Southard Street. He spotted Abby's car behind Huey's old pickup. She'd gotten home safely.

He slowed as he passed the house. Only one light was on, casting a soft glow through a second-story window. Abby's bedroom, no doubt. He imagined her coming onto the balcony. What would he do if she caught him out here? He was supposed to be angry. Hell, he *was* angry. So why was he crawling past Vernay House so late at night?

He sped up, zipped around the corner. It wouldn't do for her to see him. But as he drove toward home, he realized that the sight of that one lonely light in the house made him feel even worse.

THE NEXT MORNING, early Monday, Abby received a call from Alicia Brown. Abby waited until her voice mail had recorded a message, and then got out of bed and padded to the bathroom to wash her face. She couldn't follow through on her instinct to stay hidden under the covers all day. A few minutes later, she phoned the young woman back.

"How are you doing, Alicia?" she asked when the girl picked up.

"Okay, I guess. Miss Douglas is very helpful."

"I'm glad. She's a nice lady and a good counselor."

"I saw Cutter."

Hopeful, Abby asked, "He's out of jail?"

"No, I went there to see him. He's not getting out for a long time."

"Oh. Sorry."

"He told me I was doing the right thing by giving up the baby."

Knowing that all birth mothers had to be confident and comfortable with their decision and not pressured by outside influences, Abby said, "And you're sure this is what you want to do?"

"Yeah, I am. I can't take care of a baby right now."

Concerned that Alicia might regret choosing closed adoption, Abby asked her again, "And you haven't reconsidered at least a semi-open adoption agreement?"

"No. I know a lot of mothers think that's best. They

don't want to sacrifice their baby completely, but I need to, Miss Vernay. I can't go through life just having pictures and talking once in a while with the adoptive parents. I've got to make a clean break."

Perhaps if Abby had been face-to-face with Alicia, she would have argued in favor of a more open agreement. But the girl seemed certain, and for that Abby envied her. Right now, Abby questioned her own decision to give her baby up. And she was beginning to question her ability to counsel anyone experiencing the same life-altering situation. The choice that had seemed right to her all those years ago was now fraught with doubts. And sadness.

"I'm glad you called," she said to Alicia. "You sound like you'll be okay."

"Yeah. I will. I'll talk to you again in a few days."

TWO DAYS LATER, on Wednesday morning, Abby and Huey sat on the front veranda having coffee. Though he kept studying her as if she might spontaneously combust, Huey drank with his usual gusto. Abby sipped hers cautiously, not knowing how her stomach would react to the caffeine.

Since Sunday night, she had kept pretty much to herself, only emerging from her room to encourage Huey with his painting. Without supplying details, she'd told him that she'd confessed everything to Reese. That wasn't exactly true, though. She hadn't told Reese that she'd been getting school pictures of Jamie every year, a condition of the semi-open adoption agreement she'd signed with the adoptive parents, Ron and Deborah Ingersoll.

If Reese ever spoke to her again, if he even came close to forgiving her, perhaps she would tell him, as long as he agreed to certain conditions. But she couldn't tell him now. His wounds were too fresh. He'd been too angry, too desperate to reclaim his son. She didn't know how far he would go, and her first obligation was to her child.

Thankfully, on this beautiful Key West morning, Abby was able to push her unhappiness to the back of her mind for Huey's sake. She told him about the possibility of him joining the ghost walk tour.

He leaned back in the old wicker rocker and said, "Is this all Burkett's idea?"

"It is. He thought of it and is supposed to talk to Undertaker about it. What do you think, Poppy?"

"I don't know. If the plan came from Burkett, there must be something seriously wrong with it."

She smiled. "That's just silly."

"All I'd have to do is dress up like Armand and stand on the porch?"

"Pretty much. And I'm sure you could ad lib any way you want. And this performance would be after you sell your merchandise and paintings at the square."

He looked at Flake, who lay with his head over the top step. "Could Armand have a dog?"

"I suppose, if you kept him on a leash. Remember, if Flake bites anyone, Armand won't get sued. You will."

Huey waved off her concern. "Flake wouldn't bite anybody."

"So you're interested?" Abby asked.

"I could be persuaded."

"Well, good. Once we know how Undertaker feels, we can work out the details."

Huey grinned at her. "You don't think anybody'd be fool enough to think I was a real ghost, do you?"

"Hardly. I'm sure Undertaker will tell them you're only a representation of the spiritual being who is rumored to reside in this house." She smiled. "But I wonder… Maybe Armand will get as big a kick out of this as those folks on the ghost walk."

Huey gave her a twisted smile, as if he were seriously considering that possibility. "I guess you could thank Burkett for me, once you two patch things up."

Abby walked over to the balustrade and placed her hands on the rail. "You'll probably get the chance to thank him yourself long before I ever do."

"I'm sorry, baby girl. I wish I could do something to make this easier for you. I always said Burkett was a damn fool, and now he's only—"

She spun around. "This is *my* fault, Poppy. I hurt him."

"And you've been miserable. So what are you going to do about it?"

"I'll be fine."

"Hogwash," Huey said. "Burkett hasn't been around to see you. I guess it'll have to be you that takes the first step. You've got to be honest with yourself, though. You're head-over-heels with our police captain. And you and this situation need fixing."

Poppy was so right. "There's nothing I could say to him now."

Her dad got up from his chair. "Get your purse or whatever it is you ladies need to leave the house."

"I'm not going anywhere."

"Yes, you are. You and I are going to the Pirate Shack."

"What? You don't go to the Shack."

"I do if your future's at stake." He checked his watch. "It's nearly ten. Phil ought to be breading fritters by now."

She stared at her father a moment, decided he wasn't going to back down, and said, "If you're driving, I don't need my purse."

He let Flake in the house, grabbed Abby's hand and practically dragged her behind him to the driveway. Before she knew it, they were in his truck and on their way.

At 10:00 a.m., only two customers, die-hard local fishermen, were in the Pirate Shack, talking to Nick, who was behind the bar. When Huey and Abby came in, one of the men said, "Huey?"

"Yep, it's me."

"What are *you* doing at Phil's place?"

"None of your business." Huey spoke to Nick. "Where are—" He paused, almost as if speaking the names of his ex-wife and brother were too much for him.

Nick smiled oddly and nodded toward the kitchen. "Back there."

Huey strode to the swinging door, Abby following. "Are you sure you want to do this, Poppy?"

He pushed the door open. "No."

Phil and Loretta stopped working and stared in obvious shock. "Is something wrong?" she asked.

"What the hell?" Phil said.

Huey stood with his arms crossed. "Tell them, Abby."

"Tell them what?"

Loretta approached with a mixing bowl in her hand. "What's going on, honey?"

"I'll tell you what's going on," Huey said. "*Your* daughter is in love with Reese Burkett!"

Loretta smiled, visibly relieved. "Oh, that."

Phil walked around the food prep counter. "Really, cupcake?"

Abby stammered an answer. "I—I suppose I could be, but there are problems...."

Loretta leaned the spoon she'd been stirring with against the side of the bowl. "Has he contacted you since Sunday night?"

Abby shook her head.

"That idiot."

"Do something, Loretta," Huey said. "You're the one who let this get out of hand."

"Me? What do you think I can do?"

Abby answered for him. "Nothing! Nothing should be done. I live in Atlanta. I'm going back right after New Year's!"

Loretta set the bowl down and reached for Abby's hand. "How far has this progressed, honey? Have you and Reese...?"

Abby's skin heated to the roots of her hair. "Mother!"

"I don't mean to be nosy. It's just that sex complicates everything."

Huey held up a finger. "No talking about sex," he stated.

"No talking about any of this," Abby decided. "My rotten life shouldn't be a topic of conversation for all of you."

Phil stepped forward. "Cupcake, I love you—you know that, don't you?"

"Yes."

"Okay, then listen up. The four of us in this room, and now Reese, are the only ones who know what happened thirteen years ago. We suffered with you..." he glared at Huey "...each in our own way. We tried to support you. We went along with your decision and kept your secret. But if you've got feelings for Reese, if they're serious feelings, then you've got to make him understand. You have to show him how you felt back then. You can't give up and just quit trying."

Loretta smiled at Phil before speaking softly to her daughter. "How strong are your feelings for Reese, honey?"

Abby sighed deeply, used her thumb to wipe moisture from under her eyes, and admitted the truth. "They're pretty damn mind-blowing."

Loretta smoothed her hand down Abby's hair. "Then Phil's right. Go to Reese. Make that man open his eyes and see you for the wonderful woman you are. When are you going to meet up with him again?"

"I'm not sure. Maybe Saturday night, at the Christmas boat parade. We'd talked about going together, but that won't happen now."

Loretta smiled. "But you'll see him there. He's going to be a judge this year. And if you need any of us to go along with you to convince him…"

Abby gave her a small smile. "Heaven forbid."

Huey cleared his throat. "Have we got this settled now? Abby's going to quit sitting around the house and take action? Because I've got things to do."

Phil looked at Loretta. She shrugged. "You want a beer, Hugo?" Phil asked. "It's early, but you've earned it."

Huey's eyes narrowed. He opened his mouth and shut it again. When he answered, his voice was calm. "Sure. Why not? You're paying."

In that moment, witnessing a small miracle, Abby realized what she had to do. A risk was involved, but the possible outcome was worth it. She was going to make what would probably turn out to be one of the most important phone calls of her life and Reese's.

CHAPTER FOURTEEN

ABBY STAYED WITH HUEY at the dock until darkness had fully settled over the island. Then, after congratulating him on the sale of three paintings, she followed the trail of Christmas lights on every building from Mallory Square to the island's Historic Seaport Harbor Walk.

She passed unique decorations that made her smile. The statue beside a seashell store, a six-foot man composed entirely of sponges, blinked with red and green lights. Blue bulbs wound around a marlin above a local seafood restaurant. Someone had set a Santa hat on the metal sculpture of a seaman in the center of the harbor entrance. A large anchor by his feet glowed with red tube lights.

Weeks, maybe months, might pass before Abby managed to shake off the melancholy she felt, but for now, it was Christmas in Key West, and no place on earth quite equaled it.

She found a few inches of space among the crowd gathered along the rear patio of the Schooner Wharf Bar, the official viewing site of the boat parade. The judges and media people would be on the second-story deck alongside the bar, where they could get the best look at the boats floating by. Had plans gone as she'd anticipated, Abby would have been up there with the parade dignitaries. Now she would have to be content with watching the pageantry from sea level.

A master of ceremonies spoke through a PA system to those gathered below. He announced the arrival of a beautiful nineteenth-century, tall-masted sailing ship, one that regularly took tourists on sunset cruises around the island. Passengers and brightly lit animated figures waved to the onlookers. Christmas carols played from onboard speakers. Every mast was entwined with white lights. The MC read a short history of the proud ship and acknowledged the skilled captain at the wheel.

Abby stepped away from the throng long enough to glance up at the deck over her head. She spotted Reese immediately. Sitting next to a cameraman from a local news show, he appeared deceptively relaxed in a ball cap and island shirt. As the clipper ship pulled away, he wrote something down—his evaluation, Abby assumed. Then he peered over the water, waiting for the next entry to arrive.

Abby slipped into the crowd again, resuming her anonymity. She ordered a glass of wine, spoke to a few people she recognized, and watched the rest of the parade. She stayed to the end and cheered along with everyone else when the top three winners were announced.

Once the judges were thanked and details of next year's parade were given, she went around the side of the bar to wait for Reese. She spotted him with a group of friends in front of the building. When the group broke up, she approached, feeling as awkward around him as she had in high school. Her palms grew sweaty. She hoped the darkness hid the sudden flush to her cheeks.

Fine lines around his eyes suggested he hadn't been

sleeping any better than she had. He stared down at her, his expression unreadable. She didn't know what she'd expected, but not this awful silence. But then, she'd turned his life upside down. She clenched her hands at her sides to keep from reaching up and touching his face. She'd hurt him, and knew she wouldn't be the one he'd want help from now.

"The parade was nice," she finally said.

"I didn't expect you to come."

"I was with Poppy at the square, and figured I'd walk down to see which boat won."

"Oh. It was Bill Peterson again."

She nodded.

Another silence stretched uncomfortably until he said, "Since you mentioned Huey, I should tell you I spoke to Undertaker."

She covered her surprise with an attempt at a smile, though she should have realized that Reese was a man of his word. "What did he say?"

"He loved the idea. Wants to start next weekend, if Huey agrees. The few days before Christmas are always big tourist nights."

"That was nice of you, Reese…." She thought a moment before adding, "After everything." She kept her tone matter-of-fact, not wanting to appear needy or pathetic. "I'll tell him. I'm sure he'll agree to it."

Reese pulled a card and pen from his shirt pocket. "I'll write down Undertaker's phone number. You can speak directly to him."

And leave me out of it, Abby ended for him. She put the card in her wallet. "I'll do that. Thanks again."

They both stood there like snowmen in the tropics, about to melt away and never see each other again. These past moments had been awkward but not unbearable. Not sure how to proceed, she said, "I guess I'll be going then."

He stopped her. "Abby…"

The deepening anguish in his eyes broke her heart.

"I haven't exactly gotten a handle on my feelings about what you told me," he said. "I keep thinking of him…."

"I understand."

"And I can't let this go. I need to find out about him. What he looks like, what he does for fun."

She released the breath she'd been holding. Her decision to make that phone call was the right one. Reese was calm. Not exactly accepting of what had happened, but ready to hear more. Maybe even to try to understand. She nodded. "There might be something I can do, Reese. I'll be in touch."

A few days later, by Wednesday afternoon, Huey had a growing stack of paintings to sell and a regular gig with the Key West Ghost Walk Tour. He and Abby had painted the dog cart. And Abby had received a response to the call she'd made on Sunday afternoon. Now all she had to do was tell Reese.

ABBY WALKED IN THE front door of the Key West Police Department and approached the reception desk. "Is Captain Burkett in?"

Four words. Easy to say. Ordinarily. But on Thursday afternoon, when she said them to the desk sergeant, a middle-aged woman who smiled professionally, Abby's throat was dry. Her voice cracked.

"He sure is. Just got back a few minutes ago." The sergeant pointed over her shoulder. "Through that door and down the hallway. His office is the last one on the left."

Abby shivered in the ultracool temperature produced by

powerful air conditioners. She passed several large squad rooms with numerous desks, some of which were occupied by uniformed officers. Reese's office was across from the one labeled Chief of Police. The door to that room was closed. At least her conversation wouldn't be overheard by the head of the department.

She stopped in the open doorway. His back to her, Reese mechanically slid files into a cabinet.

After a moment, he turned. "Abby," he said simply.

"Sorry. I didn't mean to sneak up on you."

"No, no, that's okay." He came around his desk. "What are you doing here?"

"I have to tell you something."

He pulled a chair away from the wall. "Do you want to sit?"

Since her knees were shaking, she should have said yes. Instead, she said, "No, this shouldn't take too long."

He, too, remained standing. The height difference, which just days ago had made her feel secure, now made her anxious. She should have sat. "I've come to offer you a proposition, a way to learn something about your son."

His eyes narrowed. "You have?"

"I've recently had a conversation with our son's…the baby's adoptive father."

His features registered his shock. "You know him?"

"I didn't tell you that before, but…" She eyed the chair as a wave of dizziness swamped her. "I've changed my mind. I'd like to sit."

He took her elbow, led her to the sturdy metal office chair.

"Anyway," she said after a moment, "you should know something else. I've kept up on the progress of our child. I have a few photos—school pictures, mostly. And…" She admitted the truth that she hadn't even told her mother. "I've seen him on two occasions."

Reese leaned against his desk. "When? Does he know who you are?"

"No, he doesn't. I've never met him. Remaining out of his life was a condition of the adoption agreement I signed. But as I said, I've kept track of him. Contact with his parents through a third party is in accordance with the agreement. Personal contact with him is not."

A muscle clenched in Reese's jaw. "His parents?" Bitterness tainted the two words. "And you're prepared to let me in on this now?"

"Yes. But with certain conditions."

His face reflected skepticism, but his attention didn't waver. "What conditions?"

"First of all, you have to understand what my relationship has been to the family. I met and interviewed the potential parents as part of the adoption process. What it really amounts to is I chose them. When I signed over…"

She stopped, breathed. This seemed so callous. "In our contract, the adoptive parents agreed to send me periodic pictures and letters. And I agreed not to contact them on a personal level with either phone calls or visits."

"But you have? Contacted them, I mean."

"Yes. Several years ago."

"How did they react?"

"They were alarmed at first. Worried. Defensive. But I assured them I had no intention of violating the adoption terms by insinuating myself in the boy's life. I said I just wanted to meet with them again. I wanted them to know me."

"And so you got together?"

She nodded. "When Jamie—that's his name—was eight years old, I had a short face-to-face meeting with his parents in a restaurant."

Reese repeated the name softly. "Jamie. It's nice."

She tried to smile past a lump in her throat. "That was four years ago. Since then I've seen him twice. Both times I told the adoptive parents."

Reese pushed away from the desk and came toward her. "Where did this happen?"

"I watched him play in a Little League game. And two years later I saw him in a school presentation. The auditorium was crowded. I was merely one of the audience."

"He plays baseball?"

"Yes." Abby remembered that Reese had been on the Fighting Conchs baseball team in high school. That fact made her ache for him now. "I wanted to see more of him, but, well, you can imagine how strange…" She couldn't continue, so inhaled a deep breath and waited for Reese to react.

He took another step toward her. "And Jamie's adoptive parents—they were okay with this?"

"They were cautious. They still are. But I promised them I wouldn't interfere in Jamie's life in any way. I explained the circumstances that had prompted me to give him up, and that I just needed to see him."

"They must be understanding people."

"They are. They're terrific." After blinking tears from her eyes, Abby continued. "They trust me, Reese. I told them I would never violate that trust, and I meant it. They can reach me in the event Jamie asks questions about his biological parents, if he becomes curious. That was important to me—for them to know I wasn't some mental case. They've agreed that Jamie can seek me out if he ever wants to." She stared at Reese so he would have no question about where she stood in her relationship with the Ingersolls. "But they are confident that I would never attempt to meet their son on my own."

"Their son," he repeated, but without scorn. Only sadness. He waited. Forever, it seemed. His expression had changed in a matter of moments from one of tentative hope to confusion. "Where does this leave me, Abby? Where do I fit in? He's my son, too."

"Of course. And that's why I called Mr.—" She broke off, withholding Ronald Ingersoll's name for the time being. Even at this stage in her relationship with Reese, she couldn't trust him with the identity of his son's adoptive father. Not until she had Reese's cooperation. He was too hurt, too raw. The news was too fresh. He had too many investigative resources at his disposal. "Jamie's father," she amended.

Reese ran his hand down his face. "And?"

"He's agreed to meet with you. With us. Just the four of us, not Jamie."

Reese frowned. "Is this to determine if he approves of me, as he has you?"

The words sounded cold, but they were true. "Yes, Reese. Jamie is his responsibility. He only wants to protect him, as any father would." Realizing how that must sound to a man who had missed out on protecting his son, she quickly elaborated. "He understands that I've, well, reconnected with you. That puts you in the picture in the event Jamie asks questions about his birth parents."

"And how did he take the news that you'd *reconnected* with me?"

Abby couldn't lie to Reese. Telling Ronald that Jamie's

father had discovered the child's existence had been difficult. She'd promised him four years ago—prematurely, as
it turned out—that the biological father would never be a
factor in Jamie's life. She intended to keep that promise
today any way she could. But Reese was a determined
man. "He was surprised," she said. "Guarded. He asked
what it meant, if you had any legal rights."

"And you told him I didn't?"

"Reese, you don't. Florida law is clear."

"Unless I choose to challenge it. Fathers have rights
these days, Abby. There are lawyers—and I should tell
you I've contacted one—who work to establish a legal
basis for men like me, men who were never told, to prove
paternity and all that that entails."

She did know it. Many of those lawyers worked pro
bono, they were so committed to advancing the causes of
fathers who'd been left out of their children's lives. Reese
certainly qualified.

She sat forward. "This is the first step. I can't tell you
if there will be others. You can't blame Jamie's adoptive
father for being frightened of the future right now."

"For being scared of me, you mean."

"Yes. You're a very real threat. By agreeing to meet
with you, he's hoping to reduce the size and impact of that
threat. And if you meet him, I believe—I *hope*—you'll
come to accept him as I do, as a kind and decent man." She
glanced down, unable to look Reese in the eye. The sad fact
of this situation was that both Jamie's fathers fit that description. Both were kind and decent.

"When did you tell him we'd meet?"

Sensing Reese was ready to agree, she lifted her face.
"He set the date and the place. Amazingly he suggested

seeing us at their home so you can get a better sense of Jamie's life."

"That is pretty amazing," Reese said. "Of course you probably have the address anyway and the family knows that."

She did, but Abby didn't comment. "They live in Ocala. It's a nine-hour drive. Or we could catch a flight. We would meet with Jamie's parents in the afternoon. Stay over in a motel, if you'd like, or turn around and head back. If we drive straight through, we can share the time at the wheel."

"And where will Jamie be?"

"That's why this date was chosen. Jamie will be on a three-day camping trip with members of his church. Apparently, it's a yearly tradition, something to keep the kids occupied these last days before Christmas. Anyway, we'll be able to get together without him knowing."

Reese stared out the window. After remaining silent for a long time, he rubbed his nape and let out a deep sigh.

She got up and went to stand beside him, resting her hand lightly on his back. "It's the best I can offer you, Reese. You'll see pictures of him, visit his home. Maybe gain some peace of mind, something concrete to visualize when you think of Jamie, as I know you will every day of your life from now on, just as I've thought of him every day for the past twelve years." The muscles in his back contracted under her palm. He was suffering. He always would. And she'd brought this sadness upon him.

She dropped her hand and waited. Looking at his resolute profile, his taut veins, his grim mouth, she felt about as miserable as she ever had in her life. This moment hurt almost as much as the one when her baby had been taken away. And she understood. She loved them both, always had. Always would. But loving was no guarantee of happiness. Sometimes the awful weight of caring could almost be too much to bear.

He turned toward her. "I'll go, Abby. And I'll accept your terms for now. But I'm not saying this will be the end of it."

His implied threat didn't frighten her. He knew the rules. He'd given his word and she trusted him.

HUEY SIPPED WHISKEY from his glass and set the porch rocker into motion. "What time do you suppose it is?"

He and Abby had been sitting for so long she'd lost track of time, but she guessed. "I'm thinking it's near midnight, so that would make it very late Saturday or very early Sunday."

Huey nodded. "I'm sticking with Saturday. That way I can still say it's been a good day. Sold two more paintings and scared the heck out of three dozen tourists."

She smiled. "Scaring people would be a good day for you, Poppy." She held up her glass, which had been refilled twice now, and made a toast. "Here's to the magnificent reincarnation of Armand Vernay."

"So I did okay?"

"Poppy, if the real Armand does still live here with us, and if he was watching tonight, he must be jealous. There's no way he could be a better him than you were." She laughed. "You understand what I'm saying, don't you?"

Huey clinked his glass against hers. "I do indeed, baby girl. This could open up a whole new line of merchandise for me. Armand top hat thimbles. Armand bobblehead dolls. Armand—"

Abby raised her hand. "Stop right there. I don't mind getting a little pie-eyed with you, but let's be realistic. You promised to upgrade the items on your cart, remember?"

He chuckled, drank more of his whiskey. "That was something when your mother showed up tonight, wasn't it?"

Abby laid her head against the back of her chair. "For sure."

"Why do you suppose she did?"

"Honestly? I think her reason for stopping by was twenty percent for you and eighty percent for me."

He feigned a hurt expression. "I only rate twenty percent?"

"Yeah, sorry. But she's worried about my trip with Reese on Monday. She wanted me to know she was behind our decision to see Jamie's parents."

Huey shrugged. "Okay. Still, it was nice, getting that twenty percent of her attention, all things considered." He remained silent a moment before adding, "You know, Ab, I was never much of a husband to Loretta."

"No?"

"I didn't really like the job—being a husband. I wasn't good at it." He stared across at her. "I was a damn good father, though, wasn't I?"

She smiled. "The best."

"I liked that job. Always did. It's easier to assume the responsibility for someone who already believes you're pretty great than to try to measure up all the time. That's how I felt about your mother. She always wanted me to measure up, and I never did. You just loved me."

Abby raised her glass again. "Still do."

Huey leaned forward, pointed down the block. "Take a gander, Ab. It's that pickup again, going down Duval Street at a snail's pace."

She stared around him. "It's black, like Reese's truck."

"It's him, all right. The past few nights he's been casing our house pretty regularly."

"Don't read anything into it, Poppy. It's Reese's job to check out the neighborhoods."

"Not this one so much, and Burkett doesn't work on the weekends. So I doubt he'd bother with us unless old lady Howell called up the station with some complaint, which she'd have no reason to. Yessir, Burkett's been giving our street extra attention."

Abby allowed herself to hope. She'd noticed Reese driving by a couple of times, and resisted the urge to go outside and see if he'd stop. The only communication she'd had from him was a message on Huey's phone. In as few words as possible, he'd announced that he'd pick her up Monday morning at six o'clock.

Huey shook his head. "Poor guy."

She sat forward. "Who, Reese? Why?"

"'Cause he's crazy about you and mad at you at the same time. Not an enviable position to be in. I ought to know."

Abby snorted. "It's true he's mad at me. But I don't believe he's suffering too much over the crazy part." Huey smiled wryly. Changing the subject, Abby said, "How much money have you saved up in the past couple of days?"

"Some. I'm making a payment tomorrow on that property tax debt."

"Good. I'm proud of you."

He grinned. "Got to be sure you'll have something to inherit when I'm gone. Might as well be a house filled with spooks."

CHAPTER FIFTEEN

ABBY WAS OUTSIDE AT five fifty-five Monday morning. She'd slept fitfully, waking every couple of hours to cope with her own anxiety over meeting the Ingersolls again. She hadn't seen Jamie in almost two years, and she'd never been to his house. Being there, around his things, wasn't going to be easy for either her or Reese. Jamie's presence would be felt everywhere.

Reese pulled up in front of the house at exactly six o'clock. Abby retrieved her overnight bag from the floor of the porch and walked to his car. When Reese stared at the bag, she said, "I didn't know if you would want to stay over, so, just in case…"

He got out and opened the door to the cab behind the front seat. "It's fine." He tossed her duffel in the back, next to his. "I left Rooster with a friend and arranged two days off from work." He waited for her to get in the truck before he said, "We'll decide later whether we want to drive back tonight."

Reese followed Whitehead Street to Truman Avenue, a major thoroughfare through town that eventually turned into U.S. 1, which ran north through Florida and several states bordering the Atlantic Coast. For Reese and Abby, the trip would start with a three-hour drive over numerous bridges spanning several islands, before they officially reached the mainland of Florida.

There was no traffic. Truman Avenue was quiet. Abby rolled down her window and let the cool, sea-scented breeze wash over her.

They didn't talk. After an hour, he stopped at a bakery in Marathon and bought muffins and coffee. Then he suggested she choose a couple of CDs to listen to.

By midmorning, they'd put almost half the distance behind them. They'd managed to discuss a few safe topics, such as the baked goods from the coffee shop, Huey's stellar performance as a supernatural celebrity and the good fortune they'd had to encounter little traffic.

Reese drove up a service plaza ramp along the Florida Turnpike and parked. "Pit stop," he said.

They used the facilities then purchased more coffee and an order of fragrant cinnamon buns with icing. Once back in the truck, Abby searched in the wallet for another CD. Reese placed his hand over hers. The unexpected contact sent a zing of electricity up her arm. She looked over at him. "What?"

"Tell me about your decision," he said. "What you went through when you chose to give up the baby."

He had to realize this was a difficult topic for her to discuss, but he had every right to learn the specifics. "Choosing to give up a baby is the most difficult decision a young woman can make," she began. She smiled at him but he was focusing on the highway. "Next to telling the birth father years later."

Reese nodded.

"I made my decision based on a number of factors. One, I was unable to care for a baby. I had no income. My family, as you know, was stuck in financial quicksand at that time. My parents' marriage was breaking apart. Huey would have offered to help, but he wasn't the most, well…" She paused. Reese could finish the thought about her father's unreliability.

"Two, I had ambitions. I'd worked all through school to maintain an average that would get me off the island. My goal was a college education, a scholarship, a ticket away from Key West.

"And three, I truly believed I was making the best choice for the baby." She gazed through the side window, sucked in a deep breath and confessed the truth that had made her feel like such a failure at the time. "I wouldn't have been a good mother, Reese. Not then. I tried not to feel resentful of the timing, my own stupidity…" She risked a glance in his direction and added, "Your lack of attention. I felt alone, and I knew a baby wouldn't fill the void." Trapping a sob in her throat, she said, "I'm sorry, Reese. I've been sorry for so much over the years."

His gaze remained on the road, but a muscle in his jaw worked. "And what about the adoption? How did you go about establishing this agreement you made with the adoptive parents?"

She explained to him about open and closed adoptions, and the one she eventually chose, a compromise between the two. "At first my correspondence with Jamie's parents was handled through a third party. I didn't know where Jamie lived. Even the photos were sent through someone at the adoption agency." She sighed. "For the longest time I tried to convince myself it was enough. Jamie was thriving. But I was only kidding myself. So through my connections, I found him."

"And has it been easier for you since you've spoken to his adoptive parents?"

"Yes, it has. And strangely, it's been easier for them, too. They trust me. They no longer fear that someday I'll show up and lay claim to their child."

He drove for several miles without speaking, but Abby could tell he was digesting everything she'd told him. "So what should I know about these people?" he said after long minutes had passed.

"He's a dentist. She's a former hospital administrator, now a full-time mom."

"What else?"

"They belong to a church. He's active in the community, the Rotary Club or one of those service groups. She commented once that she likes to create things, crafts, needlework."

"Do *he* and *she* have names?"

There being no reason to keep their identities to herself any longer, Abby said, "Ronald and Deborah Ingersoll."

Reese flexed his hands on the wheel. "Considering what we have in common, those names should strike some kind of a chord with me."

Abby didn't respond. Maybe after today, he would feel a bond with them, as she did.

"Did they pay for Jamie?"

The question came at her from out of nowhere. She swiveled toward him. "What?"

"I've heard about money being exchanged in adoption proceedings."

She tamped down a flash of anger. "No, I didn't sell the baby. The Ingersolls did help out with medical expenses, but that's standard in most adoptions, especially when the birth mother is young and without means."

He had the decency to appear repentant. "Sorry. I had to ask. So they paid nothing but that?"

Abby went over adoption costs every day in her job, knew them by heart. "They paid quite a bit. I work for a nonprofit adoption agency and still the fees are high. I've never handled an adoption that didn't cost over ten thousand dollars."

He whistled through his teeth. "Wow."

"There are application fees, home visitation costs, employee salaries, court costs. But the government will help those who need it. In my case, aside from medical help, all I asked for was the opportunity to choose the family."

"Were the Ingersolls the only ones who applied?"

"No, they weren't. We have many couples seeking children on our list all the time. Adoption is a long and complicated process. The Ingersolls had been trying for six years." She stared out the windshield. "I truly believed they were the best candidates for the baby of all the ones applying. I still do, after meeting them a second time," she added, with what she hoped was a sense of finality.

He took a sip of his coffee. After a moment, he said, "Would you mind opening the cinnamon buns? The smell is making my mouth water."

She complied. They munched on sugary dough for a few minutes until Abby said, "You ready for more music?"

"Sure. Make it something peppy. There's a Mountain Goats in there somewhere."

She found the CD and put it in the player.

Before the music started, Reese looked over at her and said, "Thanks for being so honest, Abby."

She rested her head against the window. For the next

couple of hours, she watched billboards race by, advertising amusements in Orlando. Fun places. Big resorts that catered to families. She couldn't help thinking that she and Reese would never take their son to Disney World.

At two-thirty, Abby removed the handwritten directions from her purse. "The next exit is ours," she said to Reese.

He pulled off and headed west as she told him to. Abby glanced up at the sky, which had become threatening in the past few minutes. "It's going to rain," she said.

They passed a convenience store, a tack shop and feed-and-grain supplier.

"You can tell Ocala is horse country," Reese commented.

"Yep. It's a couple of miles before we reach the Ingersolls' development."

Reese let his gaze wander over gently rolling hills, green pastures and stands of live oaks. Paraphrasing a line from *The Wizard of Oz,* he said, "We're not in Key West anymore, Toto."

Abby smiled. "No. Not an ocean in sight and lots of open space."

They pulled into Grand Oaks, a residential area of large homes on one-acre sites. A clap of thunder rent the air, and the first fat drops fell on the windshield. "Timing is everything," Reese said, glancing up at the sky. "I hope we get there before the clouds open up."

He navigated the turns, his eyes widening as he viewed the impressive houses set back from the road. "I have to say the kid lucked out as far as digs are concerned," he said, his voice thick and raspy.

Grand Oaks was nothing like Key West. In Old Town, where Huey and Reese lived, property was at a premium, and people treasured their few square feet of lawn. Here, grass resembled plush carpets that stretched endlessly. "Maybe so," Abby said, "but I haven't seen any guys with parrots on their shoulders on the side of the road, or even one old Chevy pickup converted to a traveling porpoise. So we're not without our charms."

"True enough," Reese said.

Abby wondered if his heart was pounding, as hers was. The past minutes of almost pleasant conversation had to be masking a heightened tension in both of them. She pointed to a two-story Colonial brick house with a three-car garage attached. "This is it."

Reese drove up the paved driveway and parked in front of the double-door entrance to the house. The impending storm had darkened the sky enough that the hundreds of Christmas lights decorating the place were on even in the daylight. Two massive evergreen trees framed the front doors, their branches heavy with white twinklers.

Reese shut off the engine. "I feel like I'm in a magazine spread," he said.

Abby gave him a smile of encouragement. "I know. I feel the same way. But don't let the opulence influence you. The Ingersolls are really down-to-earth."

The rain began to fall harder. A streak of lightning zagged across the sky a few miles away. Reese rubbed his palms down his jeans. "It's now or never," he said. "Let's make a run for it." He opened his door, stepped out and waited for Abby to slide across. He grabbed her hand and they raced up the steps to an overhanging portico. Reese drew a deep breath before raising his hand to ring the bell.

He needn't have bothered. Ron Ingersoll appeared at the entrance without waiting for them to announce themselves.

He looked pretty much as Abby remembered, except for the expanding bald spot on top of his head. However, he seemed shorter than she recalled, no more than five foot seven. Or perhaps his short stature was more apparent compared with Reese's above-average height. Ron smiled, but the expression seemed forced.

"Come inside before you're soaked," he said, pulling the door wide open. "Nasty day."

They stepped into a two-story foyer with a ten-foot Christmas tree blinking next to a sweeping staircase. A grandfather clock ticked soothingly near a side table holding several family portraits in gold frames. Abby noticed Reese staring at a picture of a young boy with dark hair and deep green eyes.

"Can I get you a towel?" Ron said.

Abby checked her rain-spotted slacks. "No, we just got a few drops." She extended her hand. "Thanks for seeing us, Ron."

He shook it and then gripped Reese's as she introduced them. The two men eyed each other warily, almost like combatants on a field of battle.

"Let's go into the living room," Ron suggested, leading the way. A fire crackled pleasantly, replacing the chill that had blasted Abby when she'd exited Reese's truck. Three stockings hung from the mantelpiece, each hand-embroidered. Abby could imagine Deborah Ingersoll stitching the names.

"Make yourselves comfortable," Ron said, indicating a pair of dusky blue wing chairs. Despite the impossibility of his suggestion, Abby and Reese sat. Reese was stiff, his spine inches from the back of the seat as he crossed and uncrossed his legs.

Ron called his wife's name, and soon Deborah, wearing

a dark plaid skirt and silk blouse, her brown hair pulled back with a clip, entered the room and set down a silver tray. She greeted Abby, and then Reese.

"I was going to serve iced tea," she told them, glancing out a window. The rain was falling in thick sheets. "But I switched to hot drinks because of this nasty weather." She offered a delicate china cup to Reese. "Coffee or tea?"

"I'm good for now," he said, frowning at the paper-thin porcelain. Abby figured he didn't want the responsibility of hanging on to an Ingersoll family heirloom, under the circumstances. She accepted a cup of tea with a polite smile.

The Ingersolls sat on a sofa. "How was your drive?" Ron asked after a moment. "Long way from Key West."

"No problem," Reese said.

Abby put her cup on a parlor table. She'd navigated situations like this many times in the course of her work at the agency. She'd advised countless adoptive couples and encouraged many young women facing unplanned pregnancies. But today's circumstances were unique. Here, she participated as both counselor and birth mother.

"Well," she began. "You already know my background, the reasons I chose to give Jamie up for adoption. You must understand that nothing happening today affects your status as Jamie's parents." She looked from Ron to Deborah. "You should feel secure in that knowledge before we proceed."

The lines at the corners of Reese's mouth deepened, but he kept silent.

"As I explained over the phone, a series of events resulted in my returning to Key West around Thanksgiving," Abby said. "I encountered Jamie's biological father again, and he learned the truth about the birth."

Ron's eyes narrowed. He cleared his throat. "How did he find out, exactly? My wife and I were assured that you would maintain anonymity, that there was no reason to tell the father." He leveled a serious stare at Reese. "Sorry, but that's what we were told."

Reese didn't blink. "Things happen. Late, but they happen."

"I told him," Abby said. "I had my reasons, but I won't go into them today. The important thing is that we move ahead from here. Reese needs to know about his son. Ideally, he'd like to believe that if Jamie should ever ask about his biological parents, you would feel as comfortable telling him about Reese as you would revealing my identity. The final decision to do that is still yours, however."

Ron sat back in his chair and looked long and hard at Reese. "What is it you want to ask?"

The floodgates of curiosity opened for Reese. "What's he like? What are his hobbies? Is he a happy kid? Is he good in school? What are his goals?"

Ron sighed. "Deborah, this part is up to you. You have to feel comfortable with whatever you reveal. Do what you think is right and fair."

Abby sensed an undercurrent of animosity, as if Ron had cautioned his wife not to feel bullied. Such a reaction was justified. Surely the couple had discussed their options well in advance of this meeting.

Deborah rose and went to a bookcase in the corner of the room. After taking out a thick album, she returned to the sofa. "These are our family photos. The album doesn't contain all the pictures we have of Jamie, but it does a pretty fair job of chronicling his life." She handed the book to Reese. "If you have questions, I'll try to answer them."

She resumed her seat next to her husband and folded her hands in her lap. "But be aware, Mr. Burkett, I am appraising you as carefully as you're obviously appraising us. Our primary goal is to protect our son. A great deal of research and consideration went into our decision before we agreed to let Abby into Jamie's life, even to this limited extent. Just as much, if not more, will go into our decision about you. And, of course, any relationship you might establish with Jamie in the future is dependent entirely on his desire for that to happen."

Reese nodded, with what appeared to be a grudging admiration for Deborah Ingersoll, and opened the book.

An hour later, he had viewed all the pages. He'd asked many questions. He'd smiled, frowned. His eyes had lit with pride in the accomplishments of his son. He'd even managed to drink two cups of coffee from Deborah Ingersoll's very breakable china. He'd suffered, yes. So had Abby. But the pain they both were feeling was a cleansing kind.

Abby was confident that her decision to bring Reese here had been the right one. At least when they left, he would know who Jamie Ingersoll was. He would be convinced the child was safe and loved. And he would have initiated the first step to perhaps someday being a part of Jamie's life. Reese's emotional connection to the boy showed in his face, in the light in his eyes. In the way his fingertips brushed the plastic coating of the photographs.

The only thing Abby couldn't determine was whether Reese had started to forgive her.

He eventually handed the album back to Deborah. "Thanks," he said. "I appreciate the time you've given me." He stood up. A peace seemed to have settled over him, over the entire room.

And then the front door opened, letting in the sound of the relentless rain battering the stone entry. The door slammed shut and seconds later Jamie Ingersoll appeared in the entrance to the living room. Water dripped from his ball cap, the stuffed duffel bag hanging from his shoulder and the rolled-up sleeping bag under his arm.

"Hey," he said. "Weather's terrible out in the national forest. They told us to go home. Pastor Bob dropped me off."

Reese's skin went ashen. And Abby's heart nearly jumped from her chest.

CHAPTER SIXTEEN

REESE FROZE with what he figured was a dumbstruck expression on his face. He tried to make his jaw muscles do something, smile or speak. But his whole body seemed unable to accept commands from his brain. If he'd encountered a two-hundred-pound criminal with a semiautomatic aimed at his chest, he would have reacted instinctively. Now, staring across an expensive Oriental carpet at his son, he didn't have a clue.

After long seconds, he forced himself to look at Abby. She didn't appear any more in control of her reactions than he was. Her fingers gripped the arms of her chair. Her eyes were rounded; her jaw had dropped. She'd told Reese she'd seen their son twice, both times from a distance. But she was no more prepared for this sudden meeting than he was.

Jamie, displaying the baggy-pants slouch of a typical twelve-year-old, stood in the entrance to the living room and stared at everyone.

Thankfully, Deborah filled the void with motherly concern. She hurried over to her son, took the duffel bag from his shoulder. "You're dripping wet," she said.

He removed his cap, slapped it against his leg and smiled at her from his nearly equal height. "Well, it is raining."

"Oh, so it is," she said.

He walked into the living room. "I didn't know you guys were having company."

Ron rose. He shot a warning glance at Reese. "Jamie, this is…" He trailed off, leaving them all waiting anxiously.

Reese's ability to think and speak returned. He said, "I'm a friend of your father's. A former patient."

"Right," Ron added. "This is Mr. Burkett and his friend Miss Vernay. Folks, this is my son, Jamie."

"Hey." Jamie nodded, having no reason not to accept a perfectly sensible explanation.

"Nice meeting you." Reese grabbed Abby's elbow and helped her rise. "Abby, this weather is getting threatening. We probably should go." What could have been the most cowardly announcement under the circumstances was actually the most courageous. The last thing Reese wanted to do was cut and run. His instincts told him to stretch out the moment until this unexpected twist of fate brought him even closer to his son.

"You might want to wait," Jamie said. "It's really coming down out there." He looked through the big picture window. "It'd be cool if it was snow."

The grown-ups responded with polite laughter at the absurdity of snow in Florida. Reese couldn't take his eyes off the boy. He was tall for his age, slim, with thick dark hair that probably went every which way when it wasn't plastered to his scalp with rainwater. When Reese was that age, he, too, had been unable to keep his hair neat.

A shudder from beside him forced Reese to draw his attention from his son. Reese tightened his hold on Abby's arm. "I really think we should brave the elements while we can," he said to her.

She bobbed her head in answer.

Reese reached out to Ron, shook his hand. "Nice to see you…again."

"Same here," he said.

They were behaving with such congeniality that Reese thought Ron might add, *Come back anytime.* But he didn't. Ron was wishing this agony would end.

Keeping a firm hold on Abby, Reese walked to the doorway. He stopped next to Jamie and the woman the boy called Mom. "Thanks for the coffee, Deborah," Reese said.

She kept her arm around Jamie's shoulders, even though his damp jacket was soaking her blouse. Her eyes were wary. "You're welcome."

He focused on Jamie. "Merry Christmas."

"You, too," Jamie said.

Reese gazed at him a moment longer, knowing he must appear a fool. An odd comparison struck him. At that moment, he figured that studying a great work of art on a museum wall must be a lot like what he was doing now. He wanted to drink in every detail of this little man whose appearance was so like his own. He wanted to memorize each feature, from Jamie's dark eyebrows to his square jaw. What if Reese never saw him again? In that case, how long was too long to keep looking at the boy now?

A quiver rippled through Reese, and he concentrated on the floor to break the visual contact. Abby tugged on his arm. "Thanks for the hospitality, Deborah," she said.

Reese waved off-handedly at the family that included his son. "So long."

He opened the door. The rain had let up a little. He put his arm around Abby and hurried with her down the steps to the driveway. Behind them, the Ingersolls' door closed with what seemed a deafening thud, shutting the two of them out.

Abby climbed in the passenger seat and Reese ran around to the driver's side. He got in, started the truck and pulled away. They were a half mile away from the house before he realized that other sounds were slowly invading his consciousness besides the drone of the engine and the steady ping of rain on the rooftop—Abby's sobs.

Rain streaked down the windshield, the wipers barely keeping up. Their persistent hiss added to the melancholy chorus inside the truck. Reese's own vision was blurred, from what, he wasn't sure anymore. *Damn,* he thought, wiping a finger under his eye. *Get a grip,* he ordered himself.

An hour later, he took a ramp at a turnpike exit. He hadn't spoken a word. Neither had Abby. She sat with her head against the window, her eyes cast down to her lap. The rain was heavy again, the sky unnaturally dark for early evening. Restaurants and hotels bordered both sides of the busy exit, their lights bright and welcoming. This was Orlando, where families came for fun. Reese drove into the parking lot of a large, well-lit motel and jammed the gearshift into Park.

Exhaustion had overwhelmed him sometime during the past ten miles. He knew he shouldn't drive. He knew Abby couldn't. Drawing a deep breath, he said, "I think we ought to stay over."

She nodded.

"This place okay?"

Without checking her surroundings, she said, "Fine."

He drove under the protective arch, glanced into the lobby, where a Christmas tree sparkled with white lights and shiny red ribbons. "I'll sign in," he said. "Two rooms."

She didn't say anything.

He returned a few minutes later and handed her a plastic key card. "We're just down the walkway from each other. They're all outside entrances, so we'll get wet one more time."

She cradled the card in her palm but didn't look at him.

He parked close to their rooms. "There's a restaurant in the lobby. Do you want to go down for something to eat?"

She turned her head slowly, her eyes dull and vacant in the darkening shadows. "Do they have room service?"

"I suppose they do."

"Then if you don't mind…"

"No. Anything is fine." He was relieved. Given their silence the past hour, how could they possibly keep up a conversation in a restaurant? Still, he struggled to shake off what seemed an almost desperate disappointment. He wanted to reach out to her for… What? Hell, he didn't know. She'd caused this heartache in him. But she was here. And she understood it.

She got out of the truck and retrieved her bag from the backseat. Before shutting the door, she said, "You'll want to get on the road early, won't you?"

He didn't know. His mind didn't have space for practical thoughts at the moment. "I suppose," he said.

"Okay. I'll be ready by seven." She tucked her bag under her arm, ducked through the rain and disappeared into her room. After nearly a full minute of staring after her, Reese went into his.

ABBY SHUT THE FOAM BOX that still held half the sandwich she'd ordered from room service. She threw that and an empty soda can into the trash container and settled on the bed with the TV remote control in her hand. It was nearly ten o'clock. She was emotionally exhausted, but her body wasn't tired. Whenever she shut her eyes, two faces blurred into one—her son's and Reese's.

They had so many similar traits. Reese, too, must have seen them. She wondered if he was curious, as she was, whether he and Jamie were alike in nonphysical ways. Did Jamie love dogs? Did he like to fish?

She punched buttons on the control, and eventually chose CNN. One of the reporters was hosting a special on global warming. She set the volume low and watched, only minimally involved. The steady recitation of scientific data was all her mind could handle right now. The rain continued, pounding the concrete walkway outside her door. Abby didn't care if the storm ever abated. Maybe the monotonous sound would make her sleepy.

After a few minutes, she heard a knock on her door. She jumped up from the bed and peered out the peephole. Reese stood in the glow of her security light, his head bowed. She glanced down at the jersey lounging pants she'd thrown on along with a pale blue tank top, and figured her clothes didn't matter.

She opened the door. A gust of wind pelted her with raindrops. It was so cold, unnaturally so for central Florida, that she wrapped her arms around her chest.

Reese was drenched. Water dripped from his hair and ran down his face onto the front of his light jacket. He shivered, his shoulders hunched.

When he stared at her, she said his name and waited. After a moment, he breathed, "I want… I need…"

"You're freezing," she said, pulling on his arm. "Come inside."

He allowed himself to be tugged over the threshold and to the center of the room. Abby went back to close the door, wiping her damp palms on her pants as she did so. Turning back, she saw that rainwater clung to his eyelashes. He pushed at the hair hanging over his brow, and the wet strands fell back onto his forehead. At this moment he seemed more like his son than she could have imagined.

"Why are you out in this weather?" she asked him.

"I've been walking, thinking."

"Oh, Reese."

He looked down, as if realizing for the first time that his clothing was sopping wet. He shifted his feet, stepping sideways. "I'm soaking the carpet."

"So what?" She wrapped her hands around his arms, over his jacket sleeves. She wanted to do more for him, to do *everything* for him, but she didn't know what he required, what he expected, and, most of all, what he would resent.

And then he gazed deeply into her eyes and let out a long breath. "It hurts so bad, Abby. You felt it at the house, too. The awful hurt."

She nodded. "Yes, it hurts."

His gaze didn't waver. She kept her hands on him until he touched her waist, his fingers cold and damp against the bare flesh above her waistband. "I don't know what to do. I've never had a feeling like this. The helplessness, as if there's no solution, no way to cope…"

His fingers flexed. She felt the sensation deep inside— a sudden and inexplicable melding of the cold of his skin and the heat of his touch. An undeniable urge flowed through her, making her legs tremble and her heart ache. This was her chance. If Reese couldn't forgive her, then at least she could help him heal. She grabbed his jacket by the shoulders and yanked it down. It fell at his feet and she said, "Wait here."

She went into the bathroom and turned on the shower. When she came back, she unbuttoned his shirt, dragged it down his arms and loosened the fastening of his jeans. He kicked off his shoes and toed his socks off. She helped him shimmy out of his pants and underwear. When he was naked, she ran her splayed hands around his rib cage. Taut muscles below his shoulder blades rippled under her fingertips. His breath caught.

She led him to the shower, slid back the curtain and urged him in. Water cascaded over his shoulders. He raised his face into the spray. Letting emotions dictate her actions, Abby shed her own clothes and got into the shower. His eyes connected with hers through the mist. He smiled slightly and opened his arms. She stepped into them and held on tight, her face nestled into the column of his throat. She murmured comforting words into his ear. "It'll be all right, Reese. Trust me."

He pressed his lips to her neck and left warm kisses along her flesh. She entwined her fingers in the hair at his nape and breathed in the scents of rain and what remained of this morning's aftershave. She wanted to quell his pain, make him think of something besides leaving their son, just as she needed the same from him. He spoke softly. Many of the words she couldn't make out, though she was certain he said, "I'm sorry."

"So am I, Reese. So very, very sorry."

She stood with one leg between his and her fingertips digging into his shoulders. The water sheltered them, enclosing them in soothing warmth. They swayed for moments until he pressed fluttering kisses at the corners of her mouth. She responded with a fierce kiss of her own. His tongue entered her mouth, circled, withdrew and returned to flick against the insides of her cheeks.

When he palmed her breasts and teased the nipples with his thumbs, she shuddered deep inside. His erection throbbed along her thigh. And what had begun as an act of comfort became primitive and needy. Steam rose around them, warming her and exciting her senses. The spray tingled on her skin, spiking her desire to have him complete what could not be stopped. She guided him between her legs. "Now, Reese," she said hoarsely.

"Abby, this is the first I've felt anything but emptiness in days. But are you sure?"

She pulled his head down. "Yes, I'm sure." He plunged inside. Her need spiraled and crested in one blinding flash that obliterated every other emotion but the one she was feeling at that moment. He clutched her tightly, pinned her against his chest as if he were trying to connect with every inch of her body. He jerked convulsively, groaned against her mouth and finally exhaled a long, slow breath. Afterward he held her for precious seconds until their breathing returned to normal.

She reached behind her and twisted the faucet. Water trickled down her body, cooling her heated skin. Reese pulled a towel from the nearest bar and gently patted Abby dry all over, even where she still pulsed between her legs.

He quickly dried himself, tossed the towel on the floor and stepped from the shower. Taking Abby in his arms, he carried her to the bed and threw the covers back. He laid her down and slid in beside her. And with care and exquisite tenderness, he explored her body, nearly bringing her to a second peak. And then he was inside her again, moving rhythmically with steadily increasing thrusts until waves of pleasure rocked her body.

More content than she ever remembered being, Abby

sighed with completion. Yes, the heartache would still be there tomorrow. But she refused to let anything invade this moment. For now, in Reese's arms, she could believe that he'd forgiven her.

THE CNN REPORTER'S VOICE buzzed in the background—accompaniment to Reese's steady breathing. He wasn't asleep, but lay quietly with his arm around Abby's shoulder, his cheek against her hair. She'd waited for him to say something after the lovemaking that had left the sheets tangled around their bodies. But he'd rolled to his back, fitted her securely inside the curve of his arm, and remained silent.

Fifteen minutes passed. He pulled away from her and said, "I'd better go."

She touched his shoulder, not wanting to break the contact. She hadn't expected this reaction. "You don't have to. You can stay."

He slid to the edge of the mattress and sat up. "I should. We'll talk tomorrow."

Feeling suddenly alone, even before he left, she watched him reach for his briefs, which he'd shed next to the bed. He tugged them on, stood and retrieved his jeans. "If you think that's best," she said, her mind struggling to accept his decision.

He zipped the jeans but left the button open. Then he slipped his arms through his shirtsleeves, picked up his jacket and dangled his shoes and socks from his hand. Grasping the doorknob, he turned and said, "Abby, thank you."

Thank you? His voice was even, calm, devoid of emotion, when just a short time ago he'd whispered in her ear with the unabashed huskiness of passion. His simple expression of appreciation might have seemed appropriate if she'd waxed his squad car or taken his dog for a walk. But not for what had just happened between them. Shame and guilt overwhelmed her, along with the cold blast of wind coming in the open door. She reminded herself that she'd hurt him deeply. Maybe a thank-you was all she deserved. Maybe shame was what she should feel, a punishment for what he'd suffered. Still, she repeated, "Reese, if you don't want to be alone, you can stay."

"No. I'll see you in the morning. Things will be clearer then."

Abby tucked the sheet securely under her arms. She would have buried herself beneath it if she hadn't feared she would reveal too much about how he'd made her feel. What had these past two hours been about? She felt even more distant from Reese than she had before he'd knocked on her door. "Fine," she said. Their relationship was much clearer to her already.

He stepped onto the walkway, but leaned in one more time before closing the door. "Don't forget to lock up."

She didn't look him in the eye. "Right. I wouldn't want a stranger to come in here." After he left, she decided that that was what had just happened.

CHAPTER SEVENTEEN

THOUGH DREAMS PLAGUED HIM, Reese slept through the night. When he awoke, he checked the digital clock by his bed: 6:15. He rose and filled the coffeemaker. While he showered and dressed in clean clothes, he thought about Abby. He didn't regret returning to his own room last night. It had been the right thing to do. If he'd stayed with her much longer, he knew what would have happened—again. Even now, remembering caused an instant physical reaction.

He'd come to her door confused, hurt, and for the first time in years without a direction for his future. The last thing he wanted was for Abby to think he was using her for some sort of temporary gratification to soothe his wounds, though in her eyes, that was exactly what she must believe he'd done. He'd gone to her for comfort and she'd freely given it—to Reese Burkett, the jerk who accused her of betraying him.

He'd left her with a promise. That things would be clearer in the morning, as if he'd planned on divine revelation to tell him what to do about his feelings for Jamie, for her. Now, with the sunrise, all he'd really decided was that he had to honor Abby's pledge to the Ingersolls to stay away from his son. As far as his feelings for her were concerned, they were strong and seemed to be in a constant flux.

Okay, maybe he'd used her last night, but he'd also known that no one else on earth could have satisfied his needs the way she had. Only Abby. And that realization scared the crap out of him. The woman who'd caused his misery was the only one who could help him. Where did he go from here?

After stuffing his still-damp garments into his duffel, he wandered down to the lobby, where he thought he might find Abby. She was there, nibbling on a bagel, part of the complimentary continental breakfast. Reese poured himself another coffee and sat opposite her.

She appeared tired but still beautiful. Yesterday had been hard on both of them. She'd been as blindsided as he was by the unexpected appearance of their son. He tried smiling at her, but realized how ineffectual the attempt was. "You okay?" he asked.

She narrowed her eyes as if she, too, found his forced cordiality out of place. "Sure. Fine."

"You ready to go?"

"I'm packed. I'll just go to the room and get my bag."

"Great. I'll settle the bill. We should be back in Key West by late afternoon."

She gathered her used dishes and set them in the bin provided. "Suits me."

Ten minutes later, they were in the truck, heading down the turnpike in light traffic. Reese set his cruise control, rolled his shoulders to get comfortable. He and Abby should talk. He had a lot to say, which was uncharacteristic for him. But the topics weren't easy, and he didn't have any idea how to start.

His feelings for Abby were complex. He owed her, but also resented her. Bottom line, he wanted to forgive her. But this morning he wasn't sure what to say to her.

She put a CD in the player—a repeat of yesterday's efforts to break the silence. They were definitely back to the tension of the day before. Only, this was worse. Now the anticipation of meeting the Ingersolls was over. Reese had had his shot with them, and he had no idea if he'd measured up. He'd seen his son, been close enough to hug him, but because of the promises he'd made to Abby, he felt as distant from him at this moment as if they were continents apart.

The CD finished. Abby ejected it and reached for another. And Reese thought his brain would explode if he had to listen to one more country singer croon about the misfortunes of life. When she started to pull the next disc from its plastic sleeve, he said, "Don't, please." She looked up at him, her eyes wide, questioning.

He set the CD case on the floor. "Abby…"

She waited. He drummed his fingers on the steering wheel while he searched for the right words to break the tension. Finally, he glanced at her and inquired, "How do you think things went yesterday?"

Her reaction was one of disbelief. She'd obviously expected something else. "At the Ingersolls'?"

"Yeah."

"In my opinion, it was pretty darn weird."

"Mine, too."

"The entire incident was uncomfortable, dishonest and painful."

"Yeah." He held her intense gaze until prudence forced his attention back to the highway. "But before Jamie arrived, what did you think? Did the Ingersolls approve of me?"

She exhaled a long breath. "I can't say, Reese. I suppose they did. You didn't do anything to make them believe you wouldn't keep your word."

He eased into the left lane and passed an eighteen-wheeler. "About that…"

Abby leaned forward to stare at him. "What? You're not going back on the agreement? You can't do that."

"No. But I don't like it."

She sat back in her seat, crossed her arms.

He tried a different approach. "Obviously, they like you."

"No. They trust me. And because of that trust, they're giving you a chance."

"I realize that. But if Jamie ever asks about his biological father, do you think Ron and Deborah will feel comfortable telling him about me? As comfortable as they would about revealing your identity?"

She chewed on her bottom lip. The silence stretched for at least a mile—maybe the longest mile of Reese's life. Finally, Abby smiled. She wasn't looking at him, so Reese assumed it was a generic smile. Still, it helped. "Yes," she said. "I believe they'll be fine about telling Jamie that you're his father…if he should ask."

A torrent of questions flooded Reese's mind. "How might he ask? And when? You know about this stuff. Do adopted kids ask in their teens, or more when they reach adulthood? Are they basically resentful? Will it matter that we all lied to him yesterday? Because that really bothered me. What if—"

She placed her hand on his arm. "Reese, I don't have all the answers. Each case is different. I imagine that all adopted kids are curious, but some never ask about their birth parents. Many do, and often meetings are arranged when the kids are mature and better able to handle the consequences of hooking up with them."

She kept her gaze on his face. "I want to give you the

benefit of my years of experience in this field, but you have to accept that, legally, there is only one set of parents. And for Jamie, they are Ron and Deborah. That will never change."

He understood that, but he wasn't ready to give up all hope. So he said, "But most do ask?"

She shrugged. "Yeah, most do." After a moment, she said, "Here's what I believe might happen. That one day—and don't ask me when—your phone will ring. You'll pick it up, and a bright, young voice will say, 'Hi, remember me? We met that rainy day. I was wondering if maybe we could get together, have a little talk.'"

Reese rubbed his forehead, trying to relieve the anxiety of the past twenty-four hours. Could she be right? Could the reunion happen just that way, as two acquaintances connecting on a vitally intimate level? Should he allow himself to hope? He noticed Abby's smile was still in place, but it was definitely for him now. He nodded, accepting her prediction of a happy conclusion, a promising beginning. "Ya think?" he said. "Really?"

"Sure, why not?" Her hand was still on his arm, and she gave it a squeeze. "He's our son," she said. "For better or worse, he probably inherited my curiosity. It was the trait that made me search him out—made me search you out on that beach."

Reese's thoughts flashed back to that night, as they did so often these days. He smiled to himself.

"And he might very well have inherited your courage to take risks," she said. "Something you do every day on your job, especially with Huey."

Reese chuckled.

"And if Jamie's really lucky," Abby continued, "he got

wisdom from the Ingersolls, because I'm afraid you and I are sorely lacking in that area."

"I can't disagree with you."

"If Jamie does decide to contact you—I mean *when* he decides to—a new chapter in your life will open up," Abby said. She removed her hand from his arm. "But I have no doubt you'll be ready for it. And maybe all this sadness you've been feeling will become just a bad memory."

All at once, imagining facing that day without Abby beside him was hard. "And what about you?" he said. "Will you be one of the characters in the new chapter?"

"Me? No. If Jamie decides he wants to meet me, I suppose we'll arrange for it to happen in Ocala or Atlanta. I'd have to take my cue from him."

Reese paused, letting her answer sink in. He didn't know why it surprised him. She lived in Atlanta, yet picturing her going back there, maybe disappearing again for years, seemed to knock him off his emotional center. "How long are you staying in Key West?" he asked after a moment.

"Through New Year's."

"Tomorrow's Christmas Eve. You're going back in just over a week."

"It's plenty of time to accomplish what I came for. Poppy will make another payment on his taxes from the profit on his paintings. I'll be confident that he's going to be okay, at least for a while."

"And that's all you care about? How Huey will get along after you leave?"

She stared, until Reese felt like squirming because of the asinine, petulant question he'd just asked. He'd sounded like a jealous kid, not wanting to share the spotlight with anyone else. But damn it, that was the truth of it.

"That's why I'm here, Reese," she said. "To take care of Poppy and to make sure you didn't arrest him."

He smiled. "But you wouldn't consider staying, moving here permanently?"

Her eyes narrowed, and when she tapped her foot on the floor mat, he gripped the steering wheel until his hands hurt. "What made you ask that?" she said.

"I don't know." He truly didn't. "You grew up here. It's not such a dumb idea, is it?"

She stared out the side window as if the barren landscape dotted with struggling scrub palms was the most fascinating thing she'd ever seen. After a moment, she said, "Well, it seems like a strange, impractical idea to me."

When she'd confessed about Jamie, and Reese's world had changed, he would have agreed. Now, having Abby stick around was beginning to feel right. Last night he'd completely lost himself in her, forgetting everything but the sweet comfort of her body against his.

Today the feeling was still present—for him, at least. On this monotonous highway, heavy now with truckers and vacationers racing to get somewhere special in the next thirty-six hours, last night could have been a distant memory. But it wasn't. Reese's mind was flooded with sensory data of Abby—the scent of her in the shower, the silky feel of her hair, her warm breath heating his skin.

She was sitting no more than a couple of feet away, her face unreadable, her posture rigid. But all Reese could think of was pulling off the road and gathering her close to re-create what they'd had the night before.

He rotated his neck, relieving tension, and uttered the words he had to. "Are you ready to talk about last night?"

For an uncomfortably long moment, she simply stared at him. And then she said, "No, I don't want to talk about it. Besides, you've already thanked me. What more is there to go over?"

Whoa. He refocused on the traffic, specifically a six-figure rolling castle of a motor home ahead of him, and waited for the monster to move back into the right lane. What did she mean? Of course he'd thanked her last night. He'd been damn grateful. And he'd be just as grateful if it happened again.

"Don't make too much of it," she said. "We were reacting to what happened."

He didn't respond. When the silence in the truck made Abby want to crawl out of her skin, she risked a glance at his face. It was stern.

After a moment, he blinked hard and said, "Has it occurred to you that maybe I want to turn that night thirteen years ago, and last night, into something now?"

Unshed tears burned in her eyes. She wanted to believe him, but in the past week he'd given her no reason to. "Maybe it occurred to me at one time," she said. "But not now. We're just wrong together. You know it and I know it, and nothing will ever make us right."

He looked out his side window. "Not if you don't try."

"Me? I have. But I don't believe you will ever trust me." A horrible, weighty truth broke her heart, yet it had to be brought out. "Maybe you shouldn't forgive me—and if you can't, I don't blame you. But my decision about Jamie will always stand between us."

She closed her eyes to avoid facing the flash of reluctant agreement in his eyes. He had to agree that what she'd just said was a sad but indisputable fact in their lives. "I don't need that kind of pain, Reese," she said. "Where Jamie's concerned I have enough already."

Neither one of them spoke again. An hour later, it was nearly dark and they were in Key West.

"You want me to drop you off at your house?" he asked.

"That's fine."

He drove the back way to Southard that avoided the traffic on Duval Street. It was December twenty-third, and the main thoroughfare would be packed with tourists.

He pulled in front of Vernay House. The outside lights were on, but the interior was dark. "Looks like Huey's not here," he said. "I'll walk you inside."

She stepped out of the truck and grabbed her bag. "That won't be necessary."

He stared at her. "Nevertheless…"

"Wait. Never mind. There's a note on the gate."

Abby tore a paper from the latch and held it up to the streetlamp. "It's from Huey. He says he's on Duval Street."

"I'll take you. I'm going right by there."

Abby dropped her bag at the foot of the porch steps and got back in the truck. "Thanks."

"No problem. I don't feel much like going home yet, anyway. I might as well hang out downtown myself. The department can use a couple extra hands."

Being with a cop had its advantages. Soon, Reese had pulled into a lot behind a popular nightclub and parked his truck in a loading zone. He and Abby navigated the holiday crowd. "I wonder where Huey might be," Reese said.

"Since he almost never comes here at night, and especially not when it's crowded like this, your guess is as good as mine."

They didn't have to look far. Dozens of people had

gathered in front of the town's largest department store, forming a circle around, of all things, Huey's renovated, bright red dog cart, with its newly polished brass trim and working coach light.

Abby stared in wonder. "Wow, I can't believe what Poppy's done!"

"It's great," Reese said.

The old carriage sat at the edge of the street beside a miniature forest of artificial trees and animated figures. Its metal fittings sparkled. Plus, a string of lights had been draped around the exterior and a Christmas wreath hung in front of the driver's box.

"How did he get it here?" she asked, walking closer.

Reese chuckled. "I'd say Santa Claus drove it."

Reese's height provided him a better view, but when Abby got closer, she saw what had made him laugh. Santa sat in the driver's seat as if he'd just flown in from the North Pole. "It's Uncle Phil," she said, and then noticed Flake beside him, with an elf cap tied under his muzzle. "And he's got Poppy's dog up there with him." So that was why Huey was here. He wouldn't let his brother use the carriage and his dog without being somewhere nearby, watching over his interests.

Reese nudged her forward. "You're missing the best part."

Abby skirted a group of children accepting candy canes and small wrapped packages from Santa, who was pulling everything out of a giant green bag beside him. She looked up to smile at Uncle Phil, and gulped in surprise. The generous Saint Nick wasn't her uncle.

Dressed in the traditional red suit and black boots, but sporting his own natural beard, was her father. He dutifully cautioned all the kids to put the discarded wrappings in the trash bins, and then explained how Santa didn't always use his reindeer to get where he was going. Sometimes all he needed was a miracle dog with a good sense of direction. The kids ate up every word as if each one were coated with sugar.

Abby sidled up next to the cart and smiled when Huey noticed her. "Aren't you the versatile one," she said. "First, as Armand, you're the ghost of Christmas past and now you're Christmas present. I can't wait to see what you come up with next."

Huey answered with a deep "Ho, Ho, Ho," and reached into his bag. "I might have something in here for you, baby girl," he said, and handed her a colorful box.

Reese put his hand on Abby's shoulder. "Kind of makes you believe in miracles," he said.

"I guess."

"I'm even sorry there's no Mrs. Claus up there with him."

Abby spun around at the sound of her mother's voice. "Mom, what do you know about this?"

Loretta smiled at Reese. "Just that your father and Phil put this whole thing together."

"My father?" he said.

"Yeah." She spoke softly so the kids around them couldn't hear. "He furnished all the candy and toys, and arranged for the kids at the high school to wrap everything. Then Phil went to Huey about borrowing the dog cart. Somehow Phil talked him into playing Santa."

Abby refocused on a refreshingly jubilant Santa. "No way."

Huey leaned over and whispered to her, "I couldn't let one of those Elvis or Barbra impersonators do this. The kids would have seen right through it." Announcing that

Santa was taking a ten-minute break, he climbed down from the cart. "I need coffee, Loretta," he said, hiking up his baggy pants. "You're going to accompany me to the Pirate Shack."

Loretta put her arm through his. "Absolutely."

They started to walk away, but Reese stopped them. "Wait a minute."

Huey turned around.

"You and my dad are partners in this deal? How did that happen?"

Huey shrugged. "Frank and I have always been victims of our women," he said, grinning first at Abby and then Loretta. "Either that or it's been about money. Let's just say we came to terms. Have you been in the house since you got back?" he asked Abby.

"No."

"Don't be alarmed. There's a bunch of supplies in the kitchen."

"What do you mean?"

"I had to buy some food and plates and stuff."

"What for?"

"I lost my head earlier and invited people over for Christmas Eve dinner. You and I have to straighten the place up in the morning."

Dumbfounded, Abby said simply, "Okay."

"I'm going to deep-fry a turkey," Huey said. He laughed at the expression on Reese's face. "Don't get your briefs in a twist, Deputy Do-Right. I'm not going to set the neighborhood on fire. And you won't get any complaints. I even invited that cranky Edna Howell. You might as well come, too. Your dad's going to be there."

"My father is spending Christmas Eve at Vernay House?"

"Said he was."

"Those must have been some terms you came to. Do my parents still own the marina? Am I still their first-born child?"

Huey dismissed the questions with a wave, and Reese leaned close to Abby. "Is it okay with you if I show up?"

"Sure. In fact, you shouldn't miss it."

"Well, okay then. I accept," he said to Huey.

"Your mom's not coming," Huey stated. "She's got some garden club event…if you believe that."

"We'll be there," Loretta said. "Closing down the Shack. Phil said he wouldn't miss it for the world. Huey has criticized his cooking all these years, so he wants the chance to pay him back."

Abby's curiosity got the best of her. "Wait a minute, Poppy."

He walked over to her, leaving Loretta on the sidewalk.

"You and Uncle Phil?"

Huey grinned. "He's showing some human traits." He leaned down so he could confide in her. "You remember that mysterious payment made on my property taxes, the one I thought was an error?"

She nodded. "Are you saying Uncle Phil…?"

"Shh…don't let on to your mother. She'll use that information against me for the next twenty years."

Abby smiled as Huey rejoined Loretta and they headed toward the Pirate Shack.

"You two watch the dog cart and Flake," Huey hollered from down the block. "Don't let him get into those candy canes. He's had too many already."

Reese patted the dog as he spoke to Abby. "I thought his breath smelled a lot like peppermint. You might want to take him for a good long walk before he settles down for the night."

She grimaced. "Good advice." Running her hand over the smooth, shiny surface of a coach lantern, she said, "Do you feel like we've walked into an alternate universe?"

"Yep. Imagine me spending Christmas Eve at Huey Vernay's."

"An interesting picture." Abby was eager to get back to the house and have a long talk with her father, though she already suspected the reasons for his transformation. With his paintings, he'd found a purpose for his life. She took some of the credit for that discovery. And he'd found a darn good dog. That was purely fate.

"You don't have to stick around with me," she said to Reese. "I can keep an eye on things until Huey gets back."

"If you're sure. The stores are open late tonight, and I've still got my Christmas shopping to finish."

"Just like a man. Everything last minute." She smiled, planning to hit the stores again herself. She needed to add a couple of gifts to her list, something for Frank and maybe a bottle of cologne for Mrs. Howell.

She'd already done most of her shopping, including purchasing a Swiss fish filet knife set for Reese before she'd told him about Jamie. Afterward, she'd figured she'd take it back. Now she wouldn't. And she'd just thought of another gift for him—something risky, considering their relationship, but one she wanted him to have, since it would probably be his last reminder of her.

Reese squeezed her hand. "See you tomorrow night."

She watched him walk away and was grateful that the chill that had gripped them the last hour of their journey had melted with the holiday cheer of Duval Street.

She didn't like being angry with him. She wished the same spirit affecting their families would heal her and Reese's relationship.

He stopped and shook hands with a couple of officers on bicycles. They kidded around, smiling and laughing for a minute, and then Reese sauntered off into the crowd. He seemed as at home with strangers as he was with lifelong friends.

Abby leaned on the side of Armand's old dog cart and put her arm around Flake. She couldn't help feeling a bit jealous that Reese so easily fitted in here at Key West, the place she'd called home until a nearly impossible decision had forced her away. Could she come home again? Many people had managed it, but she'd always felt it would never work for her. The pain had been too deep, the secret too big.

Flake licked her cheek and Abby smiled up at him. "What am I going to do?" she asked. "I don't enjoy having these feelings about Reese anymore—all the guilt mixed with unrealistic yearning. What I want is for him not to resent me for the rest of my life. I want a free ticket to start over with him." She scratched Flake under his snout. "But what I *really* want—don't laugh—is for him to love me. And I'm afraid a wish of that magnitude will take a real-life Santa Claus to make it come true."

CHAPTER EIGHTEEN

BY ONE O'CLOCK Christmas Eve, Abby and Huey had made their home shine with glass cleaner and furniture polish. But since the old place still lacked sparkle, Abby now stood in a long line at Kmart, her cart crammed with Christmas decorations at twenty-five percent off. The woman in front of her turned away from the conveyor belt, where her basket was loaded with snacks, and said, "You realize that two days from now, those same items will be half off?"

Abby nodded. "I know, but I don't mind, really." She lifted the box with a seven-foot prelit tree onto the belt. She would have paid full price if that was what it took to fill her family home with holiday cheer, because this was the first Christmas in years that it mattered.

She and Huey were ready at seven o'clock when their first guests arrived—Loretta and Phil. Loretta hugged Abby and kissed Huey on his cheek. Phil presented him with a bottle of wine and a basket of conch fritters, which he swore were not prepared in week-old grease.

Reese and Frank arrived next, with an armload of baked goods from Martha's. Frank announced that Ellen sent her regrets, while Reese looked down at the floor, obviously uncomfortable with his father's lie.

Abby didn't mind Ellen's absence. This night wasn't

about her. This was about the members of the two families who'd decided to put aside bad feelings at the time of year when forgiveness was most possible. Maybe Reese would never be able to forgive her, just as she would never completely forgive herself, but for tonight they could pretend.

Mrs. Howell, in a flowing red satin dress, vintage 1960, and diamonds dripping from her ears, brought her "famous" fruitcake, to which she admitted having added two cups of bourbon before leaving the concoction to ferment in her pantry from June on. Abby decided that she would limit her alcohol intake to Phil's merlot. When Huey announced without chagrin that Flake would love it, Abby assigned Reese the job of keeping the dog far away from the cake.

Everyone commented on Abby's hasty decorating. Huey's pledge to keep the neighborhood safe from flaming turkey wildfires proved reliable. The meal was delicious. At eight-thirty, Huey got up from the table and told everyone it was showtime. He disappeared up the stairs and returned a few minutes later dressed as Armand. He and Flake stepped onto the porch just as Undertaker and his tourists strolled by for a special Christmas Eve ghost walk. Huey's guests sat on the veranda and pretended to be victims of Armand's unscrupulous salvaging activities.

When the show was over, Reese went to his truck, retrieved a colorful Christmas sack and approached Abby. "Walk with me, okay?"

They sat on the bench in the backyard beside the bougainvillea, which was sparkling with white lights. Music from Duval Street drifted over the fence. Abby recognized the rock beat. "Isn't that the Barenaked Ladies' holiday album?"

"I believe it's their 'Green Christmas' song," Reese said.

"Probably coming from the Bilge Bucket. They blasted that song last Christmas Eve about this same time. Apparently, they're making it a tradition." He laughed. "There's nothing quite like a Key West Christmas."

Abby smiled. He was so right. This was a Christmas she would never forget, for reasons that both cheered and saddened her. When she'd told Reese about Jamie, the awful weight of that guilty secret had been lifted from her shoulders, but new regrets had taken its place. She had to accept that she and Reese might never mend the past or be able to live with the decision she'd made.

"So what are we doing here?" she said. "Did you want to talk?"

"I thought we might, but mostly I wanted to give you my gifts."

"Oh! I have gifts for you, too." She ran into the house and returned with two packages. Handing them to him, she said quickly, "Go ahead. Open them. This might truly be the last time you ever speak to me."

He laughed, and the spontaneous sound warmed her inside and out. He was impressed with the set of knives, saying they were just what he needed. Whether or not it was true, Abby was pleased. When he began opening the second gift, she held her breath. She still had no idea how he would react. But if she knew Reese even half as well as she believed she did, he would appreciate her gesture.

He tossed the wrapping to the ground and held the portrait under the lights, to see their son's face smiling up at him. Jamie's expression had been captured in a moment of sublime joy, taken with Abby's zoom lens when she'd seen him perform in that school play two years ago.

Reese stared at the photo. "Abby, how…?"

"Before you say anything, read the back."

He turned the frame over and read aloud. "'Dearest Reese. No matter what else, we did create something amazing.'"

Tears gathered in his eyes, which he tried to hide by blinking hard. "When did you get this?" His voice hitched. "Where…?"

She explained the circumstances, adding that she'd brought the photo with her to Key West because she never went anywhere without it. She'd had it duplicated the night before. "Maybe this will help sustain you until that phone call," she said.

He smiled. "And he'll call. I know it."

"I believe that, too."

"Thank you, Abby. I'll always treasure this." Reese set the photo beside him on the bench and held her hand. "Will you go out with me New Year's Eve?"

She sat back and considered the unexpected invitation. December thirty-first was a week away. Did that mean he didn't want to see her until then? "Reese, I'm not sure. I'm leaving the next day, and…"

He released her hand and rubbed his jaw. "I wasn't just asking about this New Year's. I was sort of making a standing date for the next fifty years or so."

"What are you talking about?"

"If we get tired of the celebrations in Key West, we can go someplace else."

She grinned, what she figured was a giddy, lopsided expression that made her appear ridiculous. But she didn't care. For the first time in many years, she was enjoying riddles. "I don't have any definite New Year's plans for the next fifty years, so okay, sure. It's a date—or dates."

Seeming pleased with himself, he said, "Good. That's

settled." He reached behind him and removed two wrapped packages from the sack. "Here are your presents."

She took the first one he offered. It was shaped like a book. It felt like a book.

"It's a book," he said. "A little hard to disguise. I bought it last night."

She opened the wrapping and read the title: *The Magic of the Keys and Key West. Why We Keep Coming Back.* She flipped through the illustrated pages, and stopped at a photograph of Vernay House as it had looked years ago, before she and her mother had moved out and Huey had stopped caring about the property. "I'd forgotten how beautiful this house used to be," she said. She glanced up at the back porch rafters, their paint cracked and peeling. "It's in a sad state tonight."

Reese hid a smile behind his cupped hand. "It's Christmas, Abby. No time to be sad."

"I know, but…"

"Guess what I did today," he said, his smile mischievous.

"I can't imagine."

"I met with the head of the Community Improvement Board."

"You didn't! You said you were going to resign from that committee."

"I am, but first I wanted to suggest a plan."

She frowned at him, ready for bad news, but not really believing she was going to hear it.

"I did some investigating. Turns out that the CIB actually does some improving around here. They regularly repaint the sign at the Southernmost Point. They arranged for a new roof on the Wreckers Museum. They do some good."

"As well as some general hassling of citizens," she couldn't help pointing out.

"That, too. Anyway, I'll have to attend at least one meeting before I step down, the first one in January. That's when my proposal will go up for a vote. According to Harry Myers, the head of the committee, the proposal should pass."

Completely intrigued, she closed the book and laced her fingers together on top of it. "And what is your proposal?"

"I'm suggesting that Vernay House be given a new coat of paint and benefit from a few repairs to its exterior." He stood and appraised the roof. "Maybe fix some leaks up there, patch a few window moldings, shore up the carriage house. Things like that."

"Why would the committee do that?"

"Because I'm going to talk Huey into opening the place to visitors during a couple of the island's historic festivals each year, when we have an influx of tourists. This house can be part of the historic buildings tour, and the CIB can keep the profits from ticket sales."

Abby could barely contain the excitement building inside her. It was a wonderful idea, one that would preserve her home and restore her pride. Unfortunately, a gigantic obstacle to the plan was right now changing out of his Armand costume. Huey would never go for the public traipsing through his house. "It's a good idea, Reese. Maybe if I approach Poppy at the right time, I can convince him—"

"Nope. I don't want you to talk to him about this. You've had enough problems since you've been here, and you've done plenty to help him. I'm going to do it. Huey and I have some common ground to build on." Reese grinned down at her. "You being the most significant example. I can make him go along with it. Trust me."

She did. And then she hugged the book to her. "Maybe the next time I visit this house it will look a lot like it did in the picture. And I'll have you to thank for it."

He smiled. "Speaking of thank-yous, I'd like to bring up that idiotic one I gave you at the motel. My timing was terrible, but my intentions were the best. I can be dense sometimes, Abby. I didn't realize how those words might have sounded the other night."

"Don't worry about it. I hardly noticed."

He chuckled. "Right. The truth is I *was* thankful. You brought me in from the cold that night, and I'm not talking about the weather. Still, after what happened, for me to say 'Thank you' was the asinine statement of a thick-headed dunce."

He reached for the book, set it beside her and grasped her hand. "I wanted to stay with you. God, if you only knew how badly. You may not believe this, but some sort of twisted nobility made me leave. I didn't want you to think I'd come to you just for…well, for sex. Though it was pretty darn great."

He put his finger under her chin and raised her face. "That happened to us once before. It was just sex. Only I didn't know at the time that it would linger in my mind as something a whole lot more. If I ever get the chance to make love to you again, I want it to mean what it did two nights ago, when it meant everything."

Abby swallowed, prayed the words would find their way past the constriction in her throat. Prayed his answer would be the one she hoped for. "Reese, are you saying that you can forgive me?"

He rubbed the back of her hand with his thumb. "I'm saying that forgiveness works both ways. Can you forgive me for not understanding what you went through? For not appreciating how hard it was for you to put the baby up for adoption?"

"There's nothing to forgive—"

"Yes, there is. You made the hardest decision a mother ever has to make. And you made it with good judgment and careful consideration. When Jamie comes to us, as he will, he'll arrive on our doorstep as a well-adjusted, confident, fulfilled individual. And while we didn't raise him, you're the one responsible for that."

She'd never thought of her decision in just that way. And for Reese to tell her meant so much now. She gazed down at his hand, strong and comforting on hers, and felt the first tears fall. She sniffed, trying to stop the flow, but they had to come because they were good tears. Healing ones.

"I was afraid you were going to do that," he said, giving her a handkerchief. "Abby, the forgiveness stuff—it's done. Okay?"

"Okay."

He handed her a second package, a small jewelry box. "But now, here's a little something extra I picked up for you."

Abby's hand shook as she unwrapped the paper and opened the box. On a bed of soft black velvet rested a gold conch shell charm hanging from a chain. "It's beautiful," she said, removing it from the box. The Christmas lights on the bougainvillea shone on a red stone glimmering in the center of the shell.

"It's a ruby," Reese said. "A small one, but it's appropriate, considering it's Christmas. And since this seems to be the year for personal messages, I had it engraved."

She turned the charm over. It felt like warm satin in her

palm. She could just make out the delicate scripted words: *To A.V. from R.B.—the 1st Christmas.* She looked up at him. "The first Christmas?"

"A bit presumptuous of me, I suppose."

"What do you mean?"

"Years from now I hope to present you with a necklace celebrating our tenth Christmas. And years after that, another one."

Abby's chest squeezed. Her throat burned and her eyes filled with tears again. She felt feverish and faint and dizzy. It was the happiest moment of her life.

"Aren't you going to say anything?" he asked.

She hooked the necklace around her throat and laid her hand over the shell. The warm tropical breeze that she suddenly longed to feel every day of her life washed over her. "Reese, if you're really saying what I hope you are, that we have a future after tonight, I need to hear the words."

"Abby, my darling, our future started thirteen years ago, and I don't see an end in sight. And who knows? This New Year's Eve could be special for us."

"It could?"

"I plan to ring in the New Year in bed with you, with hopes of doing exactly that for a long time. And if by some miracle you're pregnant next Christmas, I'm going to be right here holding your hand." He smiled, his whole face lighting up. "We're not getting any younger for this parenting job."

She laughed. "So you're suggesting we should try the baby thing again?"

He nodded. "Not a bad idea, if you approve. And this time we'll get it right. And when Jamie calls us, maybe we'll introduce him to a brother or sister or two."

She picked up the book and read part of the title aloud. *"Why We Keep Coming Back."* Blinking hard, she said, "And we do, don't we?"

"We do. Until we finally realize this is where we were meant to be."

This night had changed everything for her. Brought her full circle with Reese and brought her home. "I have to go back to Atlanta for a while," she said. "I have cases, young women who need me."

"I understand that, and I'll be patient. Those women are lucky to have you on their side. But you might consider that we have girls right here in Monroe County who could use your help, too."

A burst of heat spread through Amy's body. Reese loved her. He admired her.

With his hands cradling her face, he kissed her. "But you will hurry home, won't you?"

Home. Just a few weeks ago, Abby had told her father she'd never return to Key West. Now no place else on earth could feel as much like home as this island. "You bet."

Still holding her close, Reese said, "I'm glad this matter is settled, because I've got more shopping to do. I've opened an account at the jewelry store."

He kissed her again as the music of a Key West Christmas once more filled the air. This time Elvis crooned "I'll be Home for Christmas." And Abby knew exactly how he felt.

* * * * *

Here is a sneak preview of
A STONE CREEK CHRISTMAS,
the latest in Linda Lael Miller's acclaimed
McKETTRICK *series.*

A lonely horse brought vet Olivia O'Ballivan to
Tanner Quinn's farm, but it's the rancher's love
that might cause her to stay.

A STONE CREEK CHRISTMAS
Available December 2008
from Silhouette Special Edition

Tanner heard the rig roll in around sunset. Smiling, he wandered to the window. Watched as Olivia O'Ballivan climbed out of her Suburban, flung one defiant glance toward the house and started for the barn, the golden retriever trotting along behind her.

Taking his coat and hat down from the peg next to the back door, he put them on and went outside. He was used to being alone, even liked it, but keeping company with Doc O'Ballivan, bristly though she sometimes was, would provide a welcome diversion.

He gave her time to reach the horse Butterpie's stall, then walked into the barn.

The golden retriever came to greet him, all wagging tail and melting brown eyes, and he bent to stroke her soft, sturdy back. "Hey, there, dog," he said.

Sure enough, Olivia was in the stall, brushing Butterpie down and talking to her in a soft, soothing voice that touched something private inside Tanner and made him want to turn on one heel and beat it back to the house.

He'd be damned if he'd do it, though.

This was *his* ranch, *his* barn. Well-intentioned as she was, *Olivia* was the trespasser here, not him.

"She's still very upset," Olivia told him, without turning to look at him or slowing down with the brush.

Shiloh, always an easy horse to get along with, stood contentedly in his own stall, munching away on the feed Tanner had given him earlier. Butterpie, he noted, hadn't touched her supper as far as he could tell.

"Do you know anything at all about horses, Mr. Quinn?" Olivia asked.

He leaned against the stall door, the way he had the day before, and grinned. He'd practically been raised on horseback; he and Tessa had grown up on their grandmother's farm in the Texas hill country, after their folks divorced and went their separate ways, both of them too busy to bother with a couple of kids. "A few things," he said. "And I mean to call you Olivia, so you might as well return the favor and address me by my first name."

He watched as she took that in, dealt with it, decided on an approach. He'd have to wait and see what that turned out to be, but he didn't mind. It was a pleasure just watching Olivia O'Ballivan grooming a horse.

"All right, *Tanner,*" she said. "This barn is a disgrace. When are you going to have the roof fixed? If it snows again, the hay will get wet and probably mold…"

He chuckled, shifted a little. He'd have a crew out there the following Monday morning to replace the roof and shore up the walls—he'd made the arrangements over a week before—but he felt no particular compunction to explain that. He was enjoying her ire too much; it made her color rise and her hair fly when she turned her head, and the faster breathing made her perfect breasts go up and down in an enticing rhythm. "What makes you so sure I'm a greenhorn?" he asked mildly, still leaning on the gate.

At last she looked straight at him, but she didn't move

from Butterpie's side. "Your hat, your boots—that fancy red truck you drive. I'll bet it's customized."

Tanner grinned. Adjusted his hat. "Are you telling me real cowboys don't drive red trucks?"

"There are lots of trucks around here," she said. "Some of them are red, and some of them are new. And *all* of them are splattered with mud or manure or both."

"Maybe I ought to put in a car wash, then," he teased. "Sounds like there's a market for one. Might be a good investment."

She softened, though not significantly, and spared him a cautious half smile, full of questions she probably wouldn't ask. "There's a good car wash in Indian Rock," she informed him. "People go there. It's only forty miles."

"Oh," he said with just a hint of mockery. "*Only* forty miles. Well, then. Guess I'd better dirty up my truck if I want to be taken seriously in these here parts. Scuff up my boots a bit, too, and maybe stomp on my hat a couple of times."

Her cheeks went a fetching shade of pink. "You are twisting what I said," she told him, brushing Butterpie again, her touch gentle but sure. "I meant…"

Tanner envied that little horse. Wished he had a furry hide, so he'd need brushing, too.

"You *meant* that I'm not a real cowboy," he said. "And you could be right. I've spent a lot of time on construction sites over the last few years, or in meetings where a hat and boots wouldn't be appropriate. Instead of digging out my old gear, once I decided to take this job, I just bought new."

"I bet you don't even *have* any old gear," she challenged, but she was smiling, albeit cautiously, as though she might withdraw into a disapproving frown at any second.

He took off his hat, extended it to her. "Here," he teased. "Rub that around in the muck until it suits you."

She laughed, and the sound—well, it caused a powerful and wholly unexpected shift inside him. Scared the hell out of him and, paradoxically, made him yearn to hear it again.

* * * * *

Discover how this rugged rancher's wanderlust is tamed in time for a merry Christmas, in
A STONE CREEK CHRISTMAS.
In stores December 2008

Silhouette®

SPECIAL EDITION™

FROM *NEW YORK TIMES* BESTSELLING AUTHOR

LINDA LAEL MILLER

A STONE CREEK CHRISTMAS

Veterinarian Olivia O'Ballivan finds the animals in Stone Creek playing Cupid between her and Tanner Quinn. Even Tanner's daughter, Sophie, is eager to play matchmaker. With everyone conspiring against them and the holiday season fast approaching, Tanner and Olivia may just get everything they want for Christmas after all!

Available December 2008
wherever books are sold.

HARLEQUIN® *Romance*®

Marry-Me Christmas

by *USA TODAY* bestselling author

SHIRLEY JUMP

A *Bride* FOR ALL *Seasons*

Ruthless and successful journalist Flynn never mixes
business with pleasure. But when he's sent to write a
scathing review of Samantha's bakery, her beauty and
innocence catches him off guard. Has this small-town
girl unlocked the city slicker's heart?

Available December 2008.

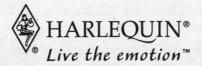

HARLEQUIN®
Live the emotion™

HARLEQUIN®

American ★ Romance®

HOLLY JACOBS
Once Upon a Christmas

Daniel McLean is thrilled to learn he
may be the father of Michelle Hamilton's
nephew. When Daniel starts to spend
time with Brandon and help her organize
Erie Elementary's big Christmas Fair, the
three discover a paternity test won't make
them a family, but the love they discover
just might....

*Available December 2008
wherever books are sold.*

LOVE, HOME & HAPPINESS

www.eHarlequin.com

HAR75242

HARLEQUIN® *Super Romance*®

COMING NEXT MONTH

#1530 A MAN TO RELY ON • Cindi Myers
Going Back
Scandal seems to follow Marisol Luna. And this trip home is no exception. She's not staying long in this town that can't forget who she was. Then she falls for Scott Redmond. Suddenly he's making her forget the gossip and rethink her exit plan.

#1531 NO PLACE LIKE HOME • Margaret Watson
The McInnes Triplets
All Bree McInnes has to do is make it through the summer without anyone discovering her secrets. But keeping a low profile turns out to be harder than the single mom thought—especially when her sexy professor-boss begins to fall in love. With her!

#1532 HIS ONLY DEFENSE • Carolyn McSparren
Count on a Cop
Cop rule number one: don't fall in love with a perp. Too bad Liz Gibson forgot that one. Except unlike everybody else, she doesn't believe Jud Slaughter killed his wife. Now she has to prove his innocence or lose him forever.

#1533 FOR THE SAKE OF THE CHILDREN • Cynthia Reese
You, Me & the Kids
Dana Wilson is *exactly* what Lissa thinks her single father needs. Dana is a single mom *and* the new school nurse. Lissa's dad, Patrick Connor, is chair of the board of education! Perfect? Well, there may be a few wrinkles that need ironing out....

#1534 THE SON BETWEEN THEM • Molly O'Keefe
A Little Secret
Samantha Riggins keeps pulling J. D. Kronos back. With her he is a better man and can forget his P.I. world. But when he discovers the secret she's been hiding, nothing is the same. And now J.D. must choose between his former life and a new one with Samantha.

#1535 MEANT FOR EACH OTHER • Lee Duran
Everlasting Love
Since the moment they met, Frankie has loved Johnny Davis. Yet their love hasn't always been enough to make things work. Then Johnny is injured and needs her. As she rushes to his side, Frankie discovers the true value of being meant for each other.